IF I LIVE

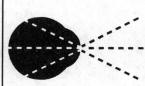

This Large Print Book carries the
Seal of Approval of N.A.V.H.

IF I LIVE

TERRI BLACKSTOCK

THORNDIKE PRESS
A part of Gale, a Cengage Company

Farmington Hills, Mich • San Francisco • New York • Waterville, Maine
Meriden, Conn • Mason, Ohio • Chicago

Copyright © 2018 by Terri Blackstock.

If I Run Series #3.

All Scripture quotations, unless otherwise indicated, are taken from The Holy Bible, New International Version®. NIV®. Copyright © 1973, 1978, 1984, 2011 by Biblica, Inc.™. Used by permission. All rights reserved worldwide. www.zondervan.com

Thorndike Press, a part of Gale, a Cengage Company.

Thorndike Press® Large Print Christian Fiction.

The text of this Large Print edition is unabridged.

Other aspects of the book may vary from the original edition.

Set in 16 pt. Plantin.

LIBRARY OF CONGRESS CIP DATA ON FILE.
CATALOGUING IN PUBLICATION FOR THIS BOOK
IS AVAILABLE FROM THE LIBRARY OF CONGRESS.

ISBN-13: 978-1-4328-4825-5 (hardcover)

Published in 2018 by arrangement with The Zondervan Corporation LLC, a subsidiary of HarperCollins Christian Publishing, Inc.

Printed in the United States of America
1 2 3 4 5 6 7 22 21 20 19 18

This book is lovingly dedicated
to the Nazarene.

1

Casey

Fried rice isn't worth dying for.

I never should have come inside. I should have stuck with fast food so I could use the drive-thru, order into the box, and get my food through a window. But I needed to use the restroom and wash my face after hours on the road, and I was sick to death of burgers, fries, and salads. I stopped at a Chinese restaurant nestled within this shopping center, figuring not many diners would be here this time of day. The lights are usually dim in Chinese places, so with my long brown wig and the glasses I'm wearing to hide my eyes, I thought I could pull it off. But the media has shown multiple sketches of how I might be disguised.

The circular booth in the corner is full of college students. A girl looks at me, then whispers to her friend, and now everyone at the table is staring at me. One of them gets on the phone.

Trying to look calm, I amble toward the front door. The waitress runs after me. "Food almost ready!"

"I'll be right back," I say, though I have no intention of returning.

Outside, I hurry up the sidewalk. I reach for a door to the anchor store and glance back. Two of the girls have darted out of the restaurant and are talking animatedly on their phones. I glance toward my car. I can't get back to it now. If those girls see me get into it, the police will know what I'm driving, and I'll have to get a different one. I'm running too low on cash. I couldn't have gotten this one without Dylan's help.

I go into the department store and look around for somewhere to hide. In the back corner of the store, I see the sign for the fitting rooms. I slip through the door and find an empty dressing room with a door that locks. I lock myself in and sit on the bench to catch my breath for a minute, my mind racing through options.

The college girls saw me enter this store. Any minute now the police will be here and I'll be arrested. My heart pounds, and the sutures on my shoulder feel like they're ripping. I wonder if they're getting infected. I readjust my sling, but then I realize it's a dead giveaway. It may even be how the students spotted me. I take it off and stuff it into my bag.

I also pull off my wig and pull my dyed black hair up into a ponytail. Keeping my arm close to my ribs, I find my baseball cap in my bag and pull it on, ponytail through the back, and take off my glasses. I shrug off my outer blouse, leaving only a tank top beneath it. I shove my sunglasses on and consider myself in the mirror. I do look different than I did five minutes ago.

Fatigue weighs me down — probably from blood loss when I was shot a few days ago — but I have to keep moving. I hang my purse strap over my good shoulder, then pile the clothes hanging in the dressing room over my arm as a prop. Never mind that they don't fit me or look like anyone in my generation would wear them. I just need to look like a normal shopper until I can get out the back door.

I venture out of the dressing room, careful with my wounded arm. Feigning interest in a sale rack, I glance around for the girls. I don't see them, so I look out the front window. I see a blue light flashing. They're here.

I head toward the back, hoping I can find a door somewhere. There's a swinging door with a sign that says "Employees Only," and I drop the clothes hanging over my arm and push into the back room. I hurry past boxes and racks of clothing, a broom closet and a mop bucket, and an employee bathroom. I see a back door for deliveries.

I open it and look both ways up the alley. There's no police car here yet. No one is out here.

I cross the alley and walk, as weak and winded as a heart patient, through a patch of woods that takes me uphill until I have a view of the parking lot. I sit on a stump behind a cluster of trees, watching the college kids talking to the cops and taking selfies with police cars in the background. This will be all over social media within twenty minutes. Cable news will pick it up, and maybe even network news. This town is ruined for me now. I have to leave.

I keep walking through the trees. On the other side of the woods, I come out in a bad area. There are men loitering on corners and lightly clad women approaching cars stalled in traffic.

I see a girl with a curly blonde wig on, wider than her small shoulders. I've had black hair, brunette, blonde . . . I've had a red wig, a blonde wig, a brown wig. None of them have had frizzy curls. No one would be looking for that.

I walk down the hill through the trees and wait for the girl to come back to the cracked sidewalk. "Excuse me," I say. "Can I talk to you?"

She looks like she's too busy for me, so I add, "There's money in it."

I have her attention now, so she turns to me. "What is it, honey?"

"I like your hair. Is it a wig?"

"Yeah," she says, touching it. "Thanks."

"I wondered if I could buy it off of you."

The woman laughs. "What? You want to buy my hair?"

"I'll give you two hundred cash."

She hesitates. "Four."

"Two fifty."

She huffs. "I paid a lot for it. I'm not just giving it away."

"Okay," I say, digging for my wallet. "Three hundred. Take it or leave it."

She sees my other wig in my bag. "What, do you collect wigs or something?"

"Yeah, it's kind of my thing. I'm an actress."

She grins and takes her hair off, revealing short-cropped brown hair with blonde highlights. She could be a soccer mom with that look. She ruffles it so it doesn't look so flattened and reaches for the cash. "I really liked this wig," she mutters.

"Surely you can get another one for a lot less, right?"

"I wouldn't sell it if I couldn't."

"Thanks," I say. "I really appreciate it."

I take the wig and stuff it into my purse, which is full to the brim, and when the girl turns away, I go back into the woods. I dust it off, inside and out, then put it on. It feels big and floppy. I look into my phone and see that it doesn't really look that bad. I actually kind of like it. With my sunglasses on, I don't think anyone would guess it was me.

I sit on the ground for a while, wishing I had gotten my food before I had to run. I'm starving, but it'll be a while before I can eat.

After a couple of hours, I need to use the facilities again. I go back through the woods to where the wig lady worked the street and see a convenience store with barred windows. I go in and try the bathroom door, but it's locked, so I have to ask for a key. They have a TV on behind the register, and I already see my face and the footage of me in the restaurant. They're warning people that I'm in the area, and that I may be armed and dangerous.

The cashier doesn't even look at me. She

hands me the key and I hurry to the ladies' room. I take a mental inventory of what they'll know from security video in the restaurant. My purse, for sure. It's big and black and nondescript, but I unload everything into the sink, turn it inside out so that the plaid lining is on the outside, and put everything back. I look down at my shoes. They're gray sneakers. Surely those won't stand out any more than my jeans will.

I realize only then that the bandage on my shoulder is visible without the shirt I was wearing over my tank top. And I don't have a different shirt to put on.

Someone knocks on the door, and I yell out, "Almost finished!"

I look in the mirror again and sigh, then pull out the shirt I took off earlier and sling it over my wounded shoulder like a towel.

I hear more sirens, see blue lights flashing on the glass in the window above my head. Are they still looking for me?

I'm sweating as I open the door and step out. The woman waiting snatches the key out of my hand and shoots inside.

The cashiers are still distracted with the police cars driving by and the news of drama in the area. I see a rack of T-shirts, so I grab one and a pack of peanut-butter crackers, step up to the counter, and clear my throat. One of the cashiers glances at the stuff instead of at me. "This all?"

"Yes," I say.

She rings me up, gives me a receipt. I throw the T-shirt over my shoulder too and go outside. Around the corner of the building, I pull the T-shirt on over my tank and throw my blouse and the long brown wig into a trash can. I stuff a bag I find in there down on top of my things to cover them.

At least now if they search me, there won't be immediate evidence that I'm the one who was seen in the restaurant.

I go back through the woods, hoping I can get to my car. The police cars should be gone from the shopping center for now. Have they quit looking for me?

Spent, I walk down the hill and around the stores to the front parking lot and, without hesitating, head purposefully to my car. I get in and don't even look around before I pull out of my space.

I see one police car across the parking lot, but his lights are off. I don't see the driver anywhere outside. I pull out of the lot into traffic and drive away.

When I'm far enough away, I let myself breathe.

2

Dylan

My car is still sitting in Dallas, right where Casey left it before she was shot by a child molester who dealt drugs. Dex drops me off at it and I glance around for some sign of Keegan and Rollins, the detectives determined to kill Casey before she exposes them, but I don't see them. The car is parked on the street behind the house where Casey got shot. From where we sit, I can see between two houses to the molester's yard and driveway. There are no police cars there. In fact, it looks as if no one is home. The truck in the backyard that would have proven some of his crimes has been moved. I hope the police towed it to their lab.

"You need to replace that phone, Pretty Boy," Dex says just before he drives away. "You need to have the same number Keegan will use to reach you."

"They'll figure out it's a different phone

15

when they can't track me anymore."

"But they won't know what you did with it. You can claim it got broken or lost."

I appreciate that Dex is worried about it, since I duct taped the phone to the bottom of an eighteen-wheeler to throw Keegan and Rollins off my trail. If I hadn't done that, both Casey and I would be dead by now.

"I guess I can replace it and use the same number."

"Go to the cell phone store. They can transfer the number in minutes. If Keegan doesn't have the serial number or whatever it is he needs to track the new phone, you'll buy yourself some time."

Dex leaves, and I head to the cell phone store and do what he suggests. Keegan is probably ballistic that I led him on a wild-goose chase. I would love to have seen the look on his face when he realized he'd been duped.

Once I have the phone, I fight the urge to call Casey on her burner phone or send her an e-mail on our secret account. I need to keep my contact with her as infrequent as possible to give her a chance to get farther away. I can't give Keegan any opportunity to get close to Casey again.

Instead I do what Keegan might expect and give him a call. He picks up on the first ring. "Where are you, Dylan?" His voice is sharp, angry.

"I'm in Dallas," I say. "My phone broke, and I was so busy going after Casey that I didn't have a chance to replace it until now."

"I noticed that," he says. "You missed all the fun."

"I was there before you were," I say, because I know that he knows it already. "I showed up right after the gunshot and I took off after her. When I didn't find her, I went to the hospitals, checked every one, showing her picture around, seeing if she had checked in for that gunshot wound."

He hesitates a moment. "We know she went to a convenience store bathroom," he says. "She was gone before we got there, but the blood trail ended. She must have patched it up or had somebody come and pick her up."

"I don't know," I say. "She seems like a loner. I doubt she has friends who would break the law to rescue her."

"I wouldn't put anything past her," he says. "I wouldn't put anything past you. Maybe you're the one who helped her."

The muscles in my neck tense, and I feel a headache coming up the back of my head. "I didn't let her escape," I say. "I told you I was looking for her."

"So why did they think you were me? Those people that shot her."

"I didn't tell them I was you," I say. "I just showed up and they acted like they'd been expecting me. So what's the deal with those people?"

"They were arrested by Dallas police," Keegan says. "Can you believe that? Somebody finally helps us get close to her, and now Dallas is hampering our investigation by arresting them for some kind of child abuse."

"Some kind of child abuse?" I ask. "You mean the molestation of a seven-year-old girl? Trading her for drugs?"

"Okay, they had it coming. But it sure threw a wrench in our case. Automatically they're sunk as witnesses. But I've got lots more. People she worked with, people who knew she was involved with that guy Cole Whittington who ran off a cliff, people who rented a room to her."

I don't bother telling him that Casey had nothing to do with Whittington's death. Casey was trying to keep the man alive. "So the Trendalls are in jail? And their dealer? All of them?"

"That's what I said."

"Child's in foster care?"

"My understanding. So are you heading

18

back home?"

My acting skills aren't what they should be if I'm going to keep lying to him, so I'd better get off the phone. I quickly tell him a few more things I plan to do to find Casey in Dallas, and he accepts that. He sounds eager to get off the phone too. He doesn't really want or need my help. He wants to have no one else but Rollins there when he finds her, so they can do whatever they want to her. Then he can claim that she was armed and fired on them, and they had to shoot her.

When I get off the phone, I ask myself: What would I be doing if I were honestly chasing her? I would probably pay a visit to the Dallas police detective again, as though I don't yet know about the Trendalls' arrest, or where little Ava is. If nothing else, I can at least put Casey's fears about the little girl to rest.

3

Casey

I don't even know what town I'm in, but I check in to an off-brand motel and change my bandage. The TV plays while I try to nap, the news channel cycling the latest alerts every fifteen minutes or so. It gets old.

I doze until a new breaking alert pulls me awake.

". . . possible indictment for Casey Cox. Let's listen in to the district attorney of Caddo Parish in Shreveport."

I sit up and squint at the screen, then grab the remote and turn it up. The camera locks onto the man standing at the bank of microphones. I've seen him before, in some election or on the news talking about me. I'm not sure where. I've already missed his opening sentences.

"We have just completed a grand jury investigation into Casey Cox's part in the murder of Brent Pace in May. Our grand jury has returned an indictment against Ms. Cox, who went missing just after the murder."

I let out a rush of air as though someone had punched me in the gut. I knew this would happen, but now I've gone from fleeing arrest to fleeing a felony indictment.

"We believe Miss Cox went to visit Mr. Pace during her lunch break on that day, and that, when he answered the door, she stabbed him multiple times."

I'm not shocked that they believe this. I saw the brutality of his murder, after all. It just sickens me that so many believe I could do such a heinous thing to my closest friend.

"She went into the house as he lay bleeding, and she left footprints, fingerprints, and other physical DNA. She then took the knife back to her car, where it was later found, along with Mr. Pace's blood, which was apparently on her hands as she started her ignition and opened and closed her door. The blood trail continued at her apartment, as she tracked it up the stairs to her place of residence. She changed clothes and fled in a taxi to the bus station, where she took a bus to Durant, Oklahoma, with some stops in between, and later to Atlanta, Georgia, then to Shady Grove where she lived for some time."

It's chilling to hear him tracing my steps like this. I go to the window and look out, expecting the parking lot to be swarming with cops. But it's not.

"Many of you are aware of Miss Cox's actions in Shady Grove, but I would caution you to consider the brutality of the murder she committed before she went there. After the events in Shady Grove, which are not relevant to the Pace murder, she fled again to Dallas, Texas. Most recently, she was sighted in Dallas, but she evaded capture once again. We believe that Casey Cox is armed and dangerous, and that she is particularly good at disguising her appearance. Her eyes are particularly notable, however, so we advise citizens to go by the almond shape of her eyes and not the hair or makeup she might be wearing. She is five feet five inches tall, about 120 pounds, and we believe she is recovering from a gunshot wound to her right shoulder."

I touch my shoulder and look in the mirror.

"We advise citizens who see Miss Cox to contact the police at once and not try to capture or follow her on their own. Again, she may be armed and dangerous."

I sigh. I don't own a gun or a knife. I don't

even have a pair of nail clippers. "Finally, Miss Cox, if you're listening, we advise you to turn yourself in to the police department closest to wherever you are, because continuing to evade the law will make it worse for you. We will find you, and when we do, we will see that justice is done."

Make it worse for me? How much worse can it be than being killed before I can tell the truth? I shiver at the way he's addressing me, and I fight the urge to turn off the news. He cannot see me, I tell myself. He can't trace my television signal. He's just trying to get into my head.

I back against the wall across from the TV and stand there as the reporters question the man.

"Was Casey Cox involved in the death of Cole Whittington in Dallas, Texas?"

"That death is under investigation. I can't comment on that case at this time."

I groan. They *know* the Trendalls did that. The truck is ample evidence. "Are there investigations into other deaths in places where Casey Cox has been?"

"Again, I'm only here to comment on the Brent Pace case."

"That would be no," I bite out.

"Have you been able to isolate a motive in the death of Brent Pace? Witnesses say they were close friends, and we know he did call her that morning. Do you know whether he invited her to come over on her lunch break? Do you know yet if they'd had a fight or anything that might have prompted such violence?"

"We haven't yet found the exact motive."

"What about the timeline?" Macy Weatherow, one of the local Shreveport anchors, asks. "The ME said Pace was killed at least a couple of hours earlier than Cox's lunch hour."

"That was an approximation."

"But is it possible that someone else killed him, since we know Cox had been at work all morning?"

I catch my breath, relieved that at least one person is questioning my guilt.

"Cox fled. The murder weapon was in her car." He turns to the next reporter's question, as if that settled that.

The murder weapon was *planted* in my car. To this day, I have never seen it.

Macy's voice rises above the questions shouted by others. "Friends describe Miss Cox as a kind and stable person. Some of her actions in Shady Grove and also in Dallas seem to bear that out. She rescued a kidnapped girl and her child, she allegedly talked a man down from committing suicide . . . How certain are you — ?"

"As I said, her DNA is at the crime scene, the knife was found in her car, Mr. Pace's blood was on her car and in her apartment."

"But some are saying that she may have just found the body, that if she'd murdered him she would have at least tried to cover it up."

"If she wasn't the one who did it, why wouldn't she have called 911 to report finding his body? Instead, she fled and has evaded capture ever since. That's all for now," he says, backing away from the microphone.

But another reporter draws him back. "How does the indictment change things? It doesn't put you any closer to finding her."

"Until now she was a person of interest in a murder. Now she's the main suspect, and the indictment charges her with a Class A felony and a Class E felony. Thank you, everyone."

The DA leaves the podium and walks away as people shout more questions at him.

I slide down the wall until I'm sitting on the floor. My phone rings. I pull it out of my pocket and see that it's Dylan. Of course. Who else could it be? No one else has this number.

It occurs to me that he's in trouble too,

now that I'm indicted. His helping a person under indictment automatically moves him into another category of crime. I don't want him to get in trouble too.

I let the phone ring to voice mail. He doesn't leave a message, but sends a text instead. You've been indicted. Have you seen the news?

I don't answer.

Are you ok?

I turn the phone off and take the battery out. I have to sever the link between us before it gets him killed or imprisoned. Too many people with ties to me have had catastrophic consequences already. I have to end this.

It would be so easy just to turn myself in. I could walk into the TV station here . . . or the police station. I could let them arrest me.

But then Keegan and Rollins would show up to take custody of me, and I would probably wind up dead.

It's insane, how trapped I am. Until I was twelve, I always believed anything bad that happened could be solved. Life had a way of working out. Justice prevailed. There were people like my dad who made sure of that.

But when I found my dad dead, lies blended into truth. What was up turned down, what was in went out, what made no sense was suddenly assumed. Evil people were believed over a stupid twelve-year-old girl, traumatized by her father's alleged selfishness.

I kept all of that inside me for ten years until I shared it all with Brent. He went after it like a hound with a ham, and it cost him his life.

A while later, I check my secret e-mail account. Dylan has left me e-mails.

I don't know if you're okay. I need to talk to you. I figure you've heard about the indictment. Call me back, anytime, day or night. If you don't, I'm probably going to go ahead and turn everything we've got over to the DA. At least it'll be a way to stop where all this is heading.

We need to strategize. I've learned some new things about our nemesis. Please call me. I can't sleep.

I squeeze my eyes shut and let the tears drip mascara down my face. I hate the heavy makeup that runs when I cry. I hate the wig that bobs when I walk. I hate that I've lost so much weight that my jeans are too big, but I can't go shopping to buy more. I hate the homemade stitches and the unceasing pain in my shoulder.

I almost don't care what happens to me. But I do want to see Keegan and Rollins pay for their sins. They have to. Otherwise all of this — my father's death, my friend's death, and the last few months of living like a frightened criminal — is a waste. None of it will mean anything.

I drop my battery and phone into my purse. When I stand, my image in the mirror startles me, as if someone I don't know is in the room with me.

I pull off the wig — sick of it — and climb into bed, pull the threadbare blankets up over my head. I don't want to turn myself in, and I don't want to kill myself.

But I do wish I would just die in my sleep.

4

Dylan

"Dude, I can help you if you show me what you got." Dex is sitting on my couch, studying the evidence I've pulled up on my computer. "Any way we can spread all this out, look at it all together?"

I can't even sit, I'm so agitated. "When I was in CID, we used to have these big whiteboards with all the evidence on every case, all the connecting dots, every significant item we logged. You could easily see what you had with a glance. Sometimes we'd just stare at them, and something would click."

Dex reaches down to scratch his prosthetic leg, a gesture I find interesting. He talks of phantom pain in the amputated limb, so I guess he also has phantom itches. "Hey, you remember that case you were working on, that sergeant who was poisoned?"

"Yeah, Sergeant Mintz. A hated man. Had

so many persons of interest I thought we'd never get to the bottom of it. Every member of his unit had said they wanted to kill him at some point."

"So how did you track all the evidence on each of the guys with motive?"

I think back and recall the large whiteboards lined up on each wall of our office. "We had a different board for each person of interest, with everything we gathered about each one. Lines connecting, overlaps. Issues they'd had with him. That case was tough because we knew the kind of poison that was used to kill him, but being in a foreign country, we couldn't get cooperation from business owners where the poison might have been bought. We even found the place we thought they probably got it, and they had security footage, but for a while we couldn't get even that."

"But you did get it, right? Eventually?"

"Finally, we did. Then the guy who we thought the video showed buying it wound up having an alibi. He was on a mission when the murder happened." I walk to the longest wall in my apartment and envision setting up whiteboards in here. "It helped that it was all up there on the boards, and we could figure out which soldiers were tight, which ones might have teamed up to pull this off, which ones had an integrity deficit and might be drawn to others like them."

"Right," Dex says. "I remember. Turned out there were two guys who had sociopathic tendencies."

"Yeah. There had been complaints from some of the others that they had shown unnecessary cruelty on some of their missions. We started tracking them and found out they were getting heroin from a local dealer. We searched their bunks and found some residue of the poison. We got both of them."

"And they were court-martialed?"

"You bet they were. They're still serving life sentences."

"So why don't you have any whiteboards, man?"

I sigh and drop down next to him on the couch. "I've thought of that, but I can't have any of this out in plain sight. What if Keegan or Rollins drops by? I wouldn't be able to hide it. The apartment's not big enough. And if, God forbid, they figure out what I'm doing, they could raid the place and find the evidence easily."

"What if you made it something you could roll up? Only pull it out when you're working on it? Like rolls of paper?"

I stare at the wall again, trying to imagine

if that could work. Actually, it could. "Yeah, maybe."

"You could take pictures of it too, send them to Casey so she could study it. It might help both of you figure out what else you need to get this over the finish line and get her name cleared."

I nod. I feel like I'm working handicapped, since most of what I'd normally do in an investigation can't be done.

"So how is her shoulder?"

I sigh. "I don't know. She isn't taking calls."

"Hey, I did the best I could, but it's not my best work."

"You did great."

Dex pushes up from the couch with his good hand, and points to me with his hook. "Come on, let's go."

"Where?"

"To Office Depot. We'll find something that can work. You need your tools, dude. You gotta get this done."

"Okay. Let's go."

We go to the office supply store and peruse the supplies I might be able to use for my board. I drop some rolls of white paper into my cart. Then I grab some different-colored markers.

Dex limps up to me as I'm checking out.

"That gonna work?"

"Yeah. I can keep the papers rolled up when I'm not using them."

Dex grins. "I don't think I've ever seen you so excited about office supplies, Pretty Boy."

He's right. I can't wait to get them home.

Back in my apartment, I unroll the white paper in rows and tape them to my wall. When I'm done, my whole wall is covered with one massive worksheet. When I finish working on it each day, I can roll it up and take it with me, hidden in the trunk of my car, then quickly put it back up the next time I need to see it. Dex is a genius.

I get to work with my notes and all the evidence we've found, all the people we've compiled evidence against, all those who've served as witnesses. I think better of putting up the names of Alvin Rossi and Gus Marlowe, who have been hiding from Keegan's group, and instead I put the names of the cities where the retired cops are living now — Jackson and GR for Grand Rapids. If Keegan ever discovers my makeshift whiteboards, I don't want them to be at risk.

I work all day after Dex leaves, and into the night, making lists and connecting dots, circling overlaps. I print out pictures and

Scotch tape them to the paper where I need them.

Yes, it does give me a much clearer picture. I take snapshots of the wall and e-mail them to Casey. Then I turn my couch and coffee table to face that wall, and I sit there with my feet up and my hands behind my head, staring, my gaze darting from one clue to another.

We need a smoking gun linking Keegan and Rollins to one of the murders. I look at the names of three people who have been murdered — Andy Cox, Brent Pace, Sara Meadows, at least. There has to be something somewhere. Until I find that, I can't be assured that Keegan and Rollins will pay for those murders. They'll only be charged with extortion and money laundering, and they may even skate on those. That's just not enough.

Armed with renewed purpose, I get to work, wedging my mind through the cracks that I see opening. Casey is depending on me. I will find something. I have to.

But later that night, as I dip in and out of sleep — in that limbo where memories lie in wait like more IEDs — my mind reminds me why I will fail.

A phone rings in some other place . . . my

childhood home, which looks like a war zone.

What has my mother done now?

I take the call and throw on my clothes and then head out to help her since she said it was an emergency.

Wishing I had at least brought along a cup of coffee, I drive toward where she waits.

It's always an emergency. I survived two IED explosions when most of my buddies came home in body bags, but my mother's dramas are the dominant forces in my days.

I turn a corner and see her. She's driven her car into a ditch, and she's staggering along the road in front of it, ranting on her phone. There's a parking lot on the other side of the ditch, so I slow until I see the entrance and turn in. I park behind her ditched car, and her yelling into the phone continues as I get out of the car.

"Mom!" I say, but she doesn't hear me. "Mom!" I shout.

She swings around, dropping her phone. She curses and goes after it, stepping into mud. "What took you so long?"

"Are you hurt?" I ask.

"Do I look hurt? Just help me get the car out so I can go home."

I stand on the other side of the ditch from her, looking helplessly at her car. The front

35

end is smashed, the hood looks like it's been folded in half. "It's not drivable. We have to get a tow truck." I look around. "Did you call the police? Was there another car involved?"

"I don't know," she says, as vague as ever. "I'll get in and you try shoving it from behind while I gun it."

I go back to the parking lot entrance and cross to her side of the ditch. She's standing partially in the road. People are swerving into the other lane to keep from hitting her. "Mom, step onto the grass. Come on."

She wipes the mud from her phone onto her baggy jeans leg, then tries to make another call.

"Who are you calling?"

"Your father!" she shouts, as if I'm the one who's the problem here. "But he's probably still passed out and won't answer. He could get me out."

"Mom, nobody can get you out of here, least of all Dad. I'm calling a tow truck."

Her breath reeks as she leans toward me and screams, "I need that car, Dylan! Get it out of that ditch now! I don't have money for a tow truck!"

"Mom, lower your voice."

"If you'd get up out of that bed now and then and get a job I might have cash for a tow truck, but no, you got the PTSD and can't do nothing, and I'm left holding the bag! No wonder they kicked you outta the army."

My jaw tightens, and I feel myself going rigid. Instant, white-hot rage. "I didn't get kicked out. I was honorably discharged."

"Because you were a mental case!"

"I'm not the one who just drove my car into a ditch," I bite out. "Mom, go sit in my car and I'll take care of this."

"Don't you call the police!" she says. "I'm warning you, don't do it!"

I figure there's no reason to call them since no one else was involved, so I watch her wobble to my car and finally get in on the driver's side . . . like I would ever consider letting her drive me home after this.

I do a quick Google search on my phone and find the name of a tow truck company. I call them and they tell me they'll head this way.

My mother has fallen asleep, her head against my headrest, her mouth hanging open. I'm going to have to wake her up to move her to the passenger seat, which I dread. She'll scream at me all the way home.

I lean back against my fender, waiting for the tow truck as her voice echoes through my brain. *Mental case . . . kicked you out . . .*

The heaviness in my chest jolts me up, and I gasp for breath. I'm drenched with sweat. But relief eases through me as I orient back into my own place, where her drunken mantras can't reach me.

I'm not a mental case.

I'm not going to fail.

I'm also not alone. God is on the case with me, fighting this battle. As I cling to the image of his sword slashing the evil around me — and around Casey — I fall back to sleep and, this time, dream of victory.

5

Dylan

My alternate burner phone rings as I stare at my evidence board. I click it on. "Hey, man."

"Dude," Dex says. "I was just reading the newspaper online, and you know how they update during the day when they have a new story?"

"I guess," I say, though I rarely go to the site to read the news online. I'm pretty much a paper kind of guy.

"So they just put up a story about a guy they found murdered in town this morning. A German guy who owns a dry cleaners. Turns out he's one of the business owners I saw Keegan talking to when I was following him."

I'm quiet for a moment, trying to absorb what he's saying. "One of the guys you thought was an extortion victim?"

"Yeah. I mean, I didn't hear what they

were saying, but I saw him go in and talk to the owner. I watched through the window. I saw the owner give him an envelope, and I could tell it was cash because Keegan seemed to be counting it. He was just one of many, but I remember him. Now he's dead."

I get up from my perch on the arm of my couch. "Okay, good catch," I say. "This could be something."

"They said he was found like three hours ago."

"Body could still be at the crime scene. I want to go see if I can get in."

"What if the dynamic duo are assigned to that case?"

"We'll see."

"You want me to tail them some more?"

I think about that for a moment. "I don't know. They'll probably be hypervigilant today, looking over their shoulders. Maybe today's not the best day. Let me get back to you."

"All right. You know how to find me," he says.

I thank Dex and hang up, then I pace my floor, trying to think. I open my laptop and go to that online newspaper site and find the guy's picture. I print it out and stick it to the paper on my wall, write "Extortion

Victim." I go to the stack on my kitchen table and look through it for the report Dex gave me about the people he thought might be extortion victims Keegan contacted on the days Dex was tailing him. I scan down the list and find the man who was just killed. I get the address of his business. "Good work, Dex," I whisper, then grab my keys and head out.

The police cars are still there when I get to the site, and the property is taped off, along with the street in front of the building. I park curbside as close to the crime scene as I can get and look at the surrounding businesses. There's a sandwich shop across the street, a liquor store next to it. Next to the dry cleaners is an alteration shop.

There's a camera outside the sandwich shop that might have security video. I wouldn't be able to get it, since I have no official connection to this case, but there are other ways to get information.

I walk along the crime scene tape, then cross through the rubbernecking traffic to the sandwich shop. I go inside. It's crowded with reporters sitting by the window, watching the activity across the street. There are no empty tables.

I walk to the counter and check out the

41

employees. There's an older man who looks to be in a sour mood, but he has an air of gravitas, so I go to his end of the counter and lean over. "Excuse me," I say. "You the owner?"

"Yes," he says. "The line is over there."

"No, I just need to ask you a few questions."

I show him my police credentials, and he comes closer. "I've already talked to the police. I don't know anything. I don't want any trouble."

"I'm not police," I say, realizing that if he's one of the extortion victims, he could have a sharp distrust of cops. "I'm a PI. I'm working with police on a related case, and I wondered if you could tell me if anyone has pulled the security video from your camera outside."

"Yes, they got it," he says.

"Could you tell me if it showed anything? What time Mr. Brauer got to work this morning? Anyone who might have gone there before it opened?"

He looks from side to side, then shakes his head. "I didn't look at it. I don't know what they got."

I don't really believe him. "What time did they take it?"

"About an hour ago."

"So he was found at seven thirty this morning. You're open for breakfast, right? So you saw the activity and didn't think about checking your video?"

He's sweating now, and he looks scared. "I didn't think about it. Do you want to order something or not?"

"Can you at least tell me what time Mr. Brauer usually comes to work?"

"He gets there around six thirty every morning. Opens at seven."

"Did you see anyone going in there before he opened?"

"No, I didn't see anything."

"Did anyone come in here for breakfast who might have been over there?"

"No, no one."

This man is irritating me. "You're sure of that? You know for a fact that no one who came in here had anything to do with him? How would you know that?"

"I know my customers."

I'm not going to get anything out of him. He must be afraid I'm one of Keegan's henchmen and that if he reveals anything, it will result in his death too.

"I'm busy," he says. "Have a nice day." He disappears to the back.

I sigh and look around, hoping another employee might talk to me. I get in line and wait my turn. When I get to the front, I order a club sandwich. As I'm paying, I ask the girl, "So what's going on over there?"

She looks around, as if making sure her boss doesn't hear her. "The owner of that dry cleaners was murdered," she whispers. "Employees found him when they came in." She leans toward me. "Shot. Scares me to death. I came in early this morning too. It could have been me."

"Was he shot inside or outside?"

"Inside. They found him in his office. Execution style, is what I hear. He was a nice man too. Came in here for lunch every day. His poor wife."

"Has she been here since he was found?"

"Yes, the police notified her and brought her down. It was horrible. I could hear her screaming all the way over here."

The wife. I have to talk to the wife. She would know if he'd been threatened. If she knows about the extortion, then maybe she'd be willing to help me.

"I'm scared to work here now," she whispers. "What if the killer comes back?"

She flits off to prepare my order, and I stand there with my back to the counter, looking through the plate glass to the cleaners across the street. When she brings me my bag, I take it and go out to the crime scene tape, where media people are clustered. I scan the uniformed officers, looking for someone I know. Finally I see a guy I went to school with. I didn't even know he was a cop. I walk the perimeter of the tape.

"Banks," I say.

He turns, sees me, and laughs out loud as he reaches for my hand. "Dylan! Great to see you, man."

"You too. You in a uniform. Who would've thought?"

"I know, right? I heard you were in the FBI or something."

"The military version," I say. "Army CID. But I'm out now. Discharged last year. I'm contracted to help the department on a case right now."

"Working solo, huh? Sounds nice."

"Can be. Were you the first responder on this case?"

"No, I didn't get here until later." He lowers his voice. "Owner shot in the head, probably with a .38."

Keegan would carry a .38, like most cops. But he wouldn't have used his department-issued weapon.

"Any shell casings found?"

"Not to my knowledge, but the CSIs are still working and I don't know what they've got. I haven't been inside."

45

"Does his family have any idea who did this?"

"No, his wife was out-of-her-mind upset. Brutal."

"Where is she now?"

"Someone took her home."

I look around at all the activity. "Who are the detectives assigned to the case?" I ask him.

"Stamps and Logan."

I think about that for a moment. Keegan would have manipulated the evidence to keep them from figuring out it was him . . . "So has Keegan been by? Rollins?"

"Yeah, some of the other detectives have come by. Curiosity, I guess."

Boom. So Keegan made sure that any hair follicles, any sweat, any prints they found of his had a reason to be here.

"Dylan! How ya doing, man?" I turn and see Kurt Keegan, Detective Keegan's son, who I also went to school with. We were pretty good friends in high school, but I haven't seen him but once since I got back stateside.

I shake his hand as if nothing has changed. For all I know, he's tight with his father and is part of Keegan's criminal circle. But he was always a good guy when I knew him, nothing like his dad. The pull of money is

46

always a change-maker, though.

I shoot the breeze with him, hoping he doesn't mention to his dad that I was at the scene.

"So I hear you've been working on Brent's case," he says. "My dad was a little irritated that they hired you."

"We're helping each other out," I say, evading.

"Yeah, I bet. He likes to micromanage. I would imagine you're butting heads. Just hang in there. We should have lunch sometime. Catch up."

I give him the same number his dad has and tell him to call me when he has some time. I don't know quite what to think of what he said. Is he feeling me out for his old man, or is he really clueless?

Later, I look up his address and drive by. He lives in an apartment not much better than mine. There's a vehicle in his parking space, a pickup that's probably five years old. If he has money, he's not spending it on things like that. But then, neither is Keegan. His toys are all carefully hidden and are owned under aliases. Nothing I've seen yet has implicated Kurt, but I'm not stupid enough to think that his dad left him out.

I hope he calls me so we can have lunch. If he's involved in Brent Pace's death — or anyone else's — I'll take him down too. I have no nostalgic allegiance to murderers.

6

Casey

The Craig's List ad I answered is for someone to "earn up to $2,000 a month working from home," and I figure the fewer people I encounter per day, the better off I'll be. I did a phone interview already with the wife of the attorney who is hiring. She didn't tell me much about the job I'll be doing, but she asked me to come in for an interview with her husband.

I take special care on my makeup and wear my frizzy wig, hoping neither of them will recognize me from the news. At least my voice isn't recognizable, since the media has only been showing my pictures.

In a strip mall, I find the office. "Billy Barbero, Esquire," says a bronze sign next to their door. It's not an upscale law firm, just a one-man show. And when I step inside, I realize just how downscale it is. His wife, the woman I talked to on the phone, is probably fifty, wearing a pair of jeggings that don't flatter her fleshy thighs, and a baggy Metallica sweatshirt. Her desk is covered with binders and stacks of paper, with only a small area cleared out for her to write on.

"Hi," I say. "I'm Liana Winters. I have an appointment with Mr. Barbero?"

"Yes, I talked to you," she says, looking around her desk for something. She pulls a clipboard out from under some notebooks and hands it to me. "If you don't mind, fill out this application so we'll have all your info. He's with a client right now, so it'll be just a minute."

As I take the clipboard and sit down, she yells out, "Billy, Liana Winters is here!"

I look up, startled. Through the door, he yells back, "Who?"

"The girl we're hiring!" she yells back.

I'm encouraged that she's already identified me as the new hire, but I can see that it's not a conventional law office. I fill out the application with fake information about Liana Winters, including employment history. I don't know what will come in handy for this job, since I'm not sure what it entails, but they could clearly use a receptionist or administrative assistant. I truly was an office manager at my job before Brent's murder, and I was good at it, so I

50

write that down with a fake address and hope they won't try to check my references. Somehow, I don't think they're organized enough.

When I'm almost done, the door opens to his office, and a young woman with a service dog — a German shepherd — comes through the door. She looks a little like Natalie Portman, but she's wearing dark glasses. She must be blind. "Marge, can you call my ride for me?"

"Sure thing, hon."

The man I assume is the attorney is in a wheelchair — the narrow kind with no armrests — and he wheels out rapidly behind her. He has long gray hair to his shoulders and is wearing a T-shirt and jeans with a hole in the knee.

Marge calls for the ride as the blind girl says some parting things to the attorney, and I wait quietly, finishing my application. When Marge hangs up, she says, "He's not answering, sweetie."

"Figures," the blind girl says. "He knows I need him. Maybe he's heading this way. I'll wait outside and keep trying him."

She lets the dog lead her to the door. Once she's out, I get up and step toward the attorney. "Hi, I'm Liana."

Barbero shakes my hand. "Come on into

51

my office," he says. "Help yourself to our coffeemaker if you want some coffee. It's all DIY around here."

I don't really want any, so I decline and follow him in.

His office looks like a tornado hit it. Binders are stacked halfway up the wall, filling every space behind his desk. Half of his desk is covered with papers, but he does have a clear space in front of where he parks his chair.

"So . . . Marge hired you, did she?"

"Um . . . I guess she did."

He looks down at my application, nods approvingly, then says, "So let me tell you what we do here."

"Okay."

"I represent disabled clients. The gal you saw in here is one of them. We sue establishments that aren't following the Americans with Disabilities Act." He stops and chuckles. "We have hundreds of lawsuits in progress all over the country. Unfortunately, one of my best researchers just passed away. Pneumonia, nasty case. Didn't expect that."

"I'm so sorry," I say.

"Anyway, we need to replace him."

"What does a researcher do?" I ask.

"I need you to find violations of the Act. Hotels that don't have wheelchair-accessible pools, mainly. That's our biggest money-maker and they're easiest to find."

I nod. "So you want me to go around to the local hotels?"

"No, ma'am," he says. "Not physically. You'll use Google Earth or Google Maps. Pick out a city and zoom in over every motel listed in the area, and if you can't see the pool lift beside the pool, we'll sue them."

"Really?" I ask. "It's that easy?"

"Yes, indeed," he says. "The law's the law."

He types something on the computer, finds a Google Earth satellite image of a pool behind a hotel, and shows me what a pool lift looks like. "It's rectangular, like this. If you see anything like this, just skip over it. If you don't see one, call the motel and ask them if they have a pool lift. Then give me the name of the hotel and their address and phone number and I'll sue them on behalf of one of my clients."

I think of all the motels I've stayed in, and I've never seen a pool lift. But I haven't been looking for one. "So . . . you don't have to be a customer of the motel to sue it?"

"Nope. Under the law we can sue them without ever going to the place. It's an important service to the disabled community."

I stare at the satellite image. "I think I can do this."

"All you need is a good Internet connection. You'll get paid by the number of leads you give me. Ten bucks a lead."

It seems easy enough, but I won't know how much that will make me until I try it. "I can start right away."

"Then welcome to your new job," he says, reaching out his hand again. I shake it and get to my feet. "Just e-mail your leads to us, and keep up with them yourself to make sure Marge pays you the right amount. She's kind of a mess. You can bring them here if you want to make sure she gets them."

"Okay, I will. I look forward to working with you, Mr. Barbero."

"Call me Billy. We're not formal here."

"Okay, Billy."

He wheels out behind me as I go back into the front office, smiling. "Thank you, Marge," I say.

"When's she starting?" she asks him.

"Now. I think she'll be a go-getter. Good hire."

I'm feeling good about this when I step out of the office. I'm walking to my car when I see the blind girl and her dog waiting on the sidewalk.

I walk over to her. "Excuse me, I heard you were having trouble getting in touch with your ride."

She looks just to the left of my face. "Yeah . . . who are you?"

"I'm Liana Winters," I say, confident because she can't see my face. "The Barberos just hired me to be their researcher. If you still need a ride, I'd be happy to give you one."

"Really?" she asks. "That's fantastic. I can pay you. I can't get Uber because I can't see the app. I ought to get Billy to sue them. I was going to call the cab company next, but Siri isn't cooperating on my phone."

She introduces me to her dog, Butch. He seems friendly, but focused. I lead them to my car, not certain how much help they need. I clean off my back seat and put my emergency bag into my trunk so the dog will have room, then I open the door for her.

She seems about my age and has a friendly expression on her face. I'm sorry she can't see, but I'm glad she can't see me.

She lets the dog in, then easily gets into the front.

I slide into the driver's seat. "Where to?"

She gives me the address. "What did you say your name is again?"

55

"Liana Winters," I say. "And yours?"

"Claire."

"So you're one of Billy's clients?"

"Yep. He was a godsend. He saw me in a Starbucks getting coffee, and asked me if I wanted to earn some cash."

"So you work for him too?"

"No, he kind of works for me. I'm a plaintiff. He uses my name on some of his lawsuits. He has a stable of disabled people whose names he uses. Gives us a cut."

"Oh." I'm quiet for a moment, not sure if that sounds legitimate. I hope she's not being taken advantage of.

"I figure we're helping disabled people everywhere, you know? The lawsuits just make it more possible for us to have access to things. And it's a good living for me."

I decide not to judge their motives or intentions. It must be legal or they wouldn't be doing it, I tell myself.

She lives in a nice neighborhood in a fairly new house. I pull into the driveway, and she gets out and opens the back door for Butch to hop down. "Thanks so much for the ride. It wasn't awkward and painful like rides can sometimes be."

"Glad to. Anytime."

"Really?" she asks. "Because I'm always looking for people to drive me."

"Sure." I tell her my phone number.

She hands me her phone. "Will you put it in my contacts list so Siri can find you? That is, if she's in a cooperative mood."

I navigate to her contacts and type my info in. Before giving it back, I grab a Kleenex and wipe off my prints. I hand it back to her, still holding it with the tissue. She doesn't notice as she takes it.

"I need to do some shopping for my niece's birthday party. You can work in the car if there's an Internet connection nearby."

"Yeah, that would work fine."

She pulls a ten out of her pocket and hands it to me.

"You don't have to pay me," I say.

"Yes, I do. If you don't take my money, I won't call you again."

Grinning, I take it and stuff it into my purse. "Okay, then."

"I'll call you about the shopping."

"Sounds good," I say. "Bye, Claire."

I watch as she gets into her house, then I back out of the driveway and head home, smiling that I've made a new friend. I like her company, and I like even more that she won't be able to see me on the news.

I feel like God has provided once again. I whisper a quiet "Thank you."

7

Dylan

I'm striking out in my investigation of the dead Mr. Brauer, so I wait until the day after the funeral, then pay a visit to his house. There are three cars parked in the driveway, so it looks like someone is home.

I park my car on the street, hoping that Keegan and Rollins don't happen by and see it. It also wouldn't be good if she told them I talked to her, but that seems unlikely, especially if she thinks they might have had something to do with her husband's murder.

Then again, I could be barking up the wrong tree entirely. It could have been a random robbery, a drug deal, or something else that has nothing to do with the police department. But my gut tells me that's not the case.

I knock on the door, and after a moment, a young woman cracks the door open, keeping the chain lock engaged. "Yes?"

I decide not to show her my police credentials, because anything police-related is likely to spook them. "Hi, my name is Dylan Roberts. I'm a private investigator. I was wondering if I might have a word with Mrs. Brauer."

The girl studies me, then says, "She's already told the police everything she knows."

"I know, but I'm not with the police force. I'm kind of coming at this from a different angle." I lower my voice. "I'm working on a case that may intersect with this one. It's very important that I talk to her."

She frowns and lifts her eyebrows, then says, "Wait here just a minute." The door closes and I wait on the porch, hoping they're not calling the police to check on me.

After a few minutes, an older woman comes to the door and unlocks the chain. She has deep lines on her forehead and red blotches under her eyes. She peeks out suspiciously. "What do you want?"

"I wondered if I could talk to you privately," I say quietly. "I'm investigating a case that has led me to believe that there are some dirty police officers on the force. I'm trying to figure out if your husband got crossed up with them."

She opens the door now and steps out, looks from left to right as if searching for anyone who might be staking out her house. Finally, she says, "Come in."

I step inside and she quickly closes the door behind me. She turns to the girl, who I assume is her daughter. "Go check on the food in the oven," she says in a German accent. "I need to talk to him alone."

Now that we're under the lights, the girl looks college aged. She disappears into the kitchen, leaving us alone. Mrs. Brauer gestures toward a chair, and I lower myself into it. She sits on the couch adjacent to me.

"Have you talked to the police?" I ask her.

"Yes. But not about what had been happening. I cannot trust any of them."

"Why don't you tell me what happened?"

She pauses and seems to think about it, then lets the words spill. "He goes to work at six or six thirty every morning to get things set up before the first employees arrive. He always keeps the door locked behind him. That's what makes me think he knew this person or he would not have let them in."

"Was the lock broken? Any sign of forced entry?"

She shakes her head no. "Whoever it was

came in through an unlocked door. My husband would not have unlocked it just for anyone. Not for a stranger."

"Mrs. Brauer, can you tell me if you were having any financial problems?"

"Yes, we *were* having problems." Tears spring to her eyes, turning the whites pink. "That's why he couldn't pay."

"Couldn't pay who?"

"The cops." She gets up and walks to the door to the kitchen and peers in to make sure her daughter isn't listening. Then she comes back to the couch and her voice lowers even more. "They came every month and demanded payment. Thousands of dollars for protection, they said. But we did not have it. Business was slow, and we had a daughter in college, and he couldn't pay. They warned him there would be consequences."

"So when did he tell them he couldn't pay?"

"Two days ago," she says, her eyes taking on a distressed, panicked look. "He came home worried. He didn't sleep that whole night. He told me he wanted me to get out of town, but I wouldn't go. I didn't want to leave him. He thought they would make an example of him. He told them he needed more time to get the money, but this was the second time in a row he had told them that. They had been there two weeks before and had given him that extra amount of time. He was really scared. He tried to get a second mortgage on our house, but it was turned down. We didn't have enough equity."

"Did he ever tell you who the police officers were?"

She rubs her forehead, then says, "Detective Keegan and another man named Rollins. When they come they're not in police uniforms. Just plain clothes. It's terrible what they do to the businesses. We're struggling to make ends meet as it is, and they take our profits so that we can't even support ourselves. And now they've done this to send a message to all the other businesses around. Every business owner around us knows who did it, but no one will tell you because they're scared themselves."

Her pitch is rising, and she gets up, grabs a tissue from a box near the couch. She wads it up and wipes the tears on her face. "Do you have any power to stop them? This should not happen. This is America."

"I'll do my best, but I may need your testimony," I say. "Your husband isn't the only one who's been killed. I'm very close to having enough evidence to turn over to the DA. But I'm going to need your help. Would you be willing to testify?"

She hesitates, but then she lifts her chin. "Yes, I would. If I can help get that scum off the streets, yes, I will testify."

"Mrs. Brauer, is there anyplace you could go for a couple weeks? I'm worried for your safety."

"I've thought about that," she says. "I want to leave town. I really want my daughter out of here. I cannot let her know too much because I am afraid she could not stay quiet. They would kill her."

"I think that would be a good idea. Someplace they wouldn't think to look for you. Just until they're exposed."

She looks at the floor as if trying to figure out where she could go. "All right," she says. "Do you want to know where I'm going?"

"I don't have to know," I tell her, because I want her to feel safe. "But it would be good if you could keep in touch with me in case I need you. Give me a phone number or something."

She nods and goes to a desk in the corner, writes down the number on a Post-it note, and hands it to me. "This is my cell phone number. Do you think they can find me through that?"

"Maybe," I say. "It might not hurt for you

to get a different phone, just in case. A different phone number. You can get a temporary phone at Walmart or a drugstore." I cross through the numbers she's given me and write down my own burner phone. "When you get one, text me the number. I think that will be safer. Buy the card with the minutes in the store. Don't activate it with a credit card."

She puts her hand to her head again and pulls her bangs back as if her temples throb. "I should have made him leave town. I should not have let him go to work."

"These people are ruthless. They're brutal. I would advise you not to talk to anyone else at the police department for now."

"I know. How can I trust any of them? I wouldn't have trusted you if you hadn't brought it up to me."

"Just keep it quiet. It's very important that they not get a heads-up that we're on to them."

Her face turns red, and veins pop out on her temples. "We should have just paid, even if we couldn't pay our mortgage or the tuition. I'd rather be bankrupt than have my husband dead!"

"Mrs. Brauer, don't do that to yourself. You didn't cause this."

I get to my feet, slide my fingers into my

pockets. "I'm so sorry, Mrs. Brauer. I can't imagine how hard this is. But I'm going to do everything I can to help." She walks me to the door and hovers there as I step out onto the porch. "Don't give up," I say.

As I walk back to my car, I say a silent prayer for her safety and her daughter's, and anyone else who matters to them. I pray that God will keep them under Keegan's radar.

As I pull away in my car, I look back at the house. The lawn is manicured, the house well maintained. Hardworking people who deserve better live there. And now the husband is dead because these maniacs are willing to abuse the power their badges have given them.

I can't let that stand. People need to be able to trust their police. If it's the last thing I do, I'm going to make sure the Brauers get justice.

8

Casey

I start my job right away because I need money so badly and because I want to make a good impression. In my motel room, I get a list of all the motels in the towns Mr. Barbero directed me to, and one by one, I zoom in with Google Earth to get an aerial view of the pools.

Most of them don't have pool lifts, if I'm looking at them right. It surprises me, because I thought these leads would be harder to find. Surely this many people wouldn't be in violation of the Americans with Disabilities Act.

Before I call any of them to verify, I look up the Act and skim through it, looking for anything about a pool lift. I finally find it, and see that it is a requirement for any business with a pool.

I find the phone number of the first lead — a small, privately owned motel with about thirty rooms — and I call. A woman answers. "Hi," I say. "I was considering making a reservation there, but I may be with someone in a wheelchair, and I wondered if you have a pool lift."

"A what?" the woman asks.

"A pool lift. You know, it helps people in wheelchairs get into the pool?"

"Um . . . I don't know. Just a minute."

I wait as the woman puts me on hold, and finally, after a few minutes, a man picks up. "Hello, this is the owner. May I help you?"

I ask him again about the pool lift. "Are you making a reservation?" he asks.

"Not yet," I say. "I was just checking your facilities."

Silence.

Feeling awkward, I say, "So you don't have one?"

I wait a moment. "Hello?" I say, and realize he's disengaged from the call.

On the form I'm to fill out for Mr. Barbero, I write, "Hung up when I asked." I call back a few minutes later and ask the woman who answers for the owner's name, and she gives it to me. I jot it down.

I wonder if he's going to get sued.

I go to the next one, and this time the person I talk to says, "Look, I know what you're doing. This is one of those Google lawsuits, right? If you want to make a reservation, then make it. We will have a pool lift here for you."

"So you don't have one now?" I ask, wincing slightly.

"When would you like to come?"

I pause for a moment, then he says, "I have two kids in college. Do you even have a conscience?"

That jolts me. I frown, feeling accused of something I don't understand. "Yes, I . . . I'm just checking —"

"This is criminal," the man says. "Yes . . . I have a pool lift, okay?"

"But you said —"

"Sue me!" he shouts into the phone. "I have a ten-thousand-dollar pool lift. Waste your time if you want!"

I hang up, and for a moment I stare at the motel in question on my satellite view. What is going on? Have I gotten myself into something that will dig me into a deeper hole?

I'm writing down what he said, when Claire calls me. I pick up. "Hi, Claire."

"Liana?" she says. "Listen, I know this is short notice, but I wondered if you could take me to run some errands."

I look at my work and consider whether I should leave. I'll take my computer with me and do the Google searches in the car wherever we go. I'll hold off on the phone calls until after I identify the motels that aren't complying.

My stomach feels a little sick as I go pick up Claire. I pull into her driveway and call her. Instead of answering, she comes right out with Butch. She walks to my car and puts Butch in the back seat, then hops into the front.

"I'm sorry for the short notice," she says, "but you said to call you. I figured you might need the cash."

"Yeah," I say. "It's fine. Where do you want to go?"

"I need to go to the drugstore and then the bank."

"No problem." She gives me the address to the drugstore, and I pull up in front, open her door for her, and watch as she feels her way along the wall to the automatic door. I back into a parking space so I can watch for her to come back out.

She told me she might be in there about fifteen minutes, so I sign onto the store's wifi guest signal and do some more searches. I find a couple of motels with pool lifts, but they're the bigger ones. The smaller ones are almost inevitably without them. I write them down, find the owners' names, and jot down their phone numbers to call later when I'm feeling less unsettled.

When I see Claire coming back through the door, I close my laptop, pull up to the door, and roll my window down. "Right here," I say, and she lets Butch pull her toward my car.

When they're back in, I take her to the bank. When she's done there she offers to buy me lunch.

"I'd love to," I say, "but not as your treat. I'll pay for my own."

She suggests a little café, and I quietly slip my arm sling off before we go in. I keep my sunglasses on as we head to a back table. People might assume I'm blind too. I take a seat with my back to the other diners.

"This is fun," she says. "I don't usually get to eat out during the day." When the server brings our drinks, she sips hers, then asks, "So how do you like working for Billy?"

"I'm not sure."

I tell her what happened with the guy who asked me if I had a conscience. "The thing is, I kind of feel sorry for that guy. I mean, he made me feel like I was doing something wrong. Billy doesn't sue people based off that info alone, does he? I mean, does he give them a chance to rectify things first? Like, before he serves them with a lawsuit, does he give them a grace period to get a pool lift?"

"He should," Claire says. "I mean, I've always assumed that the goal is to get them equipped with what disabled people need, not just to slap them with a suit."

"But he sues an awful lot of people, doesn't he?"

"Yeah, he does. A lot of businesses are in violation of the Act."

"So when he sues someone for something that could impact a blind person, he uses your name?"

"Right. He has others with different kinds of disabilities, and he's disabled himself. But I guess he can't file every suit in his own name."

"So do you get a percentage of the settlement or the award?"

"No, I just get a flat fee. I never know how a case turns out or what he gets."

So he could be raking in millions. I draw in a deep breath. "I don't know. I just kind of feel like I'm doing something dishonest. Maybe even illegal."

"It's not illegal," she says, and there's an edge to her tone. "The Act is very specific. If it were illegal, he wouldn't be winning the cases."

"But I'm acting like I'm going to check in

and need a pool lift, when it's not true. I'm literally setting them up. I mean, if I were disabled and I checked into a motel where I didn't have access to what I needed, then I could see complaining about it. But I'm not disabled, and here I am finding people to sue, when there may not have been anyone at all inconvenienced by this. And if they're not given the chance to fix it?"

"I didn't say they're not. I said I didn't know."

I soften my voice so I don't seem accusatory. "That man mentioned Google lawsuits. It's a thing. I looked it up, and it's where attorneys do exactly this. They use Google Earth to find businesses violating the Act in random cities they've never even been to, and they sue them without ever going to the place. This owner has kids in college."

"Wow, you really got a lot of information from him, didn't you?"

I sip my drink. "I just don't want to take advantage of real human beings, you know?"

"Neither do I. But if you don't like it, you don't have to do it."

Our food comes, and we're quiet until the waitress leaves. She eats a French fry, then leans forward. "You know, you may be over-thinking this. Billy and Marge are great. Unpretentious, humble people."

"Yeah," I say. "It's just that I knew this couple who sued people for fraudulent things, and they were terrible people."

"I get it. But this isn't fraudulent. If he sues them for not having a pool lift, then they'll have to get a pool lift."

"They'll also have to pay a lot of money in damages, and that could put some of them out of business."

"I don't think he's trying to put anyone out of business. I'm sure it's all above-board."

"Yeah, probably."

She stares in front of her for a moment. "That's some conscience you got there."

I breathe a laugh. "Yeah, I guess. I'm just . . . I've been learning about Christianity. Honesty is a big thing. I'm just really not wanting to . . . you know, make God mad."

She laughs. "Believe it or not, I don't want to make him mad either. I go to church too."

I don't say it, but I don't think Christianity is so much about going to church. "I'm new at this," I say. "You've probably had all this figured out for years, but I'm still at the blow-my-mind phase. Like, seriously? Jesus let them crucify him for my sins? And that one act is something that can cleanse me now? Two thousand years later?"

Her eyes are fixed just to the left of my temple. "Yeah, that is wild, huh?"

"I mean, I heard this preacher talk about Jesus praying for us. Interceding, I think he called it. And I think that might be the first time I realized he's real, today. Alive . . . you know?"

I can see from her expression that it's been a long time since she's thought of it that way, and I wonder if I've gone too far. She seems to consider that for a moment, then she says, "It's fun to see someone discovering that for the first time. It becomes old hat to some of us."

"How could it ever be?" I ask, astonished.

"I don't know," she says. "Maybe we kind of get immunized."

"Immunized," I say. "Yeah, that would explain it. You hear it so much that you start tuning it out. If I convert, I don't want to get that way."

"If you convert? You sound like you've converted already."

My heart sinks, and I know I can't explain to her why I've hesitated. "I guess I'm in the consideration phase."

She looks down at her drink. "I know I'd probably qualify as lukewarm. I actually didn't realize that until just now. But I can give you one piece of advice. Don't wait."

Her cheeks blush as she says that, and I realize she means this sincerely.

"Seriously," she goes on. "It's not complicated. If you're this pumped about Jesus . . . take it now. This feeling might fade if you don't, and you might never go all the way. You don't want that to happen. It sounds like he's wooing you."

"Knocking at the door," I say, because I read that part in Revelation last night.

"Yeah. Let him in."

I didn't expect this lunch to go here, but we both get quiet as we eat. We don't pick up with the Christian talk again, but her words hang in my mind for the rest of the day.

9

Casey

They say that walking through the forest does something to your brain, releasing hormones that give you a sense of well-being that lasts for days. I don't know if that's true, but being around people does that for me. The sound of other humans, a smile exchanged, the brush of shoulders in a crowd, the sound of voices, all contribute to my inner peace.

Except when people are staring at me because I look like that murderer on TV.

I pull into a parking space at the mega-church near my motel and look toward the front doors. It's an old movie theater converted into a church. I know about it only because they advertised their midweek service on a commercial during reruns of *Andy Griffith*. The commercial showed a dark room with the stage lit up, so I'm hoping I can slip in a few minutes late and disappear into the darkness.

I check my wig in the mirror. Maybe if I hurry inside I can keep my sunglasses on until I get to the dark auditorium.

There are a few people in the front area, talking to each other as they greet guests, so I smile and hurry past them, saying a quick hello, as if I belong here and they should know me.

The sanctuary is just as it looked on TV, with theater seating and the lights turned down. The audience is singing, and the stage is lit up as a music group leads them.

I slip into a back row and push the theater seat down. The words to the song are shown on the screen up front. I don't know this song, but I listen and study the words, relishing the sound of a few hundred voices. I wonder if heaven is something like this, with thousands, millions of voices singing prayers to God. I wonder if I'll get to hear that someday.

After one verse of the song, I pick up the tune, singing along with the others. Peace does seem to flow over me, greater than the peace I've ever felt in a forest.

I wonder what it would be like to know these people and be a part of this group, to be recognized in a good way when I walk through those doors, to be depended on like family.

I can't even imagine what that's like.

I wonder if Dylan is like that at his church. I try to picture him shaking hands and hugging people, looking down at his open Bible as his preacher teaches, writing notes in the margins. People are probably always trying to fix him up with single Christian women. I've never asked about that.

What was I thinking, to imagine a future with him?

The pastor comes to the microphone and tells the crowd to greet the person next to them, and to my horror, the lights are turned up. People begin speaking to each other.

I dart out of my row and head to the exit. The people who were greeting are gone now, probably in the service themselves. No one stops me.

I don't slow down until I'm at my car. I hope no one saw me.

I cry on the way back to my motel, knowing I'm leaving a muddy trail again. I try to shake it off and hold on to the few minutes of peace I had. It'll have to last for a while. I won't let my thoughts snuff it out.

I go to my room and open my new Bible and read the passage that was marked on the screen, the passage the pastor was about to preach from. But I don't understand it.

What would he have said? I really needed to hear it.

I Google the passage and see a list of sites come up. I click on one of them and find another message by a different pastor. I turn it on and try to imagine I'm there in person, with people around me, soaking it all in.

I don't know why I didn't think of this before. I can learn so much about Christianity by listening to YouTube videos.

For the next few hours, I listen to this preacher teach on six different topics. When I'm done, I feel better about having to walk out of church.

Even if I can't go to God's house, I can still hear from him.

10

Dylan

The call from Kurt Keegan comes on Friday, and I answer with suspicion. I can't see my high school friend as an old buddy when I know he's the son of a serial killer.

"Dylan, what are you doing tonight, man?"

I try to keep my voice light. "What have you got in mind?"

"I thought we could meet for drinks at Monnogan's."

"That dive?" I tease, knowing it's the favorite club of most of the cops at the downtown precinct.

"It's not so bad. Thought I'd invite some of the old gang. Miller, Kramer, Jecowitz. A few others."

I can't let on that I don't trust Kurt, so I grudgingly agree. It'll be a good chance to gauge whether he's getting a piece of his dad's action.

I get to Monnogan's early and check out the place just to make sure this isn't a trick. I reject the table I'm directed toward and instead pull three others together and move the chairs around it. It's kind of a paranoid thing to do, a way to control the situation in case I'm about to be set up or bugged. Then again, I guess Kurt could be wired himself if he's in cahoots with his dad.

He comes in a few minutes after seven — our meeting time — and he's got a girl with him. She's pretty, blonde, the cheerleader type, which Kurt always went for. He introduces her as Grayson and says she's his fiancée.

Grayson is pretty in a collegiate sort of way, with a quick smile and intelligent eyes. She takes the seat between us as though she's already comfortable with me, which does impress me. He seems truly smitten with her, looking at her often and including her in everything he tells me. The three of us shoot the breeze as we order drinks — two beers and my trusty Coke — and one by one, some of our friends from high school show up. Every one of them has something to say about Brent's death, but I don't want to talk about it. I quickly get them off the subject and ask what they've been up to in the last few years.

When everyone is served their drinks and there's food on the table, there are five conversations going on. I watch Grayson interacting with Kurt, and I try to see his father's mannerisms in him and figure out whether he's a psychopath too. I think back to times in our school years when I did things with him. I wouldn't call him the king of empathy, but nothing in his character ever suggested that he could be a party to murder.

When he and a friend go to the pinball machine, I'm left making conversation with Grayson. "So when's the wedding?" I ask.

"In six weeks," she says. "We're counting down the days."

I sip my drink. "You having a big wedding?"

"As big as we can afford," she says.

"My sister had this humongous wedding," I tell her. "Six bridesmaids. She married a rich dude. My family sure didn't pay for it. They were barely invited. But I was glad she got what she wanted. She deserved it."

"We're paying for most of it ourselves," she says. "We both have kind of controlling families. When we take money from them, we're beholden to them. Kurt and I figured out early that we wanted to just do it within our means."

Interesting, I think. "Oh yeah? So do you guys have a big honeymoon planned?"

"We're just going down to New Orleans for a weekend. He doesn't make much on a cop's salary, and I'm a teacher, so we don't have much put away to go to Cancun or anything."

"Yeah, that probably takes a big chunk out of your budget."

"We're good to go," she says. "I ordered my dress off of eBay. It's gorgeous. I literally bought a Vera Wang for two hundred dollars. I was worried it would come looking like a Halloween costume or something, but it was absolutely what I wanted. My church is really pretty so we don't have to spend a lot on flowers to dress the place up. And some of my friends are helping me make the food for the reception."

"That's a lot of work," I say.

"It's saving us a whole lot of money. We did kind of go crazy on the cake, though. It just doesn't seem like a wedding without a nice cake." She blushes and waves her hand. "I'm sorry. I know you couldn't care less about wedding planning."

"No, it's interesting," I say. She seems like a nice girl, and her mention of her church makes me think she might be a Christian. I can't imagine that they would be scrimping quite so much if Kurt's dad were providing any of the cash. Maybe that's a good sign that he isn't involved. I really hope he's not.

Kurt comes back to the table and orders another beer. I'm still nursing my Coke, but the ice has melted. "What are you drinking, man?" he asks, ready to buy me one.

I don't want to lie about it. "Just a soda."

"You're kidding," he says. "Are you a recovering alcoholic? Did they turn you into a lush in Afghanistan?"

I shake my head. "No, I'm just not much of a drinker."

"Oh yeah. I should've remembered that about you." He looks around, as though he wants to say something that isn't overheard. The others have left the table, and Grayson is talking to someone she knows at another table.

He lowers his voice. "So tell me about the Brent Pace case," he says. "How's it going?"

"Your dad hasn't told you?"

He shrugs. "Honestly, my dad and I don't talk that much. We had a falling-out a few months ago, and I don't have a lot to say to the guy."

I'd love to dig further and find out what the falling-out was about, but I can't appear too eager. "That's too bad when you're about to get married and all."

"My mom will make him come to the wedding. But we don't just sit around and hang out, you know? Last I heard through the department grapevine, you guys were bearing down on Casey Cox. And then all that stuff in Dallas happened."

"Yeah," I say. "We've come close to catching her twice."

"Any leads on where she is now?"

Again, my gut tightens. This could be the question he's waited all night to ask. I shake my head. "Not yet, but I'm gonna find her."

"She's smart, that one," he says. "She's given the old man a run for his money. I love it when that happens."

I'm not buying it. Grayson comes back and reclaims her place between us. "So how is your mom?" I ask Kurt.

"She's fine," he says, and looks off across the room as if retreating into his own thoughts.

Grayson leans forward. "He worries about his mom a lot."

"Why's that?" I ask him.

He turns back to me and shrugs. "I just think my dad should treat her better."

I don't say anything, afraid to tip my hand. Finally, he takes another guzzle out of his beer bottle, sets it down. "He's got a mistress. I found out a few months ago. He's been with her for a few years. He goes on these trips to Dallas, lies to my mother about where he's going. Leaves her home alone. Finally I looked into it and found this woman. She's rich, so she's buying him all these toys."

I frown. He doesn't know that Keegan's the one buying *her* toys, not the other way around.

"Did you tell your mother?" I ask.

"He should have," Grayson says, sweeping her hair behind her ears.

Kurt shakes his head. "No, man. I couldn't break her heart like that. I just told my dad that I knew. I guess I hoped it would knock some sense into him, make him realize he was about to lose everything. But nothing's changed. He's still out of town a lot."

"Wow," I say, trying to keep things light. "I'd hate to be at your Thanksgiving dinners."

Kurt laughs a little. "They never were that much fun to begin with."

I'm not quite ready to let it go. "I always thought you guys were close. You followed in your dad's footsteps, became a cop . . . right?"

"But you know my granddad — my mom's dad — was a cop too. My uncles. In fact, that's probably why my dad went into

86

it in the first place. I keep telling myself that I'm following in *their* footsteps, not his."

His distaste for his father seems real, but I'm still aware he could be playing me.

He changes the subject as some of the guys come back from the pinball machines, and there's a lot of laughter and nostalgia as we talk about memorable football trips.

After a couple more hours, the guys leave one by one, until it's just Kurt and Grayson and me left.

"There's my dad's partner," Kurt tells Grayson. "Detective Rollins." I turn and see Sy slumped on a barstool. "That means Dad's probably not too far behind," Kurt says. "Maybe it's time for us to go."

They pay their tab and get up to leave. When we've said our goodbyes, I go slip onto the barstool next to Rollins. "How you doing, man?"

Rollins squints his eyes and focuses on me. "Man, are you stalking me or what? I can't go to a bar without you turning up."

"Nah, I was just here meeting some buddies. Saw you come in."

He orders another drink, offers me one, and I order another Coke. I'm gonna be up until next Tuesday with all this caffeine in my system, but it's worth it.

"I'd sure like you better if you drank with

me," he broods.

"Then who would drive you home?" I ask.

He's in a sour mood, so I settle in, hoping he'll expose something as he falls deeper into his stupor.

11

Dylan

Rollins drinks two more rounds while I'm sitting next to him, and when he decides to leave, I don't know if it's because he's had enough or because I'm getting on his nerves. My guess is he was already soggy all the way through when he got to the bar, because with his tolerance, four drinks wouldn't have put him over the top. But now he can hardly make it to the door.

I pay my tab and follow him out, watch as he goes to the wrong car and tries to get the key to turn. I watch him over my car's roof as he fumbles around, confused. Finally, I go over to him. "Can I help you, man?"

"My key won't open it," he mutters.

"I don't think this is your car."

I take his key fob and hold it over the roof, click the panic button. His horn beeps and his lights start flashing across the parking lot. "It's over there."

I put his arm around my shoulders and hobble with him over to his car. He gets the door open this time and slides behind the wheel. Part of me wants to let him go and hope he winds up in a ditch. The other part doesn't want him to cause an eight-car pileup on the road home.

"Let me drive you home, man."

"No, I need my car," he says.

"But I really don't think you ought to be driving. Remember the DUI? It would really get you into trouble with the department." Ignoring me, Rollins tries to get his key in the ignition but he can't quite find the slit.

I reach in and take his keys from him. "Come on, man. I'll drive you home in my car and you can hire Uber to bring you tomorrow to pick yours up."

Rollins doesn't seem to have the strength to fight me. When I tug on his arm, he comes out of the car and allows me to hold him up again as we walk to mine. I put him in the passenger seat and hurry around to the driver's side.

He's almost asleep when I start the car, but I don't want that. I want him to chatter. I nudge him awake. "Seat belt, man," I say. He clumsily reaches for the seat belt and I help him click it into place. "So you seem to be in a sour mood," I say as I start the car. "What's wrong?"

"Just a terrible week," he slurs. "Keegan's out of control . . . and he won't listen to me."

I'm quiet, hoping he'll go on, but he doesn't. "Have you ever thought of asking for a different partner?"

"No way, man," he says. "He's like the Hotel California. You can never leave."

I get the gist. Getting involved with Keegan is something you don't escape from. You're either in with him or you're the enemy. "I've never understood why people kowtow to him," I say carefully. Rollins seems to sober up at the thought and he looks out the window. "He have something on you?"

The minute the words are out of my mouth, I wonder if I've gone too far. Rollins looks at me, more clarity in his eyes. "He makes you do things you wouldn't normally do."

When he's silent again, I pretend I don't understand the gravity of what he's just said. "Pushes you out of your comfort zone?"

He lets it go at that, just nods his head. I keep my eyes straight ahead, praying he'll go on, but instead I hear him snoring.

I let him sleep until we get to his house.

I'd like to get inside there, see what I can see, so I take him out of the passenger seat and walk him to the door. The garage door is closed, so we go to the front and I grope around for the right key and get the door unlocked. I start to walk him inside but he stops me, wedging himself between me and the front room.

"Thanks, man. Appreciate you bringing me. Don't say anything to Keegan about this, all right?"

"Did I last time?" I ask him.

He shakes his head no. "I'm just saying." He taps my shoulder with a clumsy hand. "You're all right, Dylan." Then he closes the door in my face and I hear the dead bolt locking. I back away, waiting to see if he opens it again, but he doesn't. I wonder if he'll even make it to the bed.

I go back to my car and drive away in silence. *You can check in but you can never leave.* At some point Rollins gave in to Keegan on one of these killings, and now he's in way over his head, doing Keegan's bidding. He knows that if he ever gets caught he'll go to prison for the rest of his life.

Maybe it didn't start out that way. Maybe at one point he really wanted to be a decent cop. Now he drinks to cover up the guilt.

If I can keep making Rollins think I'm his

friend, maybe I can make those fears a reality.

12

Dylan

I'm tired when I get home. I won't have trouble sleeping tonight. I feel so good about how much evidence has come together today that I unroll my makeshift whiteboard and hang it back up.

It's hot, so I go to the thermostat and check the AC. It says it's 80 degrees. I turn it down to 72, but the unit doesn't come on. I turn it down lower, make sure it's on AC and not heat, but it's still unresponsive.

Great.

I go to the window and open it, and cooler air does breeze in. Mosquitoes are likely to come with it since there are no screens on my windows. Humidity is already settling over me.

I change into my sleep shorts and drop into bed, wearing my PTSD patch from a clinical study. It helps with my brain waves when I sleep, and when I wear it I don't have as many night terrors. I hope I can shut my mind off tonight.

I drift in and out, but after a while, a swishing sound drags me from REM sleep. I sit up, groggy. It's dark, so I can't see what made the noise, but as I reach for the lamp, I smell a strong gas smell. I switch on the lamp and see that my carpet under the window is wet, and fumes distort the lines of the window.

Gas!

I jump up and lunge for the window when something else flies in, hits the floor, and rolls across my room.

Then I see that it's a grenade.

I dive for the door and get out of the room, fling open the front door, just as the blast throws me off my feet. I hit the concrete breezeway outside my apartment. I'm dazed when I hear the crackle of fire inside.

People. There are people in the apartment below me. Next door. Behind all these doors . . .

Searing pain shoots up my leg until a flame erupts on my shorts. Slapping the flame out, I get to my feet and run into the blinding smoke. I have to get them out.

I yell at the top of my lungs. "Evacuate! Clear the building!"

Coughing, I find my way to the door next

to me, bang on it, then run to the one on the other side of my apartment. "Open up! You have to get out! Fire!"

People are coming out now, and I yell over the railing. "Check on the people below me! Get them out!"

I bang on each door as I run to the staircase and stumble down. Smoke billows out through the shattered window in the apartment below me.

"Help evacuate!" I yell to people stepping out. "Get everybody out!"

The door to the apartment below me looks like it took as much of the blast as mine did. I pull off my shirt, cover my nose and mouth, and tie it around the back of my head to filter my air. Then I get down on my knees and crawl into that place. Fire covers the walls, and the smoke makes it hard to see.

"Anybody in here?" I call out. "Just yell so I can hear you!"

I hear a woman crying, and I crawl toward her. "Where are you?" I yell. "Talk to me!"

"Here," she says, a few feet away from me to my right. The ceiling between her apartment and mine above her has burned through, and the smoke billows upward, but it's still thick here near the floor.

When I touch her, I feel blood on her

arms, her hands, and I doubt she can get out of here on her own. I get to my feet and pull her over my shoulder. She's coughing, and I feel her warm blood down my back.

"Is there anybody else in here?"

"No. God . . . help me."

I get her out the door into less smoky air. The red lights of a fire truck pull into the parking lot. "Over here!" I yell, then I cough my guts out as I stagger toward the ambulance coming behind the truck. "Help!"

Two EMTs appear and take her from me. I've never been so happy to see anyone in my life. The woman's leg looks mutilated and burnt, and her hair is singed on one side. She, too, is coughing, trying to clear her lungs. They get her to the ambulance, then others rush to me.

I double over in a coughing fit. When I can speak, I assure them I'm okay.

"No, you're not," a paramedic says. "You have burns."

"Just get everybody out," I rasp. "There may be others."

Other fire trucks arrive on the scene, and the firefighters take over, hosing the fire and evacuating the building. It doesn't look like anyone else is injured.

As they get me into the ambulance, I wish I could have run behind the building to see if I could catch a glimpse of who threw the gas and grenade into my apartment. Whoever it was is surely gone by now.

As the ambulance carries me away, something inside me sharpens. Keegan is behind this. He must know I've figured him out and that I'm going to expose him.

He wants me dead. All I have to do is stay alive long enough to expose him.

13

Keegan

Rollins is drunk again. When I bang on his door, it takes him a while to wake from his stupor and open it. I walk him to my car and usher him in. He overcompensates for his clumsiness by trying to sit up straighter and talking a blue streak. His speech is slurred, but he enunciates more, as if that sounds natural. He thinks he's got me fooled. He's clearly not aware that his breath reeks and he has a whiskey stain on his shirt, or that he's wet his pants.

"What did you say to him tonight?" I ask as I drive, staring straight ahead into the night.

"Who?" he asks.

"Dylan Roberts. When you saw him at the bar. What did you say to him?"

"Nothing. How do you know — ? I didn't hardly talk to him."

"He drove you home."

99

He turns to me, and his outrage is almost funny. "Were you watching me?"

I don't answer.

"When'd you start watching me?" he has the gall to demand.

"When you became a loose cannon. When I had to start worrying what would come out of your mouth when you drank too much!"

"I didn't drink too much. I'm fine."

"You weren't fine at the bar. You couldn't even drive home."

"Seriously, you got somebody tailing me, or you watching me yourself?"

I stare out the windshield, my jaw set and my molars clenched so tight they ache. I don't owe him an explanation.

"So I'm the enemy now?" he asks. "I'm the one you have to watch?"

I have no intention of answering. My phone rings, so I look down at it. It's the call I've been waiting for. I swipe it on. "Yeah?"

"It's done," the caller says.

"Explosion?" I ask.

"Yeah, it was beautiful. He couldn't have got out."

"Did you make sure?"

"No, man! I got out of there before the cops and fire department came. But trust me, he's dead."

"All right, good work." I click the phone off, and Rollins is still staring at me. "What explosion? What did you do?"

"Dylan Roberts," I say. "He's been in a little accident."

His eyebrows go up, and his voice sounds tighter. "Car bomb? Did you kill him?"

I don't want to correct him, because it doesn't really matter.

I turn onto the dirt road in the thick of the trees, and as a tree branch scrapes the top of my roof, he realizes something's off. "Where are we going, Gordo?"

"I have to show you something."

"What? Where are you taking me? It's the middle of the night."

"You'll see."

Sy gets quiet as we go deeper into the woods. I put my lights on bright, and when I stop, I point through the windshield. "See that?"

He squints. "No, what?"

"Come on. Get out," I say. "I'll show you. You're gonna love this."

He opens his door and gets out, wobbling unsteadily into the headlight beams. I meet him, trying to walk with a jaunt in my step so I don't tip him off. As I walk, I draw my

Glock and keep it down so he doesn't see it.

He takes a few steps forward, sees the pit I came out here earlier to dig . . . big enough for a body.

"Somebody in there?" he asks me, turning.

He sees my weapon, my barrel only a couple of feet from his forehead. His arms come up. "Come on, Gordo. Not me. I'm on your side."

"You're sloppy," I say. "I can't have you out there drunk all the time. You're a liability to me."

"But you can't. You won't —"

I pull the trigger, cutting off his words. He falls back, partially into the grave. I step forward, staying clear of the blood, and kick him the rest of the way in. Then I walk back to my car and get the shovel out of the trunk. I shovel the mound of dirt over him, covering his face first. He's not dead yet. I watch him inhale the dirt through his nostrils, making two little divots shift in the dirt. I shovel another mound over his face, then thrust the blade into his throat. I step on it, using my weight to finish him off.

Satisfied that he's out, I cover his arms, then his legs. Before covering his torso, I thrust the shovel into his ribs a few times just for good measure. He doesn't flinch. Yeah, he's definitely gone.

When he's covered completely, I spread leaves over the grave.

I toss the shovel back into my trunk. I dust off my shoes, then swipe my hands together to get the dirt off. I slide back into my seat, feeling the adrenaline pulsing through me. It's the best high I've ever felt. Grinning, I look in my rearview mirror and back out.

When I'm on the street, I turn the radio on. Buddy Holly is playing, and I sing along to "Peggy Sue" as I head home.

14

Dylan

I can't stop shaking as I sit on the bed in the ER, grinding my teeth with the pain while I wait for a doctor to evaluate the burns on my calves and thighs. I don't have time for this. I need to go back to the apartments and look for any clues that might have been left behind. Though two or three cops have come by to check on me, and a couple are still in the waiting room, they haven't been able to give me any information about any clues left behind.

I've given my story to the police, but I didn't tell them who I'm sure is behind it. Until I can prove it, they wouldn't believe me and my story would blow up in my face.

The burns on my legs are minimal compared to the wounds of the woman I got out of the apartment below me. They've airlifted her to the burn center. This wouldn't have happened to her if it weren't for me. Once again, I'm the survivor who's barely injured, and someone else is fighting for life.

"Are you kidding me?"

I look up to see Dex in the doorway. "Hey."

"What happened?" he demands to know. "I saw the fire on the ten o'clock news. Went by there and saw it was your place that was blown out." He rubs his mouth with his good hand. It's trembling. "Dude, I thought you were dead."

"Nope. Not me."

He looks at my burns, shakes his head. "Seriously, what happened?"

I sigh and try to think. "First my AC was out, so I opened my window. I never open my window. It's too humid and there's no screen. I don't remember the last time I opened it." I try to move my leg, but I wince in pain.

"Yeah, and?"

"Someone was outside my window, sloshed gas in."

"You're on the second floor."

"Yeah, they must have used a ladder. They probably knocked out my AC so I'd open the window. The sound woke me up. I was just headed for the window to look out when a grenade came flying in."

"A grenade?" Dex comes toward me. "Man, how did you survive?"

"I got out the door. Didn't get away completely unscathed. Then the woman below me . . . She was badly burned. I got her out . . ."

Dex turns away for a moment, and I can't see his face. Finally, he turns back. "So whoever did this was preying on your PTSD. A grenade?"

"Yeah. A literal blast from the past."

"That's not even funny."

"No, it's not. Sorry."

He doesn't hold it against me. "Man, if a grenade came flying at me, I'd have lost it."

"I did lose it."

"But you acted, man, just like you did that day in Kandahar. You saved people."

"One person. And she may not make it."

"That day you saved more, Dylan. You know you did. You saved me."

I don't really want to hear that right now. "I just need to get out of here. How bad do these burns look?"

Dex was a medic in the army, and he treated all kinds of burns. He looks them over. "Bad enough to need dressing. What's your big hurry? You don't have anyplace to crash."

That's true. Where will I go? "I lost my

phone. My computer. The evidence I'd compiled. It's all blown up."

"No, it's not," he says. "Remember, you have a lot of it in the safe deposit box. I can help you re-create the rest. And you took pictures, right? Aren't they on the cloud somewhere?"

That's true. I e-mailed them to Casey. That makes me feel better. I wish I could call her now, but I don't know her burner phone's number. I had it programmed into mine, and now it's collateral damage. I'll need to e-mail her after I get another phone. She needs to know how desperate Keegan is getting, even if she won't talk to me.

"You're coming home with me, man."

I shake my head. "No, I can't barge into your place. Your wife, your kids . . . I'll get a hotel. It's fine."

"Do you even have a credit card with you? Any cash?"

I sigh. "No. I was sleeping. My wallet was on the dresser. I'll have to wait till morning to go to the bank and get another card. And a driver's license."

"Then you can't get any cash out tonight. You have no choice, Pretty Boy. You're coming with me."

He's right. I should be grateful he came. "It may be a while," I say.

"Lay down, dude," he insists. "I've got all the time in the world."

15

Dylan

I've met Dex's wife, Shannon, a couple of times, but I'm not sure how she'll receive me when Dex brings me home. He apparently called to tell her I was coming, and she greets me with a careful hug. The smell of brownies wafts across their small house, even though it's four in the morning.

"I made comfort food," she says. "I hope you like brownies."

"It's the middle of the night," I say. "You shouldn't have gotten up. I hope I'm not putting you out."

"You saved my husband's life, Dylan," she says, tears glistening in her eyes. "There is nothing you could do that would put me out."

I've always liked her. I know she and Dex have had their issues, but she seems like an angel.

"Thanks for taking me in, Shannon. Once

I get my debit card replaced, I'll get a hotel until I can go back home."

"You don't need a hotel, dude," Dex says. "You need a new apartment."

"I saw the fire on the news," Shannon says. "If that blast area was your apartment, you're not going back there."

"Nobody in that building is going back there for a while," Dex says. "I'm sure the wiring is toast even in the apartments that weren't touched."

Weary, I lower to the couch, squeezing my eyes shut with the pain.

"Here, put your feet up," Shannon says, offering me a pillow. "I'll bring the brownies. You want some decaf?"

"No, thanks." I lift my feet to the coffee table.

"You're sleeping in Jared's room. You must be exhausted."

"I can sleep on the couch. Really, I don't want to displace anybody."

"Are you kidding? I've already moved him to our bed. He's zonked out, so don't give it another thought. You're sleeping in Jared's bed so you'll be more comfortable."

Her insistence moves me, and I decide not to fight it. I eat the brownies, surprised at how comforting comfort food really is. In my family, food was fuel, but most of the time we had to fend for ourselves. I eat at least four, letting the sugar energize me.

Eventually, Shannon goes to bed, and Dex shows me where the bathroom is and points me to the room where I'll sleep.

"Go to bed, man," I say. "I'm fine. You've done enough for me tonight."

"I will. But if you can't sleep, wake me up. We can watch a movie or something."

I don't know if I'll sleep, but I wouldn't wake him up for anything.

I go lie down on the twin bed and stare up at the ceiling. I would really like to talk to Casey tonight, but I don't have her number. It would be good to hear her voice, to talk through this with her. She is comfort for me like the brownies, but it's a comfort I can't have right now.

I hope she's all right.

I wonder what she would be like as a wife. Would she be like Shannon, welcoming my hurting friends as if they're family, making brownies, fussing around to make sure they feel welcome? Yes, somehow I think she would be.

I close my eyes and ask God to forgive me for my ingratitude at surviving again. I thank him for saving me tonight, for waking me up and giving me a window of time to get out of that apartment before the blast, and for helping me get to the woman in the apartment below me. I pray for her, that God will heal her and comfort her tonight.

Then I pray for Casey, that as she stands on the precipice of faith, she would understand the height and depth and width and breadth of God's love for her.

And mine too.

Love is a striking word that I don't use often. I haven't thought of it in relation to Casey Cox until now. But it occurs to me as my adrenaline fades after a close call with death, that love is just what I feel for her. I've never felt quite this way about another human being. But what if it's just the pressure and the intensity of our relationship that makes me feel that way?

I ask God to give me a chance to know her without the threat of death hanging over her. I ask him to give me the opportunity to get to know her under boring conditions, to see if anything is really there. I ask him to let me be a blessing and an example to her, whatever happens between her and me.

Tomorrow I'll get a new phone and e-mail her my new number. The craving for her voice aches through me.

I fall asleep and dream of us at the deer camp where I helped Dex treat her gunshot wound. The touch of her face on my fingertips, the feel of her lips when I kissed her . . .

Unbelievably, I sleep deeply, undisturbed by my burns or the PTSD flare-up I would have expected after what happened tonight. Just thoughts of Casey — the comfort food to my mind. Better even than brownies.

16

Dylan

The next morning I go to the bank and replace my debit card. They are able to print it so that I can use it immediately. I also go by the DMV to get a new driver's license. Then I head to my cell phone store and replace the phone that everyone knows about for the third time in a matter of weeks. I follow that by getting a burner phone at the drugstore. I activate it right away.

I wrestle with whether I should call Keegan to update him, but I decide to bag the idea. I can't make myself do it.

I drive back to my apartment, and I'm struck again by the level of damage. There's still a fire truck there, and firefighters hosing smoldering embers. I get out of my car and stand in the parking lot looking up, wondering if they would let me go in. I doubt there's much I could salvage.

Instead I walk around to the back of the building. There's a ladder lying on the charred grass under my window. As I get closer I can see that they've dusted it for prints.

I take a step closer to the building and study the ground for footprints. After all the water that was sprayed at the building, the dirt is mud now, but I walk to where it's still dry. Nothing.

I finally give up on finding prints and go back to my car. I sit there for a moment, trying to imagine what might have happened last night. Keegan knows I'm on to him. If he suspected that I was about to take him down, he would take me out first. That's what last night was about.

I wonder if Rollins got drunk because he knew it was happening.

17

Casey

I miss talking to Dylan. It's as if he's been a vital part of my days for decades, even though I've spent so little time with him. I ache with the need to resolve my case so I can go back to seeing him. But I still won't let myself talk to him, and his calls have fallen off. I get on the Internet and go to the local news site to see what new things they're saying about me that might not have been picked up on the national news cycle. Tonight I'm the lead story again on Channel 3. They're rehashing the indictment and why it's taking police so long to find me.

Then the anchor says, "In a related story . . . ," and launches into the coverage of a fire at a local apartment building last night. I watch the footage to see if anyone I know lives there. I recognize the apartments. I used to drive past them on the way to work.

But ,ow are they related to my investiga-

"Fire officials say that the fire was caused an explosion in the upstairs apartment ,f a local veteran who works as a private investigator. Sources told us that he's working with police on the Brent Pace murder case . . ."

I catch my breath and stumble to my feet. *Dylan?* Is that where *he* lives?

I listen for them to say if he was injured, but somehow I've missed it. I back it up and play the video again, and the word *explosion* reverberates through my mind. I back it up again. Was Dylan killed? When did this happen? Last night? Today?

Apparently it was in the wee hours of this morning, and it says that two people were injured, including the veteran who lived there.

I stumble to my purse, grab my phone out, and click on his number. It rings until a voice says that the person I'm trying to call hasn't set up his voice mail. I text, but get a message that it's undeliverable.

Was the phone burned up in the fire? Is he suffering in a hospital?

I consider calling his regular phone, but I don't know the number, and even if I had it, it could get him into terrible trouble. I

117

dial the local hospital closest to his apartment and ask if Dylan Roberts is a patient there. They tell me he isn't.

Tears assault me. Why did I dodge his calls for the last couple of days? I get on my e-mail, hands shaking, and type him a message.

Dylan, I just heard about the fire. Please call me. I'm praying you're okay.

I hit Send and wait to hear back, but an hour passes, then two, and I don't hear from him.

I've never felt more helpless. I have an overwhelming urge to call his friend Dex or my sister Hannah, but my better reasoning wins out and I don't do it.

Calm down, Casey, I tell myself. *Get a grip. Don't do anything stupid. He'll call. He has to.*

I navigate to another local news station and watch their footage of the fire. I hear that the downstairs neighbor suffered severe burns, but that Dylan's condition is unknown.

"Fire department inspectors are telling us that they do suspect foul play. We're told that a device was thrown through the resident's window, and its explosion caused this fire to erupt and destroy most of the building."

I'm sick, so I run to the bathroom and sit on the floor. Someone threw a bomb through his window? It had to be Keegan or one of his partners. And they'll try again.

Dylan probably doesn't have either of his phones. Everything he owns was probably burned in the fire.

What if Dylan's dead? No, he couldn't be. They would have said that. They just said the neighbor was badly injured, not Dylan. Could it be that he escaped the blast? *God, please!*

I can't stand it, so I call that number again. It still doesn't go through.

I check my e-mail, but he hasn't answered. I have to do something.

There's no one I can call, but I pack my bag, check out of the motel, and head south to Louisiana. If I don't hear from him by the time I get there, I'll have to do something drastic.

18

Dylan

When I call Dex to let him know I've replaced my phone, he says, "Listen, have you seen Detective Rollins today?"

"Last night I did. I told you I drove him home from a bar before my apartment fire."

"Interesting," he says. "I'm taking what happened to you personally, man, so I decided to tail Keegan and see what him and his buddy are up to. Off the clock. No charge."

"I'll pay you," I say. "I appreciate that."

"No, it's on me. But here's the thing. Rollins is nowhere around. So I leave Keegan and go by Rollins's house, and his car's not home. Since you said he was drunk last night, I went by the bar and his car's still there."

"He's probably hung over. Hasn't gotten it yet."

"I'm just thinking it's weird that they're

not together after the bombing. I get the feeling Keegan is looking for you. He's been to a lot of hotel parking lots, driving through looking for something . . . probably your car. But if Rollins is involved too, wouldn't he be trying to help?"

"Maybe he's not involved."

"Maybe. So you need a place to crash again tonight?"

I smile. It's good to have friends. "No, thanks. I'm gonna get a hotel. I got my debit card replaced, so I have some cash now. Thanks for the heads-up, though. I'll use our friend's method to get a room." I deliberately don't use Casey's name, just in case someone's listening via Dex's phone. "Pay cash and claim my wallet got stolen."

"Dude, you know he won't be looking for you at my house. Don't you think that's safer?"

"No, I don't. I don't want to keep your family in this mess. And I can stay under the radar."

"What about your burns? I can change the bandages."

"With one hand? No, I'm good, Dex. I can do it."

"So what about Rollins? You want me to keep watching?"

"Yeah, if you will. You're officially on the

clock now. Let me know when he sticks his head out."

I spend the morning filing a claim on my renter's insurance. My deductible is huge, so I go ahead and buy another computer — which I can't do without — and spend a couple of hours downloading my files from the cloud. My next stop is the bank where I have my safe deposit box, and I load my newest files onto the thumb drive that's stored there. Then I lock it back up.

Once I get in touch with Casey, I'll get her to send the pictures of my evidence sheet back to me.

While I have a wifi signal, I open Yahoo and go to our e-mail account, where I see the message she sent me today. She's heard about it on the news. My heart sinks. I didn't want her to find out this way.

I write back: I'm fine. Phone gone. Got a new one but don't have your number.

I find a motel and park my car at a restaurant a block away. Then I check my e-mail again. She's written back with her number. Please call! I'll answer this time.

Relief floods over me, and I smile.

As I walk to the motel, I program in her number, then click on it.

She must be holding her phone, because

she answers the second it rings. "Are you okay?"

Her voice is a gift that soothes my soul. "Yeah, just a few minor burns. Are you okay?"

"No! I almost had a heart attack when I saw the news on the website. Dylan, what happened?"

I tell her the whole thing. "I'm fine, really. I had a lot to replace today, and I'm staying under his radar. You don't need to worry."

She expels a long breath. "Dylan . . ."

The care in her voice melts me. I could get used to it. "My neighbor below me got the worst of it. She didn't have any warning at all."

"So you're the hero who saved her?"

"Hero is a stretch since she wouldn't have been injured if not for me."

"Keegan? Did he do this? Rollins?"

"Not Rollins. He was drunk. I delivered him to his door last night. No, it was a risky operation, so it was probably someone they hired. Probably thought sure they'd killed me."

"Did you go to the hospital? Did you have your burns treated?"

"Yes. Dex stayed with me all night. I'm fine. I have some dressings, but —"

"Dylan, they tried to kill you!" Her voice

123

is on the edge of panic. "You understand that, don't you?"

"Of course I do. Things are getting intense here. But I'm hiding."

"No! You have to get out of there," she cries. "You need to leave town!"

"I can't," I say. "I'm so close to having everything I need. There was another murder. One of Keegan's extortion victims. His wife told me he failed to make a payment to Keegan and Rollins. They threatened him. That ties Keegan to more than extortion. It connects him to murder. And now the grenade and the fire — I still have to find a way to link them to that. If I leave town, nothing will happen."

"This is enough!" she cries. "I don't want you dead! I can't take any more people I care about being murdered!" She's crying now, almost hysterically, and I wish I were there to hold her and reassure her. I know the full force of the other deaths is slamming her now. Her father, Brent, even Cole Whittington . . . The trauma of those deaths multiplies her worry about the attempt on my life.

"I'm not dead," I tell her. "Casey, I want you to breathe. Count to twenty. Breathe in . . . and out . . ."

I don't know if she's breathing with me or

not. There's silence, and I wonder if I've lost the connection, or if she thinks I'm being condescending.

"We're so close to this," I say in a steady voice. "I have to get them. I promise you, if it looks like things are getting too dicey, I'll take it to the DA before taking a big risk. But if we wait just a little longer, if I dig a little deeper, we can connect the dots from them to all of these murders. It can happen, Casey. You'll be able to come home. You'll have your life back."

I hear her sniffing, and finally she says, "Having my life back won't mean that much if you're not in it."

My heart jolts at the reality of that. The confession anchors me. "I feel the same," I whisper.

"I want to come there. I want to help."

"Stay," I tell her. "Wherever you are, just stay there. I'll let you know when it's okay to come. Just trust me now. And trust God. He was with me when that grenade came in, and he's with me now."

"I do trust him," she says, her voice calming. "I've been reading the Bible. It's fascinating. I don't understand it all, so I bought a study Bible with a lot of notes and stuff in it, and it helps explain things."

"That's good. Old or New Testament?" I ask.

"Both. I read from the Old for a while, and then the New. Yesterday I read all of Genesis and last night I read Matthew."

"That's a lot of reading."

"Yeah, but I honestly can't put it down. And I found all these preaching videos on YouTube."

I hesitate to ask. "So would you call yourself a believer yet?"

She pauses. "I believe, but I'm counting the cost. That's biblical, right? Jesus said to do that."

My heart sinks a little. "Yeah, he did."

"It's just that, to whom much is given, much is required."

I smile. "So now you're quoting Scripture to me?"

"The minute I surrender," she says, "I'll have to repent. That guy, the one who wore potato sacks and ate wild locusts . . ."

"John the Baptist?" I ask. "I think he wore camel's hair."

"Yeah. That guy. He said something that kind of hit me like a baseball bat. He said to perform deeds in keeping with repentance. Repenting means I'll have to come back there and turn myself in. But I won't live through that. It's certain death."

126

"You can give your life to Christ and repent without running into bullet fire right away."

"Can I? Is that what Christians in hostile countries do? When they know they could be murdered for converting? Don't they immediately put themselves in harm's way, just by professing their belief?"

I don't quite know what to say. "Where did you hear that?"

"On a video. A missionary talking about the persecution of Christians and how dangerous his work is. I think it's going to be kind of like that for me. I mean, I live in a free country where I won't be murdered for openly going to church. But my decision to believe dictates repentance, and repentance will put me in danger. So how do I reconcile that?"

I want to tell her that making an eternal decision like that will be worth whatever the cost is, but I don't want her to come back here and be killed. Maybe my own faith isn't that strong. Finally, I'm only able to say, "I pray for you, Casey, all the time. Let God dictate the timing, not fear."

When we hang up, I feel like I've been given a dose of one of those benzo drugs my doctors are always trying to prescribe for me. Talking to Casey makes me feel like

I can do this, finish this, defeat this.

I check in to the motel under the name of Baxter Jones. When I get to my room, I pull out the bandages I bought at the drugstore and change my dressings, fighting the pain. I lie on the bed and mentally replay Casey's phone call.

Her caring for me is nothing short of a God thing. He's still working in my life. I see him. It assures me that he cares about me too.

19

Dylan

I sleep until Chief Gates calls me and asks me to come in to talk to him about the bombing, and I'm suddenly suspicious that I'm walking into a trap. When I arrive at the station late in the afternoon, I see Keegan's car in the parking lot, and I can't wait to see how he plays this. Rollins's car isn't here.

I feel a little sick as I walk up the long hall to the chief's office — trying not to limp — and when I step inside, I see through the secretary's area that Keegan is sitting across from the chief's desk. I clench my molars so hard the muscles of my jaws ache.

"Mr. Roberts, he's waiting for you. Go on in."

My mouth feels dry and my throat constricts as I step into Chief Gates's doorway and see that Captain Swayze is there too. Chief sees me first. "Dylan, come on in. Have a seat, man."

I shake his hand and don't bother to shake the other two as I lower to the chair closest to the door. I can't even feign normalcy.

"How you doing, man?" the chief asks. "You okay?"

"I'm fine," I say stiffly.

"You lose everything?" Keegan asks with a note of joviality in his voice.

I don't look at him. "Nothing that matters."

"What does that mean?" Swayze asks.

His tone makes me wonder if he's in on it. "It means that I made it out. I'm okay with losing stuff."

"What about your injuries?" Gates asks.

"They'll heal," I say.

He looks me over, but he can't see my wounds under my jeans. "Dylan, we're doing everything we can to find the perpetrator. We got some prints from the outdoor AC unit and the ladder they left. We're trying to pull the security footage from businesses around the apartment complex, to possibly catch images of the person driving by. I have detectives working on all those who had access to grenades in the area. We're making some progress. I wanted you to know that."

That's more than I expected. "Who's on the case?"

130

"Steele and Johnson."

"Good," I say.

"I was just talking to Keegan about the Casey Cox case, and wondering if this attack on you could have had anything to do with that."

I keep my gaze locked on Gates. "And what did he say?"

There's a second of silence, then Keegan clears his throat. "I was telling him that it's possible. Maybe she did it herself."

I look at Keegan now. "Where would Casey Cox get a grenade?"

"This girl has resources."

"True," I say. "But this was pretty physical for someone of her size. Carrying a ladder, getting it against the building, carrying a gas can up, tossing the grenade . . . I was thinking it was probably a man. If a woman had all that stuff and was even getting it out of a vehicle, it might call attention. But a man doing it wouldn't."

I know I should modulate my tone, that I might sound too anxious to get their focus off of her, but obviously Keegan knows I'm on to him or the attempt on my life wouldn't have happened. I'm sick of this, and suddenly I don't care if he knows it.

"Again," he says. "She's resourceful. She could have had help. Figured you were closing in on her and wanted to take you out."

I'm dumbfounded that he would go that far, but I stay quiet. "Where you staying, man?" Keegan asks.

"Don't know yet."

"We want to help you find a place," he says, all sympathetic-sounding now. "Rollins and I can do some of the legwork for you."

"Where is he, by the way?" Gates asks. "I left a message, told him to be here."

"No idea," Keegan says. "I've been calling him all morning and he won't return my call. Car's not home, so I don't know where he is."

Dex's suspicion that something is going on with Rollins, coupled with Keegan's "concerns," raises a red flag for me. Keegan knows where Rollins is. Tension pulls at my temples.

"My call to Sy went straight to voice mail," Swayze said. "Maybe one of us should go by his house and check on him."

"Yeah, I'll do it," Keegan says. "Soon as I leave here."

Gates turns back to me. "What can we do for you, Dylan?"

"Find who did this."

"We have to find that girl," Keegan says, like it's settled that Casey threw the grenade. "This is getting old."

132

"It's gone on too long," Chief agrees. "Where are you on that, Dylan?"

"Close," I say. "This slowed me down a little."

The meeting is basically useless, and I feel like Keegan might have been the one to call it, to root me out. I get out to my car before he does, but he's close enough behind me that I don't leave yet. For a few minutes we both just sit there, until he realizes I'm not leaving. Finally, he starts his car and pulls away. I give him a ten-minute head start, knowing he's waiting just up the street to follow me to wherever I'm going so he can finish the job. Maybe Rollins is actually waiting here somewhere too, hidden, ready to follow me when I leave.

I get on my phone and order an Uber to meet me around the corner at a coffee shop. Then I grab my computer bag with every possession I now own, pull on a baseball cap, and walk through the cars to the shop. I order a coffee, and by the time I have it in hand, the car is there.

I have the driver take me to the motel I'll be staying in tonight. I'll come back later to get my car.

Dex calls me a little while later, and I pick up. "Hey, dude. Whatcha got?"

"Rollins is still not up, man. I've been

watching nonstop. Keegan came by and banged on the door, but he didn't wait very long. I'm suspicious, man. Something's happened to that guy. You don't think Keegan did something to him, do you?"

"No, they're too tight. I don't see it."

"Then where could he be? Not showing up at work, not at home . . ."

"Maybe Rollins has a girlfriend. Or a plane, and his own mistress in some other town."

"I'm gonna keep watching. I'm curious now."

"All right. Let me know the minute you find him."

20

Dylan

I'm driving to Rollins's favorite drinking hole to see if his car is still there when my phone chimes. It's Chief Gates. "Hello, Chief?"

"Dylan, have you heard the news yet?" His voice is somber, low.

I hesitate, and my mind instantly goes to Casey. Has something happened to her? "No, what?"

"Sy Rollins is dead."

I suck in a breath and look for a place to pull over. *What?* I half whisper.

"His body was found in a shallow grave a little while ago. Shot through the head."

"Murdered?" I ask. "Wait . . . when? How long has he been there?"

"Probably overnight."

My mind races. "Any leads?"

"We're working on it. Keegan is on the case. He won't leave any stone unturned."

I can't help asking, "You really think that's a good idea? I mean, Keegan is awfully close to things. Shouldn't it be someone more objective?"

"It's personal to him. He's like a dog with a bone. I'm putting another team on it too, but Keegan won't be able to focus on anything else for a while anyway."

I'm silent for a moment, but then I decide to just say what's on my mind. "I took Rollins home from a bar last night. He'd had too much to drink, and I was there with friends. I knew he couldn't drive. But I got him home safely and watched him go in. I don't know how he could have gone out after I left. If he went out again, someone had to come get him. You should get a team over there and check fingerprints on the door. See if there are any clues about who was there after he got home. Maybe he was shot at home and moved."

"Keegan's on it."

I grit my teeth. I don't tell him that Keegan will hide the evidence, that nothing he "uncovers" will ever point to the real killer.

"I do wonder if the fire at your apartment and this murder are related," Gates says. "It did happen on the same night."

A sudden chill shivers up my back at the thought that Rollins was being murdered while I was supposed to be burning to death. Keegan would have framed Casey again, since she's the link between the two of us. It would have been all over the media. He's probably planting another murder weapon as we speak.

My living threw a wrench into his plan, but it won't stop him.

I do feel some relief that Keegan will be distracted from Casey now, but who am I kidding? This is all *about* Casey . . . and me too. Keegan knows exactly who threw the grenade, and he knows who killed Rollins. He may have even done it himself.

"I wanted you to know," Gates goes on. "Just keep working on the Cox case. Keep reporting new findings to Keegan. I'll have to assign him a new partner when things settle down, but that might take a while."

When I get off the phone, I call Dex. "You can stop watching his house," I say. "They found him. Dead." I tell him what Gates told me.

Dex is astonished. "His partner is getting desperate. Dude, you need to watch your back. Can you rent a car?"

"Yeah, might be a good idea."

"And keep using a fake name in hotels. Maybe even let me check you in so they don't have footage of you. I'm telling you, man. That guy is gonna kill you. He knows."

I decide to take him up on it. We meet up, and I give him the cash. He leaves to check me into a motel that's off the beaten path. When he's got the key card, he drives to where I wait in a Walmart parking lot.

"Leave your car here and I'll drive you to a car rental place," he says. I don't know what I'd do without him.

Dex gets me a rental car with his credit card, in case Keegan is tracking mine. He gets the keys to a black Malibu. As I drive away from the place, I begin to worry about Casey. It's unlikely that Keegan knows where she is, which is why he's gotten desperate. She's been smart enough to stay undetected until now. But now he knows about me.

He was tracking my phone a few days ago. He probably realized I was on to him then.

I drive over to the bar where Rollins was last night. His car is right where we left it.

I park and go in, wait to get the attention of the bartender. When he comes to me, I ask if I can see the manager. He calls to the back.

The manager comes out front and I show him my police credentials. "I'm working with the police department on a homicide case," I say. "A man who frequents this bar was found murdered this morning. I need to look through your security video to see if he was with anyone when he left here last night, since his car was left in your parking lot."

He frowns. "You think it was one of my patrons?"

"Maybe," I say.

He looks worried, but leads me to his office. He's got the footage on his computer, and he navigates to it, then gets up, letting me have the chair. I fast-forward through the footage, watching everyone who came out of the bar. I find Rollins's car in the parking lot — and finally I see him coming out, and me helping him. I scan the other cars as I watch myself drive Rollins away. Headlights come on right after we leave, and a car pulls out a few seconds later.

Keegan's car.

My heart racing, I copy that part of the video onto a thumb drive, as well as the part that shows Rollins staggering out and going to the wrong car, then me guiding him toward my car. I have no doubt that this will become an issue. Keegan will use it to paint me as the killer, since I took Rollins home. But my time is pretty much accounted for the whole night of my apartment fire. His obviously isn't.

21

Casey

Back in Memphis in a new motel, I go online to check the *Shreveport Daily News,* looking for any more information about the investigation into Dylan's attack. And then I see it — *Local Police Detective Found Murdered.* I click on the article, and up comes a picture of Sy Rollins.

I suck in a breath. He's dead. One of my tormentors is dead! I touch my heart, not sure how to feel. As much as I wanted him out of my life, the idea of his death doesn't thrill me. I would much rather have watched him suffer through being exposed and embarrassed in front of the world, doing a perp walk in a jumpsuit and flip-flops into the van that transports him to the state or federal prison. I would much rather have known he was incarcerated with people he had locked up, people who might not take things so well.

But death is something I didn't expect. I read the article about how he was found in a shallow grave, shot through the head. There's even a quote by "his partner, Gordon Keegan."

"Detective Rollins was a hero," Keegan says. "I don't know what we're going to do without him." The article goes on to say, "When asked if he had any leads on who might have killed the detective, Detective Keegan answered, 'It could be any number of people who were out to get him because of the investigations he did. We'll narrow them down one by one, and when we find this person — him or her — all the power of the Shreveport Police Department will see that they're brought to justice.' "

I sit back in my chair, aware that he's just implicated me. The press won't need him to call my name. They will run with it themselves. Tears sting my eyes. If Keegan would kill his best friend and closest confidant and his partner in crime, then he's going to kill Dylan too. He's already tried. There is no doubt in my mind he will keep trying.

Dylan needs to get out of town. He should come where I am and stay off the grid with me. I have to get word to him and make a case he can't ignore.

He won't want to. Men like Dylan don't

dwell on the danger to themselves when they can save someone else. They stay in the fight until it's resolved. But I can't let him do that, if I have any pull with him at all.

I pack my bag, clean every surface so I leave no prints, and pull on my wig. As I drive away, I'll call him on his burner phone from somewhere that will ping off a tower I'll soon leave far behind. I'll use every persuasive trick I can think of to convince him.

I step out the front door of the hotel and cross the parking lot. My car is parked at another hotel a block away. I have to hurry.

When I'm halfway across the lot, a siren blares close by. Memphis police cars fly out of nowhere and surround me. I drop my purse and lift my hands over my head as the cops jump out, shielded by their doors, their weapons trained on me.

"Don't move!" one of them orders, his urgent tone suggesting that he's perfectly willing to pull that trigger.

I do as he says and call out, "I'm not armed!"

"On your knees," they yell, staying carefully back from me until I'm down. Someone comes up behind me and orders me to the ground, facedown. I smell the tar of the pavement as he tosses my purse and snaps cuffs onto my wrists behind me.

People come out of the hotel and cluster at the door, some of them filming with their phones. They watch as the police frisk me, making sure I don't have a machine gun down my pant leg or a machete under my shirt.

It's the moment I've feared, the inevitable outcome of my running.

It's the beginning of the end.

22

Casey

Everything has changed. I sit in an interview room that's way too cold, and there's a lock on the door and a guard standing watch outside it. They know I'm Casey Cox, the notorious fugitive who's evaded the law all these months. I'm prepared to tell them the rest of my story, including Keegan's part in it. But they put me in this room and make me wait. They're probably contacting Keegan right now to let him know I'm here.

I drop my face into my hands and pray some more. "Even if I die," I whisper to God, "let the truth get out. Don't let Keegan control the story."

I don't know if I'm talking to God in the right way, but I have learned that Jesus intercedes for me. And I know he'll translate my prayers into what I really need. I pray for Dylan and for Hannah and little Emma, for my mom and Hannah's husband, Jeff, and all my friends who will have to see this played out in the media. And then I pray for the media people, the ones I know and those I don't, who will cover this story. I pray for their curiosity and their doubt, and their determination to dig to the bottom of it. I pray they'll see the good in me, and not just accept Keegan's story at face value. Then I pray for the police detectives who will hear my story, that it will ring true to them. My dad had gut instincts that often served him well. Maybe these detectives do too.

As my heart finds its normal rhythm, I linger in that prayer zone a little longer, dwelling on the privilege of coming to the Creator with my pleas. Finally, I whisper, "Lord Jesus, I believe in you."

Peace washes through me. Though I'm still afraid, I know that he will not make me endure this alone. And I can pray while I'm being interrogated, while I sit in jail, and while I'm being transported to prison.

I can even pray as I'm bleeding to death.

Finally, two new detectives come in. They introduce themselves like we're going to be great friends — Leibowitz and Briar. Leibowitz has a blond buzz cut, and Briar needs a haircut. Briar is carrying a bottle of water. He hands it to me as if it's some sort of peace offering. "Please listen to me," I say, trying to keep my voice steady. "I know you're thrilled to catch me, but I'm telling you, if you know the real story it will change everything. It's not the way it seems."

The detectives exchange glances, and they pull out the chairs and look at me with nothing but patience and calm, as if they want me to believe they're on my side, always will be. But I know better.

"I didn't kill Brent Pace," I say, knowing they're videotaping me and that there are observers on the other side of the glass, watching the murderous fugitive who was finally captured thanks to their skill and hard work. "Brent was killed by two cops — Gordon Keegan and Sy Rollins and whoever works with them. They also killed my father thirteen years ago." I talk fast, trying to get in as much as I can before they interrupt me. "They set me up to find Brent's body, and I tracked blood all over the place because I was in such shock, and I left because I knew there was no way on this green earth that anyone was going to believe me, just like they didn't believe me when I found my father dead — it was ruled a suicide, even though there were clear signs of a struggle."

I stop to catch my breath. Leibowitz leans

up on the table, his eyes fixed on mine. His voice is as calm as a dog trainer trying to calm a rabid dog. "So why don't we just go back to when you found Pace's body?"

"Can we call him Brent?" I say. "Because he was my friend. I didn't call him *Pace.*"

"Tell us about that morning. What you did when you got up."

They're trying to find gaps in my testimony, contradictions prosecutors can use against me in court. "I got up like every other day and I took a shower, dried my hair, put on my makeup and my clothes, and went to work."

"Did you stop anywhere? Did you talk to anyone?"

I try to remember. There's so much about that day I have tried to forget. "I think I stopped at Starbucks and got a coffee and a muffin. I went to work and everyone there saw me. I'm sure they've already checked that out. They know exactly when I left."

"Did you talk to Brent that morning?"

"Yes, and I'm sure that's also common knowledge to everyone working on this case, including Detective Keegan himself. Brent called me that morning and told me that he had found something about my father's case that was going to help me prove he was murdered. He told me I should come by at lunch and he would tell me. He said he was loading the evidence onto a thumb drive for me."

"Did he say what was on it?"

"No, but he said it would help crack my father's case and help me prove what I already knew to be true. And *they* must've been listening. They must've had his phone tapped. When they realized he was on to them, they came and murdered him, then left him for me to find. And they put that knife in my car. It wasn't mine."

My eyes burn with tears, but their expressions are blank.

"But they didn't know Brent had put a thumb drive in the mail to me. I was able to get it a few days later. I learned from a video on the thumb drive that he had interviewed a woman named Sara Meadows, an evidence clerk at the police department. But after Keegan found that file on Brent's computer, she was shot to death. I'm telling you, the more you look into this the more dead bodies you'll find. Most recently, Sy Rollins himself was found dead with a gunshot to the head."

I take a breath and watch them for some sign that they believe me, but I honestly can't tell.

"I know some in the media have suggested

that maybe I did that too," I add, "but I wasn't anywhere near there. I've been going under the name Liana Winters. I've been living at the motel where you found me, and I've been the driver for a woman who's blind, and I've also been working for an attorney here. It wasn't me. Gordon Keegan killed Rollins or had him killed, and he will keep killing because things are getting hot."

Detective Briar stands up, slides his hands into his pockets, and jingles his keys. "So you're telling us that the police department itself is involved in these murders?"

"I know how that sounds," I say. "I'm not suggesting that the entire police department is involved. In fact, I know it's not. My dad was a good cop and there are other good cops there. But I have a lot of evidence. Look in my purse and you'll find that thumb drive. But you have to make sure that Gordon Keegan doesn't get it, and that he doesn't come here to pick me up. I promise you, I wouldn't live to get back to Shreveport and stand trial. But that wouldn't be the end of it. There are others who have this same evidence, who will release it if anything happens to me. Plug it into your computer, please. There's enough there for you to see the truth."

They look at each other, and hope flickers

in my heart. God is working on this too. It's not just me.

"You say that's in your personal effects? The evidence you're talking about?"

"Yes," I say, hopeful. "Please go get it. I tried to tell them when they were booking me, but they took it with everything else I had on me. It has an interview with Sara Meadows, facts about other cops at the time of my father's death who were beaten or threatened. Notes on an interview with the wife of a Shreveport dry cleaner who was murdered just days ago. Things Keegan has bought with the money he's made . . . a whole other life he's living."

Detective Leibowitz leaves the room to go find the thumb drive, and I suddenly second-guess myself. Is there anything on the drive that implicates Dylan? I don't think so, but it does include the pictures of his evidence board. What if there's some metadata on the photo with the location where it was taken? I should have checked that before.

Briar humors me a little longer. I can tell he doesn't know which trail to follow. The one about Brent, the one about my dad, or the one about Keegan.

"Let's go back to the day of Brent's death," he says. "So after you found the body, what did you do?"

I shake my head, not wanting him to focus on Brent and forget about Keegan.

"Look," I say, "you guys have known bad cops. I know you have. They're a blight on the whole force. My father knew of them. I'm just asking you to consider that what I'm saying is *possible.* You don't have to believe me. Just check it out. Everything I'm saying can be corroborated."

There's a knock on the door, and the detective looks up and someone motions to him. He slides his chair back. "I'll be right back."

I know it's going to be a long wait, and I sit there and freeze silently, continuing to pray, hoping they're looking through the files on the thumb drive now.

After an hour or so, a female guard comes in and puts handcuffs on me and leads me to a holding cell. Her search of me is horrifying, but I endure it as if I'm not in my body, as if I'm standing off to the side, looking away as this other person goes through the motions. I can do this, I tell myself. I've been beaten by a psychopathic kidnapper, roughed up by a drug addict who traded his child for a hit, survived having my car rammed, and even been shot. This is easy.

After I go through the degrading process

of booking, they make me change into a jumpsuit and put me into a holding cell alone. It's got a bench but no mattress, and the room is even colder than the interview room. But I'm grateful for a place where I can lie down and think. I don't know what's going on or what will happen next, but I hope Dylan gets word soon that I'm in jail. Best case scenario, he will come for me. Worst case, Keegan will.

And if he does, I'll be dead before we hit the city limits.

23

Dylan

The Paces are broken up about Sy Rollins's death. "Do you think that girl had anything to do with it?" Elise asks me in a voice that seems to have a permanent quiver in it.

I shake my head. "No, I really don't. I think I would have found her if she were back in town."

"But she's good at this," Elise says. "I try to make some sense of it — how a girl like her can do the things she's done — and I just keep coming up with mental illness. How else could anyone do what she did to Brent?"

The haunted look in her pale eyes isn't likely to disappear anytime soon. Nothing I do is going to banish it, but at least she might be less confused when the truth finally comes out.

Jim seems lost inside himself. "If she came out of her hole and killed Rollins, or did that to your apartment, she's more deadly than anybody even thought."

I can't let that stand. "It doesn't fit any part of her profile. I think it was someone else."

"How can you say that?" Elise asks. "She was brutal with Brent. Blowing up a building full of people to go after the men hunting her isn't that much of a stretch."

"I doubt seriously if it's physically possible for her to do either one of these things. I saw Rollins last night, and he was really drunk. Could hardly walk. I don't see any way she could have gotten him out of his house in that condition and taken him somewhere to kill him."

"Rollins drank a lot," Jim says. "I always smelled alcohol on his breath. Sometimes he seemed to stagger. I really didn't have a lot of faith in him to find Cox. It was almost like Gordon Keegan was covering for him, trying to keep him working. That's part of why I hired you. Rollins didn't give me a sense of confidence. I like Keegan and felt like he was on top of things. Maybe Rollins just got himself into trouble with somebody. A drug dealer or a bookie or something."

That's a theory I hadn't expected Jim to come up with, but I don't reply.

"We're glad you're still on the case,

Dylan," Elise says. "We need you now more than ever. It's worth every penny."

When they write me another check, I feel a surge of remorse. But I quickly shove the guilt back. I'm going to make sure Brent's killer gets justice. That's ultimately what they've hired me to do. And if they feel deceived after it's all over, somehow I'll pay back everything they've paid me.

I'm back in my car when my phone chimes, and I glance at the readout. It's Chief Gates. I swipe it on. "How ya doing, Chief?"

"Good, Dylan," he says. "I have some news for you. It's about Casey Cox."

I step on my brakes and pull over into a random parking lot. My gut hitches into a knot. "What is it?"

"She was just captured by Memphis PD."

I draw in a sharp breath. "She what? Are they sure it's her?"

"Positive. Someone saw her at a hotel and called it in. She was disguised, but since her arrest she's admitted who she is."

I'm dumbfounded, and I can't even speak. "You there?"

I put my car in park. "Yeah. I'm just . . . stunned." I rub the sweat beads on my upper lip and realize my hand is shaking. I'm glad he can't see me.

"There's something you should know. She's telling the Memphis detectives that Gordon Keegan and Sy Rollins are the ones who killed Brent Pace, that they also killed her father, that Keegan killed Rollins and burned your building . . . Basically, that Keegan's Jeffrey Dahmer reincarnated."

Good. She's told them. I want to ask if they believe her, if they're taking it seriously, if an investigation is under way. Instead, I say, "Really? She said that?"

"Yeah. She's claiming she's got some things in place where this will be released to the press. I just wanted you to know since she may try to convince you of it too."

"Okay. Are you going to investigate her claims?"

He chuckles. "Claims that one of my best detectives is a serial killer? Come on, Dylan."

My mind is racing. "I'm just saying, Chief — the press will want to know if you checked it out. In today's media climate, they're not going to treat it as a false claim. It's sensational. It'll dominate the news cycles for days. Maybe you could question her some more and see what evidence she's offering."

"They said she gave them a thumb drive. They're e-mailing me the files."

"Treat it seriously," I warn him. "If the press gets the files too, and you have to assume that they will, they'll expect you to have looked into them. Just see what the evidence is so you can talk about it."

"Yeah, I will. Honestly, I don't know if she's crazy or if she sincerely believes this."

"What matters is what the press will believe, right?" I know that's not true. The truth really does matter. But I need to keep him at arm's length, since I don't know whether he's in on this whole thing with Keegan. "Let me know when you get that stuff," I say. "I'd like to know what's in the files."

"Will do," he says.

"Have you told Keegan she's been apprehended?"

"Not yet. I don't look forward to telling him what she's saying. Plus his best friend is dead. His head is bound to be in that case instead of this one."

"Any way I can get clearance to go get her?"

"That's not a good idea," Gates says.

"But like you said, Keegan is distracted. I'm the most available person. You know I can do it."

"You're not on the force."

"Then put me on the payroll for a few days."

There's silence as he seems to think it over. Then he sighs. "Maybe that's the best idea. All right. I'll draw up the paperwork. Come by the office."

I hang up, so relieved I can hardly breathe. But it frustrates me that Gates isn't even considering Casey's claims. Then again, I could be just jumping to conclusions. Of course he wouldn't immediately trust the claims of a woman he thinks is a killer. And the fact that he took my advice and is sending me instead of Keegan looks good for his innocence.

How will Keegan react? He won't want me to transport her. He'll want to do it himself. He's not knee-deep in grief, as he wants people to believe. And he can't let Casey keep talking. She might make sense.

I'd better get to Memphis as fast as I can. Driving's too slow. I call the airport's charter service and learn there's a corporate plane departing for Nashville in an hour. They tell me I can hitch a ride and they'll drop me off in Memphis. They charge me twice what I've had to pay before, but to protect Casey's life I'll pay whatever it takes. I book it and pray that we depart on time, before Keegan has the chance to beat me there.

Before going to the airport, I stop by the police department to sign payroll paperwork and get quickly sworn in. It's not how I wanted to come to work here, and the chief lets me know not to count on this. It's just temporary.

All I need is one day to get Casey.

24

Keegan

I make sure my mourning for my good buddy Sy Rollins looks authentic, and that lots of my colleagues see my grief. When Chief Gates comes up to my office personally, I expect him to give me a hug, like I'm inconsolable. He stops short of that, and instead just pats my shoulder.

"You doing all right?"

"Sure, Chief. You didn't have to come up here to check on me. I'm doing fine."

"You could take some time off, you know. You've had quite a blow."

I look down at the floor, as though I'm on the verge of crying like a little girl. "No way," I say. "I have work to do. I'm not taking off."

He seems moved by my determination. "Can we sit down?" he asks.

"Sure." I gesture toward the chair across from my desk, and he slides it back a bit and lowers himself into it. I sit down in my rolling chair and cross my legs. My foot is more jittery than I'd like, but I hide it under my desk. "What's up, Chief?"

"Keegan, I've got some news," he says in a low voice. I lean in so I can hear him. "I just got a call from the Memphis Police Department."

"Oh yeah? About what?"

"Casey Cox is in custody."

My heart screeches. "Are you kidding me?"

"Nope. Someone saw her in a hotel and called it in."

I get to my feet and look around my desk for my phone, then realize it's in my pocket. "I'll head out right now."

"No, no," he says. "I'm sending Roberts to transport her. I want you to stay here. You have the funeral and everything."

I feel the heat rising to my face, my ears. "Chief, this is big. It's my case. Sy would want me to finish what we started. I have to get her!" He just stares at me, and my mind flits around, trying to hit on a solid thought. "Are they sure it's her? Not just some crackpot trying to get their fifteen minutes?"

"It's her. They sent us her mug shot. She looks just like herself except her hair is dark, but we knew that. Fingerprints match. It's her."

I wonder if she's talked, what she's said, if she's poisoned my well just yet. "Has she confessed?"

"No," he says, and he looks away as if he doesn't want to tell me quite everything. My gut twists, and I know with certainty that she has mentioned my name. I have to get there as soon as I can.

"She's just denying her involvement. Gordon, Roberts is already on his way."

I want to knock something over. "Are you kidding me? She's an escape artist. She's escaped from *him* before! Are you seriously telling me that you trust him with her? A guy who's not even on the force?"

"I hired him."

"You *what*?" I'm sweating now, but I hope he doesn't notice. "Look, Chief, I've been working on Rollins's case, and something has come to my attention that I haven't told you yet. I was waiting until I had more, but if you're sending Dylan, you need to know."

He frowns, deep lines gashing into his forehead. "Know what?"

"The last person to see Sy alive was Dylan Roberts. He drove him home from a bar. I'm not saying he killed him . . . or maybe I am. We just don't know. But it at least has to be considered."

"No, it doesn't. Roberts had an attempt on his own life last night. His apartment burned down."

"So maybe he killed Sy when he took him home, before that happened. Or maybe he thought Sy tossed the grenade and he went to confront him. I don't know, Chief, and that's why I haven't told you before now. I need to dig further. But if you're sending him to pick up a known murderer who has evaded capture for months now, and has even escaped miraculously *from him,* you need to know that this is an issue. It's very possible that he had something to do with Sy's death."

The chief just stares at me, then he gets to his feet and rakes his fingers through his hair. I note the confusion in his eyes, as if he doesn't know which way to turn. I just need to push harder.

"Call Dylan Roberts off. Let me go."

"But I've already let Memphis know he's the one coming."

"Call them back. You gotta let me do this, Chief."

He looks even older now than he did moments ago. "She claims you're the killer. She says she has evidence against you. She has this whole story about your part in all these murders."

"What?" I say, acting shocked. "Come on. They gotta be laughing that off. It's ludicrous. We're not going to let a known killer call the shots, are we?"

He slides his hands into his trouser pockets, and I can tell I've really confused him. So I double down. "Chief, she's a con artist and a killer, and Dylan may be involved in Sy's death. I have reason to believe that he's been helping her all this time. That he let her walk away in Shady Grove. We're wasting time here, Chief. You gotta let me go. I have a buddy with a plane, and I can get him to fly me over. I can have her back here tonight. Then we can sort all this out."

He finally lets out a hard sigh. "All right, Gordon," he says. "I'll make some phone calls. I'll call Roberts off."

"Tell the Memphis PD I'm not really the bogeyman."

He gives me a weak smile.

"Don't worry, Chief. Once all her crimes come out, nobody is going to believe she's innocent." I grab my jacket, shrug it on as Gates leaves the room.

As I walk out, someone says, "Where you going?"

I turn back with a Cheshire cat grin. "I'm going to get me a cute little homicidal maniac," I say, and I march out and down the stairs.

25

Keegan

I cut corners on my preflight checklist, something a pilot is never supposed to do. But I've got to get my plane to Memphis to pick up Cox before Dylan gets there. Takeoff takes too long, but I have to wait for the air traffic controller to give me clearance to take the runway.

When I'm finally airborne, I try to decide what I'll do once I get her. I have no intention of bringing her back, on my plane or otherwise. I'll rent a car when I get there, take her from the Memphis jail as if I'm transporting her back, and then do what I have to do to silence her. She can't ever make it back to Shreveport to tell her story in person.

The details of my plan hang me up. Will her death fulfill the prophecies she's made to the Memphis PD?

There are ways around that. I'll make it

look like I had to shoot her during an escape attempt. I just have to make sure there are no witnesses and no evidence. Drew Peterson stayed out of prison for years until he made some mistakes. I won't make mistakes. If somehow the media gets wind of her statement in Memphis and starts digging like a dog with a bone, I can stall — like getting a lawyer who can make sure they don't interview me.

I don't want it to go that far. If it does, people will doubt me, and my life will go south.

This line of thinking makes me wonder if I've handled everything right. I go back over the ways I hid the evidence after killing Rollins. I couldn't have missed anything, could I? What if they detect my DNA? My shaved head minimizes the possibility of a hair being left behind, but there's always the hair on my arms, or sweat, or oil from my skin . . . I covered all my footprints, but I could have missed something because it was dark. What if there's a fiber from what I was wearing? I should have burned everything I was wearing that night.

Panic rises in me, but I quash it. No. I've come this far out of sheer intellect and caution, and I can keep going. The lights below me fade into the darkness of acres and acres of woods and crops, and I hit the Mississippi River and go north, following its path, traveling low.

I work through my answers to the things Cox has already told them. The things about her dad should be easy enough. I can make the case that it was a twelve-year-old girl who was emotionally traumatized and trying to find anyone but her father to blame for his death. I'll keep talking up the mother's mental illness and how it must have been passed on to the daughter.

But what else does she know? What if she suggested to the Memphis cops that I'm Sy's killer? She can't know since she wasn't there, so I'll tell them I was with J.J. Parker that night, watching the taped USC championship game, and that he and I were awake until well past 4:00 a.m., at which point he sacked out on my couch and I went to bed. He owes me, J.J. does. I know where his bodies are buried too, since I hired him to bury them — and I know where he spent his cash. Gail will know it's a lie, but my wife knows not to cross me.

But what if it's not enough? The thought plagues me. What if I kill her and then discover that I've forgotten something? I play with the thought of keeping Cox alive and actually bringing her back. Of putting her in my plane, handcuffed and shackled. Then I fantasize about opening the plane's door and shoving her out. No, that would never work, because her body would be found. That's the key, I think. Her body can never be found. Yes! People have to think she's still hiding.

Maybe I could even set up another Casey Cox homicide, with her possessions, hair, and DNA at the scene. Adding to her kill list would distract everyone from me.

I've been flying mostly over forest, but now I see a cleared space, no trees, a long, long way from any houses, and then it dawns on me. I need to find a place like that. A cleared place where I can kill her and then start a bonfire to burn her body without risking starting a forest fire, which would draw all the wrong kinds of attention. Then I can claim she escaped and that she's still out there somewhere. As long as they never find the body, I'll be okay.

I can't help laughing out loud. The thing I've got going for me is that, once she's out of the way, even though she spun her story to the Memphis PD, everyone will want to believe me instead of her. And then when I get back, I'll find Dylan Roberts and finish him off too.

The turncoat is not going to turn on me.

26

Dylan

My flight is delayed for forty-five minutes, and each second that ticks by is like a sledgehammer through my temple. Keegan will be on his way to Memphis soon with or without Gates's blessing. I watch out the window for a Cessna taking off, but I haven't seen one.

When we're finally on our way, the smell of alcohol drifts through the plush plane as the three record executives being transported to Nashville celebrate some deal they just signed with a recording artist who lives in the area. They live large, which is why they have a King Air to fly them. Since it's a jet, I pray it'll get there faster than Keegan's Cessna.

I close my eyes, feigning sleep, and cover Casey in prayer. I try to believe that God is on top of this, that he will protect Casey from Keegan, that he hasn't brought us this far just to turn his back on us now.

But God's ways have never been my ways. Brent is dead, Keegan is still walking free, and Casey is sitting in jail. If only I had a minute of FaceTime with God to get clear marching orders.

Before we make our final descent into Memphis, I call the fixed base operator there and ask if my rental car has been delivered. The man at the desk tells me Hertz has just delivered two.

"What do you mean *two*?" I ask him.

"One for you and one for another guy from Shreveport who just landed in a Cessna."

I close my eyes. I can't believe this. Somehow Keegan beat me here. My mind races.

I'm still the one sent to bring Casey back, and the Memphis police know that. They're not likely to turn Casey over to Keegan. Then again, he's slyer than a fox, and he's persuasive.

"What are the two cars?" I ask.

"Want to make sure you get the best one?" the guy asks with a chuckle. "Looks like there's a silver Enclave and a black Tahoe. Your name's on the Enclave."

So Keegan's getting a black Tahoe. "Okay, that's fine," I say. "Just do me a favor, would you? Don't mention to the other guy that I'm coming in. He's my colleague, and we've got a competition going on. I'm trying to win."

"Will do," he says cheerily.

I click off my phone and think. Maybe I could flatten a tire on the Tahoe if it's still there when I get to the office. That would slow him down. But I would have to get there before he claims his car, and the plane is taking its migraine-inducing time to get to the tarmac.

I've broken out in a sweat by the time we slow and turn toward the buildings. I search through the window for the two rental cars parked side by side in a parking lot beside the building, where Keegan may be by now. I look for the plane I've seen Keegan in before, but the airport is too big. I can't see it. The King Air taxis to the gate where I'm getting off. And as we approach, I see Keegan's plane. He's already tied it down.

I thank the pilots and wait until the door is open, and then I jog down the steps. I'm headed across the tarmac to the FBO when I see the black Tahoe pulling away. I want to punch something.

I hurry into the office, but the guy at the desk has gone to the bathroom. I wait, pacing in front of it, but he takes his sweet time.

When he comes back, he's full of chatter. Keegan must have paid him off to slow me down.

I encourage him to do my transaction as quickly as possible, and a few minutes later I'm in my Enclave, typing the police department's address into the car's GPS. I study an overhead view and figure out the shortest route. While it's loading, I glance at my voice mail.

Chief Gates has left a message. I click on it and hear his voice. "Dylan, I'm sorry about this, but I've decided to let Keegan go get Cox. I thought he'd be tied up with the funeral plans, but he insisted that he's on this. Just stand down and come on back. We'll reimburse you for any expenses you've incurred. Sorry. Let me know when you're back in town."

I let out a yell, knowing no one can hear. How did Keegan pull this off, considering all the questions surrounding him now?

I try to think. Maybe there's enough confusion about the extradition that I could convince them I'm still the one supposed to get her. Keegan will probably get there first, but there'll be paperwork. They have to get an extradition warrant, and that takes time.

As I'm driving I call the Memphis PD, ask to speak to the detective on Casey Cox's case. A guy named Leibowitz picks up, and I burst into my pitch. "Hi, my name is Dylan Roberts. I'm working with the Shreveport Police Department on the Casey Cox case, and I'm on my way there right now to transport her. I wondered if you could start processing her extradition paperwork. I'd like to get her back to Shreveport as soon as possible."

"Uh, I don't know about that," the detective says. "We were told you were coming, but then we got different orders. We're supposed to turn her over to Detective Keegan now."

"No, no," I say quickly. "That would be a terrible mistake. She'll use that in court — that she implicated him in several murders, and you still turned her over to him. It'll be a publicity nightmare for you guys."

There's a moment of silence on the other end of the phone. "I was a little concerned about that too, but our captain wants us to comply with what the Shreveport PD has requested. Keegan is in town. He's on his way here."

"So am I." I grasp at straws, trying to think of a persuasive argument. "Look, this could put him in a bad situation and compromise the investigation. Imagine the narrative if the press gets wind of her accusations and learns you put her in his hands. It has the appearance of impropriety."

He doesn't immediately respond, so I hope he's processing that.

"I'll call Chief Gates. There's no hurry here. Just don't let him have her yet."

He hesitates again, so I try one last shot. "Look, man. I'm an Afghanistan and Iraq veteran, and I just got hired by the Shreveport PD. If I don't bring her back, then I probably don't have a shot at keeping this job."

"My son is serving right now."

I seize on that. "Then you know what it's like. You want him to get a job when he gets back, right? I was in the CID in the army — it's like being an FBI special agent — and I just got hired on with the Shreveport PD. I have to do this. And if Gordon Keegan has been accused of anything, even by someone who's taking her last desperate shot, then it doesn't help anyone if he's the one bringing her back. I'm sure he'd agree with that if he knew the whole story. Just hold on until I can get there and get Chief Gates on the phone with you."

"I don't have the authority to make this decision," Leibowitz says. "I'll have to talk to my captain. We're still waiting for the extradition warrant, so it'll take a while anyway."

He hangs up on me. I check my GPS and try to figure out how much farther I've got. Only five more miles. I wipe the sweat off my lip and my temples and call Chief Gates, praying he's still in his office. His secretary puts me right through. "Dylan?" he asks when he picks up.

"Chief, I'm in Memphis. Listen, you've got to let me get her. I'm almost there. I came all the way here. Jim Pace wants me to bring her back, and with the accusations made against Keegan —"

"I'm letting him do it, Dylan. It's a matter of honor with him."

"But it compromises *everything*!" I go into the same spiel I gave the Memphis detective. "Look, Chief, there'll come a time when she talks to the media, and if she tells them you turned her over to the person she claims committed all these murders, they're not going to give the benefit of the doubt to the cop. They're going to milk the story for all it's worth, focusing on the pretty girl who couldn't have done such a brutal thing, and it might damage the investigation."

His voice is higher pitched than usual. "On the other hand, if you take her and she somehow escapes, the narrative will be that I put her in the hands of a brand-new hire."

"But that's always been my task. I've always planned to bring her back when I found her."

"Well, you didn't find her. Dylan, I've thought it over. I'm just going to let Keegan bring her back. Your job is over here. Come on back."

He clicks off the phone, ending the call, and I throw it, bouncing it off my seat. No, I can't let this stand! I have to somehow convince them. I have to protect Casey.

I will not let Keegan kill her.

27

Casey

My toes are turning blue, but this holding cell could be a lot worse. I don't mind the cold so much. I have a thin blanket I can put around my shoulders. It's not long enough to cover my whole body, I guess because they're afraid I'll make a noose and hang myself somehow. I'm thankful for my socks. One of the trustees who brought my food told me that when I'm taken upstairs to the general population they'll issue me some socks, and they don't fit well and aren't as good as mine. She let me keep my own for now.

I'm hungry, but even that isn't as bad as it could be, because they gave me a ham sandwich earlier. That settled my stomach somewhat. I have to say that unburdening my soul and confessing everything to the police — both good and bad — has made me feel much lighter. It's only the dread of

Keegan getting his hands on me that keeps me unsettled.

But God has been with me so far, and I think I saw a flicker of belief on the detectives' faces when I told them about Keegan. At least there's doubt there, which I hope will make them look into things. I know that if Dylan knows I'm in custody, he's probably sent our evidence to some media person, or he's already taken it to the DA. And I beg God to let Dylan miraculously be the one who's sent to transport me. That would be a miracle.

I sit on the bench with my back against the painted cinderblock wall, and I doze for a moment. Then suddenly there's a clang — making me jump — and the door swings open.

"Cox, you're being extradited to the Shreveport police."

I get to my feet, confused.

I'm instantly alert as I walk out in my sock feet, looking around me, anxious to see who's waiting.

Please let it be Dylan. Please let it be Dylan.

As we round the corner to the hallway, I hear a voice that makes my blood chill. Gordon Keegan, cackling like he's a good old boy and the other detectives are his fishing buds. They're talking about fantasy football and placing bets. He's a master.

I look for an exit, but of course there is no way out. As the guard leads me to that room, I stop. She grabs my arm and her hand moves to her Taser. "Come on. Move!"

I step into the room and see him. The hair on the back of my neck rises. Tears sting my eyes. I can't look at him.

I feel suddenly hot, my ears burning, my hands beginning to sweat. I can hardly swallow, my mouth is so dry.

The two detectives have clearly already forgotten what I've told them.

"Well, if it isn't the disappearing Casey Cox," Keegan says. He glances toward one of the guards. "Go ahead and get her personal effects. I'm ready to get her on the road."

"I want a lawyer," I blurt. "Before I leave, I need to see my lawyer."

Keegan looks up. Is that alarm in his eyes? "You can get a lawyer when we get to Shreveport."

I look at him full on now, my gaze sharp. "My lawyer lives here."

Detective Briar, who seemed to half believe my story, scratches his head. "Who's your lawyer?"

"Billy Barbero," I say. Suddenly fear overtakes me. What am I thinking? I'm going to hire an ambulance chaser to represent me on a murder charge? When he doesn't even know who I am? But I can't change course now. "I need to talk to him before they take me. Please call him."

"So let me get this straight," Keegan says. "You've been interviewing her for hours? And she lawyers up now? Before you extradite her? No way. That's not gonna happen. She can get a lawyer in Shreveport. I don't have to say a word to her on the way. I won't ask her a thing. She can keep her lips sealed and just wait until we get back to say anything. But by God, I am going to take her back."

I turn my pleading gaze to the detectives. They're probably running the laws through their heads and considering whether they'll get blamed if I get off because they violated the rules. No cop wants to be the reason a murder charge is dropped — especially one of this magnitude. I double down on that.

"I could get off on a technicality if you don't let me see my lawyer. He will tell them in court that I was not allowed an attorney when I asked for one."

Keegan speaks up quickly. "Once you ask for an attorney we're not allowed to question you further. That doesn't mean we can't take you. In fact, I'm going to Mirandize you right now for the murder of Brent Pace in Shreveport, Louisiana. You have the right to remain silent . . ."

I listen to my rights with my breath held, but my eyes are locked on the doubting Detective Briar. If I can just get him to call Billy Barbero, maybe it will slow things down. Billy doesn't know Casey Cox from Adam, but he won't be able to avoid the pull into the limelight if he's chosen to represent a supposed murderer like me. It may not occur to him that I'm Liana Winters, but he'll figure it out soon enough.

My hope is dashed when Briar looks at Keegan and says, "It's your case, man. If you want to take the risk, you can make her wait until she gets to Shreveport. Her lawyer can drive there."

I close my eyes. When I open them again, Keegan's got his crow's-feet activated. He's thrilled that he's getting away with this.

Where is Dylan?

I don't have time for subtlety, so I try again. "If he kills me on the way back to Shreveport, you will know that I told you the truth. If I vanish or if I don't make it back, please look into what I told you. There are people who know the truth and have the evidence, and they will hold you accountable."

Keegan cackles like he just delivered a hysterical punch-line. "This girl's good. You got to hand it to her, boys. She doesn't let up. Come on, get her back into her clothes. Give me her personal effects and we'll be on our way."

The female guard takes me into another room and watches as I change back into my clothes. I feel like I'm going to throw up, but somehow I hold it back. Instead, I whisper aloud, "God, it's in your hands now."

The guard looks disinterested as she walks me back to the detectives and hands me over to the man who will murder me.

28

Dylan

There's not a parking space open at the jail, so I double park behind the correctional facility's transport van and run inside. The guard who's supposed to be manning the front has stepped out for a moment, so I stand at the window, pacing in the tiny area next to the steel door into the jail.

He doesn't come back out. After a moment, I bend down to the round hole in the glass positioned nowhere near the height of any adult human. "Hello!" I say loudly. "Anybody here?"

Nothing, so I look up at the camera aimed down at me and hold out my hands as if to say, "Could someone actually do their job here?"

I bend down and yell again.

Finally, the guard returns, looking irritated. "Help you?"

"Yeah, I'm here from Shreveport to take

custody of Casey Cox. Detective Leibowitz is waiting for me."

He slides a clipboard to me in a drawer under the window. "Sign in there."

I hurriedly scribble out my info.

The loud metal door slides open and I hurry through the sally port where they get new arrestees out of the transport van. At the next locked door, I look up at the camera again, then back to the front desk just beyond the windows. I hear a loud click as the lock disengages.

I go in and sign some more forms, then they direct me to the booking room. The guard there seems to be logging a new booking's personal items.

"Excuse me," I say. "I need to see Detective Leibowitz. I'm here to take custody of Casey Cox."

"They're in a meeting right now," she says. "You can sit down and I'll tell them you're here."

I can't accept that. "The meeting, it's about her, isn't it? She's about to be extradited but I need to get back there. Please, go tell them I'm here."

She seems to move slower just because I asked her to hurry. It's a power thing. She takes her time finishing what she's doing, then shuffles slower than natural around the hall and down to the corner. How long since I landed? Fifteen or twenty minutes? I check my watch.

Keegan couldn't have gotten here much faster than me, but I did see his car in the parking lot so I know he's still here. I pace in the holding area, my head splitting.

Finally, she comes back. "They'll be right with you."

"They'll be right with me?" I repeat. "What is this, a bank? I came to transport an inmate, and I need to see them now!"

She doesn't like my tone. "I told you, they'll come when they can. They're busy."

"I'm busy too. Let me just go back. It's really important that I —"

"Have a seat!" she yells as if I'm one of her prisoners.

I huff out a sigh and glance toward the bright orange plastic seats against the wall. I step toward them, then change my mind. She can just get over it. I lunge toward the doorway she came through. She jumps out of her seat and comes after me, moving remarkably faster now. "What are you doing?" she yells.

I don't look back at her or slow my step, but I'm not sure where I should go. "I'm going to get my prisoner."

"You get back in there!" she shrieks.

I don't listen to her. I just keep walking, looking for any room that has people in it, hoping they'll hear our voices and come out into the hall. Finally, I see a plainclothes man at the end of the hallway near an exit door. I hurry toward him. "Detective? I'm Dylan Roberts. I spoke to you over the phone." I honestly don't know if I spoke to him or someone else, but it does make him stop.

He looks a little sheepish and slides his hands into his pockets, but he steps toward me.

"He shot past me and came back here without permission!" the guard yells, her voice reverberating down the hall.

"It's okay," the detective says, holding out a hand to stem her assault on me. "I'll take it from here."

"I need to take custody of my prisoner," I bite out. "Is she still here?"

"I'm sorry. They just left."

I fight the urge to slam my hand against the wall. "You let Keegan take her? Are you insane?"

"I had to," he says. "Our captain talked to your chief, and that was the plan."

"You don't know what you're doing," I say. "This is going to backfire on you. *If* anything goes wrong with this extradition, you're going to be blamed."

"For handing her over to the cop who was sent to get her?"

I want to scream that she's telling the truth, that Keegan wants her dead, that she'll never make it to Shreveport. But I don't have time to tell him how I know that.

I push past him to the exit door he's standing beside. "Did he go out this door?"

"They're already gone. They just drove off."

I pause for a minute, trying to control my raging need to break something.

"She asked for a local lawyer before he took her, but he opted to take her on to Shreveport."

I'm sick at the thought of Casey in the car with Keegan. "She asked for a lawyer and you didn't let her have one?"

He bristles. "It was his call. He said he would call the lawyer when they got there."

I try to shift my thoughts. "She named a lawyer?"

"She said his name is Billy Barbero. I've never heard of him."

I make a mental note of his name. I'll get in touch with him as soon as I can, and maybe he can do something to stop the extradition. Maybe he can get in touch with Gates, and the chief can call Keegan and change the plan.

"So why won't you let me out the exit door?"

"That's only for transporting inmates. You'll have to go out the way you came in."

I'm wasting time here, so I head back the way I came, past the guard who's seething over my audacity. "Thanks for your help," I quip as I pass her.

I get to the metal doors. They take as long to open as they did on the way in, and finally I'm back in the parking garage at my car. I look to see if Keegan's SUV is still there. Of course, it's gone.

I can't believe this. When in history have the wheels of justice moved this fast? I get in my car and try to figure out what Keegan will do. Will he head back toward Shreveport in the rental car? Go back to the airport and put her in his plane? Then I realize that he won't do either because he doesn't intend to transport her to Shreveport.

She'll miraculously "vanish," and he will skate.

I'm a failure, but I try anyway, pulling out of the parking lot and heading right and trying to catch up to any car that looks like his rental. But this is useless. I have failed Casey and it might cost her her life.

When I don't find Keegan's Tahoe, I

decide on another course. I pull over and Google "Billy Barbero Memphis Attorney." An address and phone number come up, and I click on the number to place the call, hoping he'll answer even though it's night.

"Yello."

I'm surprised to hear that greeting. "Is this Mr. Barbero?"

"Yeah, that's me. Who's this?"

"My name is Dylan Roberts." I know I'm speaking too fast, so I try to slow down. "I understand you're the attorney for Casey Cox."

There's a long pause. "For who?"

"Casey Cox. She's been all over the news. You're Billy Barbero the attorney, aren't you?"

"Yeah," he says. "And I know who she is, but I never met the woman. You say she named me as her lawyer?"

"That's right." I'm confused. How would Casey have known him? Maybe he has a billboard or commercial. Or maybe he was the first listing in the phone book. "Mr. Barbero, what kind of law do you practice?"

"Mainly I represent disabled people, but I consider myself a full-service attorney. If she named me, I'll be glad to defend her."

"Full service?" I ask. "So you aren't a criminal attorney?"

"Does she need a lawyer or not? Just tell me where she is."

I feel like an idiot for even talking to this man. But he's the only option I have. "I need you to listen carefully. Casey Cox has been placed in the custody of a Detective Gordon Keegan of the Shreveport PD. She claims he is the real killer of Brent Pace, among others. I need for you to call Chief Gates of the Shreveport PD and throw around as much weight as you can to stop her transport. I have evidence that Keegan is guilty and plans to kill her."

"I'm listening," he says.

"She doesn't have much time. Don't tell him you're not a criminal attorney."

"I'll call right now."

"Threaten to call a press conference. Threaten to smear the entire police force."

"Don't worry. I'm pretty good at intimidation." He chuckles. "Casey Cox, huh?"

I roll my eyes. "Move heaven and earth, and call me back at this number."

When I hang up, I pull over and beg God to intervene for Casey. But I wonder if my faith is too flimsy these days to move the mountain of Gordon Keegan.

29

Casey

The very presence of Gordon Keegan makes me feel a swirl of nausea, and I can't seem to control the images of my father and Brent that keep strobing through my mind, as if my brain is cycling in and out of a dream.

But it's not a dream. I'm awake, and I can smell Keegan — the sweat scent mixed with too much aftershave — and I can hear him humming some song I don't know under his breath.

I lean my head back on the tan leather of his back seat, my hands bound with a plastic tie on my lap. I work them as I sit there, trying to wiggle my hands out, but he's pulled it too tight. He isn't driving toward the interstate; he has no intention of taking me to Shreveport. And he doesn't care about tainting the case that will go before the court. He doesn't intend for me to get that far.

He stops humming and looks at me in his rearview mirror. "You know, darlin', I don't like it when people file false reports about me. Did you think you were gonna turn the entire Memphis PD against me? Think again, sweetheart."

"I told the truth," I say. "That you're a bloodthirsty murderer."

He laughs with giddy delight. "And nobody'll believe a word you say."

Blood on my living room wall . . . my screams ripping from my chest . . . my cries for Daddy . . .

I close my eyes and will them to see what's in front of me now. Keegan's face is lit up under oncoming headlights. "You really are a psychopath, aren't you?" I ask. "What happened to you? Were you abused or tortured or abandoned?"

He laughs again, with his bone-chilling cackle. "If that's the story you want to tell yourself."

"Why did you kill Rollins?" I ask. "Was he balking at all the murders you'd asked him to commit? Was he threatening to go to the police? Drinking too much?" Of course he's not going to admit to anything, but I have to say it anyway.

Dad's body swaying, his head oddly twisted in the makeshift noose, the fan creaking as though it will pull from the ceiling . . . the smell of death and terror . . . blood on the walls . . . on his hands . . . signs of a struggle . . .

Sweat drips into my eyes now. My hair is wet and my heart is slamming. I know I'm losing it.

I speak again to hear my own voice. "When you killed my dad, was that quick? Or did you torture him? I know he fought back. I saw the blood. A person who hangs himself wouldn't have blood like he'd been in a fight for his life. You killed him because he was going to expose you."

His smile fades and his teeth glisten against the headlights coming toward us. "I watched him strangle to death." He looks at me in the mirror again, gauging my reaction. "Does that make you feel better?"

I think of lunging forward and looping my hands over his head, cutting my plastic tie into his throat by sheer strength, my teeth sinking into his jugular. I could kill him in cold blood now, watch his life bleed away. If I have to live the rest of my life knowing I really am a killer, I'd be okay with that. I could rest knowing that he is off this earth.

But then I second-guess my strength, the tightness of my wrist tie, my ability to sink a deep enough bite before he fights back.

"What about Brent?" I ask. "Did you stay

until he was dead?"

He seems delighted that he has the chance to boast about his brilliance. "I knew he called you," he says. "I knew you were coming on your lunch hour."

My brain takes me back to that moment when I turned the knob and pushed inside to call out Brent's name, and found him on the floor . . . My brain flashes back and forth, from Brent's death scene to me here in Keegan's car . . . then back again. I try to stay here, present.

"You didn't know he sent me a thumb drive, did you, before he even called me, just in case something happened to him. I actually got it. I'm not the only one who's seen it."

I see the grin fade from his eyes now, so I keep going. "It was probably out in the mailbox when you murdered him, and you didn't even know it. The mailman picked it up and sent it. You dropped the ball on that one."

Now I see a flicker of worry in his eyes, and he looks back at me over the seat. "Nice try, but there's no way you would've gotten any of your mail."

I smile now, because I did get it, but I can't tell him that my landlord gave it to my sister and my sister got it to me. I just go quiet, letting him wonder. Finally, when I speak again, I say, "The press is going to really enjoy getting all that the moment anything happens to me. You'll have a lot of explaining to do."

He thinks that through for a moment and sees the holes in it. "They won't know whether anything happened to you. You go missing all the time. That's what's gonna happen again tonight."

He turns onto a dark dirt road, into a wooded area. I want to ask him where he's taking me, but I know the answer. He's taking me to my death. "If I disappear after what I told the police, they're going to know it's you. They'll dig into it and they won't let it go."

He laughs again. "Not if I tell them you got away, call a BOLO, tell them you're still on the run out there, and you're armed and dangerous. Oh, and there might be another body I set up with your possessions at the scene. I have your personal effects right here, sweetie. It'll just add to your body count."

I meet his eyes in the mirror. "I've never been armed," I say. "But I am dangerous. Even dead. The wheels are in motion to release it all to the press. You didn't think I would go without a safety net, did you?"

His grin fades, and he looks away. He slows at another dirt road and turns into it, lights it up with his headlights and sees a gate that's locked there. He's trying to find a place where he can murder me. At least I know he doesn't have a shovel in this rental vehicle. He probably hasn't chosen a place yet — he's figuring this out as he goes. Maybe that can play in my favor.

Trying to stall, I bite my cheek until it bleeds, then I lift my hands together and get the blood on my fingertips. I wipe some on my face so he can see it. "I'm bleeding," I say.

Of course he doesn't care . . . yet.

"It's going to upset your apple cart. If there's blood evidence in this car, they'll seriously doubt your story that I escaped."

He looks back at me and sees the blood I'm wiping on the seat, and I'm pretty sure his face is a whiter shade of pale. He curses and swerves.

I bite my cheek again, ignoring the pain, the metallic taste spreading on my tongue. I wipe more of it on the seat and the door, then I spit it to spatter it farther.

He speeds up now, muttering profanity, and I can see the homicidal intentions glistening in his eyes, but I may have bought myself a little time. He doesn't quite know what to do.

"They'll know there was at least a struggle. Some of them will wonder if you killed me."

He gives up on the dirt road he's on, shifts into reverse, slams on the accelerator, and screeches back up the road again. He turns and drives back the way we came, his lights on bright, looking for another dirt road that he can turn into.

That's when I know I have no choice. I have to fulfill the story he was going to tell about me anyway. I have to escape. I try the door handle, but he has the child lock on.

He's probably going forty miles an hour now as he tries to find a place to turn, but somehow I have to get out of this car. If I can get him to roll my window down, he'll have to unlatch the child lock. "I'm going to throw up," I say.

"Knock yourself out."

I've never made myself throw up before, but I jab my fingers down my throat until I gag, and then jab a little harder, making myself heave. The ham sandwich comes up.

He curses again, growling that I'm leaving more evidence, and he rolls my window down.

The lock is now disengaged. I throw open the door and fling myself out. I hit the ground wrists first, slide painfully across the dirt, and roll down an embankment. I scramble to my feet and run faster than I knew I could until I'm in the trees, bushes scraping my skin, and then I go deeper, downhill into the woods.

I stop to catch my breath, wincing at the pain in my wrists and knees, and look back to see if I can tell where he is. His car has stopped and the interior dome light is on. He left his door open and came after me. I see the beam of his flashlight moving the wrong way . . . away from me. The orchestra of the forest muffles my breaths. I stay still as that beam moves in the opposite direction.

I look at the car, my backseat door and his driver's door still open. My personal effects are in there on his front seat. If I could just get up there I could get my phone.

I wait until he's far enough away, then I limp as quietly as I can back up the hill to the car, go around it and lean in on his side. I glance through the windshield. The beam is still moving in the woods. My wrist is swollen as I reach in and look for the keys, but he took them with him. The paper sack of my personal effects is sitting on his passenger seat with a label on it that has my name. I grab it, open it, and see my phone and purse. Wadding the top, I tuck the bag under my arm and cross the road and go deep into the woods on the opposite side. After several minutes of running, I look back toward the road. Through the trees I see glimpses of light and assume he's moving back toward his car. I hear the doors close, and the car begins to move, his headlights on bright.

He's searching for me, desperate. I hunker down as the light passes. He goes a couple of miles up the road and makes a U-turn and comes back, looking again. I try to think like he's thinking. He could call for backup, get the police to swarm out here looking for me, but how would he explain being so far off the path to Shreveport? How would he explain taking me to a remote place nowhere near the interstate? The blood on my seat?

No, I don't think he can take that chance. He's going to have to go with his original story even though this time, parts of it will be true. He'll have to claim it happened somewhere else, along the way to where he should have been going.

Yes, he's desperate, and he isn't going to give up easily. I got away from him. I'm not lying in a grave somewhere with my personal effects. I really am out here like a ticking bomb.

I wait him out for at least two hours before he finally gives up and leaves. I know he's probably not really gone, and then I see his car coming back up the road, the headlights off this time. I cut behind a tree again, afraid he has some kind of technology I don't know about. Infrared glasses, maybe.

But after another hour of searching, he finally disappears and doesn't come back. I walk up that dirt road — limping on a knee that has swollen to the size of a melon — until I see lights shining on the other side of the trees. It's a convenience store with gas pumps. I wipe the blood off my face onto my sleeve, tuck my bound hands under my shirt, and walk in fast until I get to the bathroom.

When I'm locked in the ladies' room in the bright lights, I dump my personal effects out of the bag and find some nail clippers. I bend my swollen wrists until I leverage the clippers just right, and I cut the plastic tie and free myself. Then I wash the blood and vomit off my face and hands and clothes. I finger-brush the leaves out of my hair. Then gathering up all my things and putting them back into my purse, I head out. I check my cell phone for bars and a charge. *Please, God.*

The battery is at 10 percent and there's

one bar out here, but it might be enough. I click on Dylan's number. He answers after the first ring, and I'm so grateful I almost can't get the words out. "Dylan, it's me!"

30

Dylan

When I hear her voice I almost run off the road. My eyes sting as gratitude rushes through me. *Thank you, God.* "Casey, are you all right?"

"Yes." I can hear wind rushing into her phone. "I got away." Her voice bounces as if she's walking, and she's out of breath. "My phone's about to die. I'm walking down Highway 14, behind the buildings. I'm behind a furniture store that's about half a mile down from a BP station right now. There's a sign on the gate that says Brainard Furniture. I guess I need to call a taxi but they'll recognize me."

"I'll be there in a few minutes."

"You're here? In Memphis?"

"Yes! I was trying to beat Keegan here. Where is he?"

"Looking for me. I left blood in his car. He's probably trying to clean it before he reports my escape."

I turn my car around and follow its GPS. "Are you hurt? Do you need an ambulance?"

"No!" she almost shouts, then she lowers her voice. "I bit my cheek to draw blood. I'm fine. Please hurry. He's desperate."

"Stay on the phone with me. Don't hang up."

"It's about to die."

I see the Highway 14 sign and I turn. "Casey, I'm coming from I-40 — are you north or south on Highway 14?"

She hesitates. "I'm not sure."

"Hold on, I'm looking for the furniture store."

"It should be about two m—"

The call cuts out. "Casey?" I've lost her, but I've figured out that I'm going the wrong way. I pull over into the left lane and turn around. Then I speed toward her, my eyes scanning the lit buildings for the BP station or the furniture store.

There it is, up ahead, on the left. I almost hit a car as I speed past it. I see something ahead in the dark.

There she is. I recognize her frame. She comes running toward me as I pull into the parking lot. I lean over and unlock the door to let her in.

She slides into the passenger seat and throws her arms around my neck. I kiss her face and realize mine is wet. I don't want to let go, but I hold her at arm's length to check her out. Her hands and arms are scraped, and both of her wrists are swollen. Her shoulder is still bandaged and there's blood dotting the gauze.

"I'm not dead," she says. "That's what matters. We have to get out of this part of town."

I turn the car around and drive back into traffic. We're quiet as I try to decide where I should go. I head back to the interstate, intending to get out of this town. When we're far enough away for her to feel safe, she seems to wilt.

"He was taking me . . . to the middle of nowhere . . . and he was going to kill me and leave me there, then stage another murder and leave my personal effects at the scene. He may be setting me up right now."

My mind races. Yes, he would do that. Find a random person — anyone — to kill, and then blame her. Something to prove she's alive, something to make people fear her even more.

"He's digging a deeper and deeper hole," I say.

"That's why he's desperate." She looks at

205

me. "Where's your regular phone?"

"I got rid of it."

"You need to get rid of the other one too. I'm afraid they'll track mine. They may have gotten the number of your burner when they had mine. I got it back because he had it in my personal effects."

I take out my phone's battery and roll my window down, then throw both mine and hers out. "I'll get new ones tonight."

"Dylan, you're going to get arrested if they know you have me."

"I can't turn you over to the police."

"I told them everything. They listened, took notes, videotaped it. But then when he came, they just handed me over. They didn't believe a word." She looks at me. "What if everyone is like that? What if no one ever believes us?"

"Someone will."

"But I don't want you to be charged because of me."

"I can live with jail," I say.

She starts to cry, and I want to pull over and comfort her, but I have to keep driving. I have to get her out of here.

31

Casey

"They may not have found my car when they arrested me," she says. "I left it down the street from my hotel and walked there. You could take me to it."

"No, we're not going anywhere near it."

I'm quiet and look at Dylan. His eyes are intense, and I can see the wheels turning as he puzzles through what to do with me. I hate this. I don't want to cause him to be arrested.

"Dylan, if we do get caught . . . if the police stop us somehow . . . tell them that you caught me. That you were taking me in."

"We're not going to get caught."

"We can't just drive all night."

"Why not?"

"Because Keegan will find out what you're driving. He'll suspect I got in touch with you. He probably has a BOLO out for you already."

"He already knows what I'm driving. Trust me."

"Maybe you could call Chief Gates. Tell him what happened, all of it. Take a chance on the truth."

"I'm not taking *any* chances with you, Casey. If he's involved, it could blow up in our faces." He takes an exit off the interstate, and I see a Super 8 motel looming ahead.

"I'm going to check in," he says. "Get down on the floorboard. Don't let anyone see you."

I unhook my seat belt and get on the floor. He pulls into the parking lot. I can't see where we are, but he's not near the entry or any overhead lights, because there's no light shining down on us. He must have parked in a darker part of the parking lot.

"Be careful," I whisper.

"It's not me they're looking for," he says. "It's you. Stay down." He gets out and goes inside.

I stay hunkered on the floor, my head down. Despair knots in my throat, stinging my eyes. But then I force my thoughts to do a U-turn.

I look where God is working, as Dylan told me to do weeks ago. And when I do, I see him.

"You helped me get word to someone in authority," I whisper. "You helped me think of planting the blood evidence in Keegan's car. You helped me escape from him and kept me hidden. You left enough charge on my phone to call Dylan for help. You had Dylan in Memphis when I needed him."

Now the tears flow, but instead of despair, I weep over the miracle of it. God was in on all of this. He's still in on it now.

This is all so tangled and so impossible, but God did the impossible tonight. He does it all the time. I'm so overcome by it that I can't formulate an elaborate prayer. I simply whisper, "Thank you."

Dylan comes back to the car after a few minutes, and he doesn't look at me. He starts it up and backs out of the parking spot. "We have a room on the back side of the building. First floor. I'll park near the door."

I wipe my face, not wanting him to see that I've been crying while he was gone. I wipe my eyes and my nose on my sleeve.

He pulls the car around, and I feel it stopping again. "There's no one out here," he says. "I'll unlock the door, then come back to the trunk to get my bag out. You head in while I'm doing that."

He gets out and I hear him unlocking the

motel room door. Then, as he opens the lift gate of the SUV, the light comes on. I open the door and slip out, then hurry inside.

In the bathroom, I look at myself in the mirror. My face is dirty. I wash it with soap, rinse it off, and pat it dry. I hear the outside door closing, so I step out.

He's standing at the window, looking out the curtains.

"Are we okay?" I ask.

"Looks like it. There were only a couple of cars parked on this side. I don't think anybody saw us, and I don't think the cameras could have gotten a good view of you."

He turns from the window and looks at me now, his hands at his sides. His face twists, and he crosses the room and pulls me into his arms. He holds me for a long time, and I cling to him. I don't want to let him go.

Finally, he steps back, and I see that his eyes are wet. He takes my hands gently, looks down at my swollen wrists and the scrapes. "I'll get you some ice."

"No," I say. "Don't leave this room."

He pulls me to the small couch against the wall, and I drop down, suddenly aware of how exhausted I am. He sits next to me and pulls me against him.

His kiss is salty, desperate, and I feel the urgency in it. I touch the stubble on his face, tears rolling down my own, and slide my fingers through his hair.

Suddenly, he pulls back, lets me go, and gets up. I catch my breath and watch him walk across the room, putting distance between us.

He turns back to me, his eyes so full of things I can't name that my heart almost breaks.

"The thing is, I'm in love with you," he says.

My hand goes to my heart, then to my mouth.

"I have been . . . I don't even know how long," he says. "I want you . . . but more than tonight. I just . . . can't picture tomorrow without you."

I'm sobbing now, unable to hold it back. I whisper, "Me too."

He takes a step toward me, but doesn't come much closer. "God is looking out for us. I don't know if you see it."

"I do," I whisper.

"I don't want to dishonor him by following my impulses. I'm in this for the long game."

I know exactly what he means, and I nod my agreement.

"So . . . I'm going to keep my distance tonight. You sleep in the bed, and I'll take the couch."

"Okay," I whisper.

Our gazes lock for a long moment, and I want to get up and go to him, touch him again, taste his lips . . .

A soft grin pulls at his lips, and suddenly I'm smiling too. He said he loves me. He wants a future with me. He's willing to wait.

"You're so beautiful," he says.

"So are you."

A lifetime of words and emotions passes through our gaze. My heart aches with gratitude.

"Your bandage needs changing," he says, stepping toward me and touching my shoulder. "You may have opened some stitches."

I pull up his pant leg and see the bandages on his calves. "You don't look so great either."

"Mine's fine. I have bandages in my bag," he says.

"I'm fine, Dylan."

"You will be." He digs through his small duffel and pulls out a box of gauze pads and medical tape. He sits on the couch sideways and carefully peels my bandage off.

I try not to wince.

"Okay," he whispers. "Good. You didn't break the stitches. You just pulled them."

"I told you I was fine."

He cleans the wound with hydrogen peroxide, then carefully fashions a new bandage. When he's done, our eyes lock again. He kisses me, then gets up and moves away from me again.

I smile. "You're killing me."

"We'll have time. This can't go on forever."

It isn't forever I'm worried about, but I don't say that.

I get up and look at the bed. "Do you think it's okay if I take a bath?"

"Sure," he says. "I'll check out the news, see if your disappearance has been reported yet."

I go back into the bathroom and start the bathwater, but before I get in, I say another prayer thanking God for tonight. If I wind up in prison tomorrow — or in a grave — at least I will have had these moments.

32

Casey

I hear Dylan in the shower before dawn, and I get up and turn on the light, check myself in the mirror. I look like someone who slept in a ditch, and I don't have makeup or anything to make me look better. Bruises from branches as I ran through the woods have browned on my face and my arms. My wrists are still sore and swollen, and my knee aches.

I make a pot of coffee, then turn on the TV and wait for the news. I don't know if Keegan has reported my escape yet, or if he's killed someone and tried to set me up . . . At least he didn't have any of my possessions to leave at the scene, so maybe he didn't. He could have gotten my blood off the seat, but that would take too long for them to identify forensically, so it might not be an immediate way to frame me.

Dylan comes out of the shower as I pour

a cup of coffee. "Hey," he says with a smile.

I hand him the cup. "Did you sleep at all?"

"A little. But I did a lot of thinking. I've got a plan."

"What?"

"We should leave now, before it's daylight, while we still have cover of darkness. Then we need to call your attorney."

"Barbero?"

"Yes. I called him last night, but when I found you, I forgot to circle back to him. He was going to try to get you out of Keegan's hands."

"Too late."

"How'd you choose that guy? He's not even a criminal attorney."

"I work for him as Liana Winters." I tell him about my slightly unethical job. "I didn't know who else to call."

"Well, maybe he can help us until we can get somewhere else."

We get back into the car, and he has me get into the back seat instead of the front, so I can hide more easily. He drives us to an all-night drugstore. When he comes out, he tosses me a bag. Inside is one burner phone.

"I thought you were getting three," I say.

"Not all in one place."

While I stay hidden in the back seat, he

215

goes into two more stores and gets more burner phones. We activate them with the minutes he's bought with them.

With one of them, he calls Dex. "Hey, buddy. Sorry to wake you."

I hear Dex's sleepy bass voice, but I can't make out what he's saying.

"Listen, I need to find a safe place. A house or deer camp or something off the beaten path."

Dex has come through for us before. He's the one who stitched up my shoulder after my gunshot wound and took Dylan in after he was burned in the apartment fire.

I hear him telling Dylan something, and Dylan writes it down. "You sure the key is there? Nobody's staying there right now?"

Dylan thanks him profusely and hangs up. He glances at me in the back seat. "His in-laws have a lake house in Little Rock."

"Arkansas?"

"Yeah. It's not that far from here. Sounds perfect. I can get you there in a couple of hours, then I'll go down to Shreveport and pay a visit to the DA. I'll explain the whole case. I'll leave you this car and get a flight down to Shreveport."

"Dylan, I'm scared for you."

"It'll be fine. By the time you turn yourself in, I want to make sure we've gotten the story out there."

He disposes of the phone he used for Dex, then heads west.

33

Dylan

I've hired a flight instructor at the Little Rock airport to fly me in his Piper Cub down to Shreveport. We can be there in about an hour.

Now that I know Casey's safe, I get ready to do what I should have done weeks ago. During the flight, I update the evidence on my thumb drive. I add the information about Keegan taking Casey to kill her, the blood she left in his car, her escape, and his vow to frame her for another murder. And I include the videotape I got from Monnogan's bar, with Keegan following us out of the parking lot the night Sy Rollins was murdered. Then I copy all of that onto two more flash drives I picked up with the phones.

From the Shreveport airport, I take an Uber back to where my car is. On the radio as I drive, I hear the alert about the manhunt going on in Memphis for the fugitive who broke free of her transporter, and I stew that the media is so clueless. They clearly haven't been informed that she warned Memphis PD that Keegan would try to kill her.

They will know soon.

I put one of the thumb drives into a padded envelope and address it to Macy Weatherow, the reporter who has defended Casey. I take it by the TV station. Shoving on sunglasses and a baseball cap — a pretty pitiful disguise — I go in and ask the receptionist to get this package to Macy.

Then I slide another flash drive into my pocket and head to the DA's office.

I think it through. If he's not there, do I want to talk to an assistant DA? I decide that I have to speak to the district attorney himself, otherwise word might leak out and ruin everything. I can't take the chance of having anyone give Keegan a heads-up.

It's late afternoon — almost closing time — when I get to the DA's office and park, and my hands begin to sweat as I get out of my car and walk up to the building. Inside, I go to the receptionist, who looks up with a smile as I walk toward her.

"Hi, my name is Dylan Roberts." I explain my connection to the police department. "I need to speak to the district attorney about a matter of great importance, having to do with the Casey Cox case."

She calls up to his office, then instructs me to get on the elevator and head up to the fourth floor. The building has twenty floors, and I doubt seriously that his office is on a lower floor, but I go there anyway. I get off and look both ways, trying to figure out where to go next.

A man approaches me. "Mr. Roberts?"

"Yes."

"I was sent to see what it is you need."

"And who are you?" I ask.

"John Appinet. I'm assistant to the district attorney."

"Are you an AD?"

"No, sir, a paralegal. Could we go in here and you can go over what you have?"

I clear my throat. "No, actually. I need to see the DA. I have information about Casey Cox that I need to give to him personally. It will impact her case going forward."

"Do you know where she is?"

I cross my arms, unyielding. "Get the DA for me. It's highly sensitive, and very urgent. Believe me, it's something he'll want to know before the press gets wind of it."

That raises his eyebrows. He looks up the hall. "Okay, just go into the waiting area and have a seat. I'll be right back."

There's another receptionist or administrative assistant behind a desk in the waiting area, and she doesn't look up as I sit down. I check my watch and look out the glass, wondering if Appinet is making it clear that this is urgent.

Several minutes later, he comes back. "This way, Mr. Roberts. I'm going to take you to DA Phillips. He's on a different floor."

I follow him back onto the elevator. As I walk, I reach into my pocket and fold my fingers around the thumb drive. I can't wait to give it to him.

The DA's office isn't as elaborate as I would have thought. It's probably bigger than the other offices here, but it isn't a corner office and probably pales in comparison to the kind of office he would have if he worked in the private sector.

The man I've seen often on TV looks distracted and disinterested as he gets to his feet and shakes my hand. "What can I do for you, Mr. Roberts? It sounded important."

"If we could have some privacy . . ."

Phillips nods to Appinet, and the paralegal leaves. When the door is closed, I sit down and pull out the thumb drive, slide it across his desk. "As you know, I've been hired by Brent Pace's family to find and bring back Casey Cox. Yesterday, Chief Gates swore me in with the police department. But in the course of this investigation, I've discovered some things about key police detectives on the force who, I believe, are responsible for Brent's murder themselves. Casey Cox is innocent, and I have evidence here that Gordon Keegan and Sy Rollins, among some others, murdered Brent and a number of others. And that a few days ago, Keegan murdered Sy Rollins."

Phillips sits up straighter, his face blanching, and takes the thumb drive. He frowns as he assesses me again, and he shoves the drive into his computer port. "Before I look at this, you have to tell me. Do you know where she is?"

"We'll talk about that after you see the evidence. Her attorney will negotiate her surrender after you see this, but Ms. Cox fears that Keegan is going to kill her to shut her up. She told this story to the Memphis police, and they blew it off and handed her over to him. Very stupid move. I have evidence that he tried to kill her and she escaped during the attempt."

He gapes at me. "What evidence?"

"Keegan wasn't taking her to Shreveport.

He took her to a remote, wooded area with every intention of killing her. Her blood is in his rental car, and she can direct you to where he took her. You'll find her prints in the dirt there and possibly more blood since she had scratches."

"You've seen her, then?"

I evade. "I've spoken to her. She told me the story, and based on the evidence that I've collected throughout this case, I believe her. Gordon Keegan is an extortionist and a serial killer. He's a cancer on the Shreveport Police Department, and it's about to metastasize. Casey's attorney will make sure that her story gets to the press, and you can imagine how they'll latch onto this. You need to know all this before that happens."

"Have you talked to anyone at the Shreveport police department about this?"

"No. I don't know who's involved, and these people are deadly. I decided to come to you instead."

"Not even Chief Gates?"

"No."

He sighs. "Okay." Not surprisingly, he seems a little rattled, and he shakes his head and tries to refocus. "Which file should I open first?"

I direct him to the overview of all the information, and I walk through it with him.

He listens earnestly, asking questions and making sure he understands. It takes over an hour for us to go over it all, and he tells his assistant to hold all his calls. When we're finally done, he's sweating. He gets up and paces across the room, his eyes studying the beige carpet as he thinks.

Finally, he turns to me. "Okay, here's what we're going to do. I'll need to issue an arrest warrant for Keegan. Your life is obviously in danger. And we have to figure out how and when we'll get Casey Cox in here. I'll need a number so I can talk to her."

I don't want to give it to him, but we're down to the wire here. He needs to hear her side of it. I give him Barbero's number instead and tell him Barbero can connect them.

"I don't want you to leave here until I've set some of this in motion," Phillips says. "I'll need to talk to you as we're working on this. I'll give you a room and ask you to stay in it until it's safe for you to leave. It's a secure room — the press and Keegan and whoever else can't get to you. Are you okay with that?"

It's such a relief to have someone in authority taking this seriously that I'll do almost anything. But I'm not sure about this. "I'd rather not be stalled here. I want to help find Keegan."

"Of course. We'll need you for that. But I have phone calls to make and I want you close so I can get your input. It won't take that long."

I'm reluctant, but in the end I say, "All right. But when Casey turns herself in, I want to be the one to bring her."

He nods, then rubs his fingers through his hair and lets out a curse. "I can't believe this is happening. It's going to be national news. International. It'll take years for our people to recover from this."

"Better to start that process now. Get Keegan and his boys off the streets."

He leads me to the secure room and has his assistant load the small refrigerator there with Mountain Dew and Coke, my two favorite drinks. It has a bathroom, so I won't have to go out. There's a TV, and the assistant gives me a wifi password. But when I click on my cell phone, I don't have any bars.

I e-mail Casey from our Yahoo address. It's done. Told the DA. He'll call you soon. They're setting things in motion. I'm safe in a secure room in their offices until they arrest him.

I press Send, but the screen doesn't change. I click it again. Nothing. I'm not sure whether the e-mail sent or not. Is something wrong with their wifi?

While I'm waiting to see if I get a response, I turn the TV to the news. My heart feels unburdened, hopeful, and I thank God. I feel like things might really work out now, that there's a chance that Casey will be vindicated and she and I might have a future together. What will that look like? Where will we go from here?

We could go to a movie, to dinner, hang out watching TV, do actual date stuff. Will our relationship work even if we don't have the pall of death and murder hanging over us?

Yes, I think it will. We're not drama queens. We don't need that kind of stimulation to connect us. She seems like a person who's simple and low-maintenance. Even though we've spent so little time together, I have a strong feeling that she wouldn't be a drain. Instead, she fills me up, even in the worst times.

Yes, that's what I feel. Filled up. Like there's been a piece of me hollowed out, and she has what I need to fill it.

I check my e-mail again. No reply. I try to send my message again, but I can't — my Internet is frozen. I sigh and chalk it up to the security in the room.

I look out through the small rectangular window with the view of a parking lot. No one is in view, and only a couple of cars are left. The staff has probably already gone home for the day.

I try to open the door. It's locked. I didn't know Phillips was going to lock it.

The hair rises on my arms, and I try the knob again. Even though I don't see anyone through the door's window, I bang on it and yell.

Too much time has passed. I don't like this. I knock on the door, hoping someone will hear me and come unlock it so I can ask what's going on. No one comes. I go to the bathroom, lean over the sink, and wash my face. I dry it off and look into the mirror.

I suddenly get the chilling sense that I've done the wrong thing. No, I tell myself. What I've done is right. I took the flash drive to the TV station. I came to the DA. I reported a series of grisly crimes. It's going to be all right. Phillips has a whole case to lay out for Gates. Or maybe he's talking to Gates's boss, the mayor, first. It all takes time.

Then I hear someone unlocking the door. I dash out of the bathroom as the door opens.

"Where have you been?" I ask. "You didn't tell me you were locking me in!"

The DA steps in, but he doesn't make eye contact with me. I see a shadow on the wall behind him.

Gordon Keegan steps into the doorway, grinning. "Hey, buddy. How you doing?"

34

Dylan

I swing and my fist hits home, right across Keegan's jaw, but they're both on me in seconds. I flail with my fists as they fight me, and I manage to stay on my feet until Keegan kicks me in the shins, sending lightning flashing through my burns that knocks me to my knees. They wrestle me to the floor and cuff my hands behind me.

"Thought you had me, didn't you?" Keegan says through his teeth as he jerks me back to my feet. "I've thought you were a turncoat for a while now. I told Rollins I couldn't trust you, but he was starting to."

I've left a gash on his jaw, and he dabs at it now, checks the blood.

I turn to Phillips. "So you're in on this too? Is that how he's gotten away with it all this time?"

Neither of them answers, and I know it's useless.

"You have the right to remain silent . . ."

I can't believe Keegan is Mirandizing me, this man who fractures the law and uses it like a weapon. This cold-blooded murderer, this psychopath, who will kill anyone in his way. I can't believe this district attorney put here by the people of Louisiana is kowtowing to him. How is that even possible?

"Where are you taking me?" I demand.

"You're under arrest for colluding with a fugitive," Phillips mutters. We step out into the hall, and I look for someone, anyone, who can help me. There's no one here, but I try anyway. "These men are murderers!" I shout so loud that my throat feels like it's going to snap. "Somebody!"

Keegan turns and punches me, his ring snagging my lip. Blood drips down my chin, but I can't wipe it away. Following Casey's example, I spit the blood toward Keegan, splattering his pant leg. He curses and smashes me again.

I don't mind that, because every drop of blood I shed will be evidence that can be used later. If they kill me, Casey will still talk to the press, and maybe someone will find this evidence.

"Casey knew I was coming here," I say. "She'll tell the press. You won't get away with this."

They exchange looks, then drag me to the elevator and push the button to the basement. It opens to a parking garage.

I yell again as they force me out, but Phillips slaps his hand over my mouth and threatens to strangle me. Keegan straps my ankles together and lifts my feet. I fight, thrashing with my knees and my head as they carry me to a car.

Keegan drops my feet and lets me stand as they get the back door open, then they shove me inside and slam the door.

I'll be okay if they take me to jail. It's just a matter of time until Macy Weatherow breaks the story. But jail isn't our likely destination. My mind races as I study the doors for an escape. I twist my body and try to open the door, but the child lock is on.

Even if I could get the door open, I couldn't get away with my feet bound. I have to wait it out or get the attention of someone passing on the street. But they turn down a back road where there isn't much traffic, and it's starting to grow dark.

"Call the lawyer back," Keegan says to the DA as he starts up the car, and as if he's Keegan's trained puppy, Phillips clicks a number into his phone. When he hears the faint sound of ringing, Keegan snatches the phone from Phillips's hand. As he pulls out of the parking lot, I hear Barbero's voice.

"Barbero, this is Detective Keegan in Shreveport. We need to get a message to Casey Cox. Tell her we've got her lover here with us, and that we advise her to call off the interview she was about to do. Got that?"

I hear Barbero yelling on the other end.

"Bring her here today," Keegan says. "Otherwise, let her imagine the consequences."

I spit blood again and yell, "Don't bring her here!"

I know Barbero hears me, because there's more yelling. Keegan cuts the call off.

Keegan pulls the car over and thrusts the phone back to Phillips. He gets out of the car, yanks open the car door, lunges across the seat, and grabs me by my throat. I feel the blood pooling in my face, my ears burning, my throat being crushed.

After a minute, Keegan lets me go, and I gasp for breath and try to swallow. I'll have bruises on my neck and inflammation in my throat at the very least. I cough, trying to breathe. Keegan's eyes are as lethal as I've ever seen them as he breathes into my face. "You try to wave a flag again," he says, "and

I won't wait. You'll just be dead and we'll be done with it. That's what I wanted anyway. The only reason you're alive is to get her to do what we want, Lover Boy."

He walks to the passenger seat and tells Phillips to drive. Phillips gets out and goes around the car. The hierarchy here is dumbfounding. Keegan is definitely the big dog, and Phillips is submissive. Keegan must have something on him, or he's paying him massive amounts of money. But petty extortion wouldn't pay well enough to split it with so many, including the district attorney. I don't get it.

"The lawyer said Casey would turn herself in at eight tomorrow morning," Keegan says. "I told him that won't work. It's gotta be today. But we have to catch her before she actually does it. We can't let her get to the police."

"Is she going to talk to the press?" Phillips asks.

"No," Keegan says. "Trust me. She doesn't want him to die."

They don't know about Macy getting the thumb drive. If she reports it tonight, they'll probably bury me alive.

I close my eyes and pray that God won't let Casey walk into this trap. She knows she can't turn herself in to Keegan, but she doesn't know about the DA. I'm almost certain my e-mail didn't go out to her. They must have blocked my Internet access.

Why didn't I realize what Phillips was doing? How did I let this happen?

My mind flashes to an image of that Afghani store owner, sweeping his front sidewalk after our IED explosion, while my buddies lay in pieces just yards from his shop.

I shake my head, telling myself to stay present. I can't succumb to another PTSD episode, but I've never been good at controlling it. I fight the nausea rising in me, the panic, the sweat drenching my clothes. The man keeps sweeping, ignoring the tragic suffering, looking away from the evil taking place right before him, the skin burning, the blood, the smell of death.

I latch onto a Bible passage that always gives me comfort. Romans 8:28. I move my lips to the words as that image of the Afghani storekeeper tries to pull me in.

And we know that in all things God works for the good of those who love him, who have been called according to his purpose.

All things . . . all things . . .

I fix my mind on that, playing the verse through my mind over and over, trusting it, believing it. Whatever happens, death or life, betrayal or escape . . . It's going to work for good.

Isn't it?

I say the verse again in my mind as the smell of smoke and scorched flesh almost chokes me. *All things,* I say as I'm there again, dragging Dex out of the fire . . .

All things. All things. All things.

My panic subsides, the image of the sweeping man and my dying friends fades like dust.

I'm here now, not on that street in Afghanistan. I force my mind to rehearse an escape. I look around, searching for anything I can use. But I can't come up with a plan that works with my hands and feet bound. As I suspected, they're driving away from the police department and not toward it, and I know I'm going to wind up in some remote location like Casey did last night, where I'll be murdered and buried.

And Casey will still be considered a murderer, and she'll never get away. All that we've been through will be worthless. She'll never get her life back. Her family will grieve for her, and they won't know if she's dead or alive.

She'll probably be dead.

No, I can't fixate on that. All things work together for good.

I think of Jesus, suffering on a cross, bleeding to death, betrayed and mocked. That, even that, worked for good. And this will too, somehow, even if it seems like the worst possible thing.

All things.

I force my thoughts back to the possibility of escape. If I have any chance at all, it will come when they get me out of this car. I watch every turn, trying to keep track of the landmarks, and eventually we wind up driving down a long gravel road, past a mechanic's shop that looks like its doors are boarded shut. The sign is rusty and fading. It hasn't been open in a long time.

Keegan pulls onto a gravel road behind the shop, and we drive through forest for several minutes. Eventually a cabin emerges from the trees. It's nicer than I expected, and I wonder if it's another of Keegan's expensive blood-money toys.

We pull up to the front of the house, and Keegan gets out and finds the house key under a rock in the garden. It must not be his house. He comes back to my door and opens it. He cuts the bindings on my ankles, freeing them.

"Get out," he says, but before I can move he draws his weapon, holding it aimed at my head just in case I try to make a move.

The DA pulls out a firearm as well, and they've both got them trained on me. I sense that either one of them would be okay if the other one shot me right here on the spot, and they could be done with part of this nightmare. But they need me alive so they can manipulate Casey.

I let them walk me in. The house looks like it could be featured in a magazine. Every detail is perfect. Keegan goes to a room in the back of the house, then comes out with a metal rod that looks like a closet rod and some louvered doors. "It's idiot proof now," he says.

"Sure you want to keep his feet loose?" Phillips asks.

"Yeah, I'm sick of carrying him. Let him walk."

Keegan leads me to a room that looks like it could be the maid's quarters. It's empty of any furniture, and the closet doors and rod have been removed.

They shove me in and lock the solid wood door. I look around for an escape. There aren't any windows in here. The floor is carpeted, and there's only one light fixture. The ceiling is ten feet high at least, so the fixture is too high for me to reach.

Casey will demand to hear my voice. If they let me talk to her, I'll tell her to run.

237

Leave the country. There's truly no one she can trust.

But I fear it's already too late.

35

Casey

The wait is killing me. It's been hours since Dylan left to talk to the DA, and he promised to call as soon as he was finished. But the workday is over, and the sun is going down, and I'm scared to death. I can't stay here in Dex's in-laws' cabin forever. Has something happened to Dylan?

Finally, the phone chimes and I jump — then I'm deflated when I see that it's just Billy Barbero.

"Hello?"

"Liana?" he asks.

"Casey," I correct.

He ignores that and starts talking. "A Detective Keegan called me. He said to tell you they have your lover."

My heart jolts. *What?*

"Are you planning to go to the press? Because if you do, I need to be with you."

My mind is reeling. "I . . . I don't know."

"They said you knew what the 'conse-quences would be."

The subtext under Keegan's message sinks to my core. They have Dylan. They're going to kill him if I talk to the press.

"Did you talk to the DA?" I ask.

"I haven't been able to reach him. I've been talking to Chief Gates, and he assured me that they will put you into a lockdown unit and limit who can access you once you surrender. But then I got the call from the detective."

"The DA must be in on it," I mutter. "He must have called Keegan. They're trying to draw me out."

"Casey, he's right about consequences. I don't recommend you talking to the press. The police could use anything you say against you."

I grab my purse and gather my few things. "What number did they call from?" I de-mand.

"Casey, listen to me."

"What number?" I yell, grabbing a pen next to the microwave.

He looks for the number on his phone, then reads it out to me. I write it on my hand.

"So tell me where I can meet you —"

I click off the phone, open my web

browser, and Google "Find My Phone." I've heard there's a way to do it even without the Find My Phone app. If you have a number, they can tell you where it's located. I once had a friend who dropped her phone as she was walking through town, and she found a website that told her right where it was.

I go through the list of Google results, trying to find something that will work. There is one website that tracks the cell phone, but it works by making the phone ring so you can find it. That's not what I want, so I go back to look for another. Most of these are paid services, and I don't have a credit card so I can't use those. But then I find an article about how to locate a lost phone or track your kids' phones. There's an app I can download.

I quickly download it and register with the app under a fake name, and I type in Dylan's number. I wait a few minutes as it buffers, then get a message that it can't find the phone with that number. I yell, but then another idea hits me. Keegan's phone — the number Barbero just gave me. I type in the number and a map fills the screen. There's a blue dot where the phone that called Barbero is, and I zoom in and study the location. My heart sprints as I see that the phone is in Shreveport, but I don't recognize the street. It's just outside of town. I try to figure out where it is in relation to the DA's office.

There's no guarantee that Dylan is where that phone is, but it's a place to start.

I clean up any evidence that I was in Dex's in-laws' cabin, then quickly disguise myself, lock the door, and return the key to where we found it. Then I get in the rental car that Dylan left me and head toward Shreveport.

I pray all the way there, every few minutes repeating the prayer as if the only way to get through to God is to catch him when he happens to be looking my way. I know it doesn't work that way. I know that he's attentive to me every time I pray, and that Jesus is sitting at the right hand of the Father, interceding for me, like I heard in church. Surely God is attentive to Jesus.

My prayers grow more frantic as I get closer to Shreveport, navigating my way to that blue dot on the map.

36

Dylan

As I wait for Keegan to kill me, I search the room for anything that can be used as a weapon. The closet doesn't have a shelf I could dislodge, and Keegan already removed the rod for hanging clothes.

I take a quick inventory. There's a light switch by the door, but with my hands bound it would be tough to do more than short out the switch. I might be able to break the switch plate and fashion it into a sharp enough object to help me fight my way out.

There's crown molding, baseboards, Sheetrock. With no tools, I can't do anything with those.

I go to the light switch and bend over, stretching my arms up, almost out of their sockets. I use my thumbnail to turn the screws, loosening the plastic plate. Yes, this could work. I could break a corner off, then another corner, and use it as a makeshift weapon. I'd only get one shot at it, since they'd probably notice it's missing the next time they come into the room.

I study the door. There are hinges on this side of it, and I wonder how long the screws are. The door sounded solid when they closed it. If it's solid wood, then the screws might be longer, and if I place them between my knuckles, they could work as a weapon. I step quietly toward it and study them, inserting my fingernail and trying to turn each of them. There's no way I can get them out without a screwdriver.

But if I break the switch plate into something I can use as a screwdriver, I can dislodge the screws from the hinges. If I ever hear them leave, I'll be able to dislodge the door and escape. But if they don't leave . . . if they come for me . . .

I look around once more. The only other thing in here is the carpet. Yes! The carpet.

I go to the doorless, shelfless, rodless closet and sit down with my back to the wall. I slide my fingers behind me to the edge of the carpet and pull it up from the floor. It comes up pretty easily. I pull it back until I feel what I'm looking for.

The wooden tack strip with small nails sticking up to hold the carpet in place. I grab the wood that's nailed to the subfloor, and I manage to get one end loose. I pull the other end and get it free too.

I tuck the carpet back down, hiding what I've done, and swing the three-foot strip. Yes, it could do a lot of damage if I use it right. And maybe the nails will help me cut the plastic ties on my hands. I try, but I can't apply enough pressure to cut through.

I pull up my pant leg where I still have dressing on my burns. There's no way to hide it against my leg because the tacks will get caught on my jeans. I stick it back under the carpet, leaving the rug loose so I can grab it when I need it.

When they come to kill me, I can at least fight.

Casey will demand proof of life, and that's why they're keeping me alive. They're using me to lure her here.

I hope Casey is keeping her head down. When Barbero told her that Keegan had me, she probably went ballistic. I hope she's thinking clearly and not just doing what they say.

But she will. She's brave and selfless, and she will put my life above her own.

I know her.

The thought brings a stinging mist to my eyes. I don't know when anyone ever in my life has put me first like that. My mom and dad sure didn't. My sister and I were pretty much just trying to survive — every kid for himself.

She loves me. I close my eyes and replay those words we exchanged last night, when I told her I was in love with her and, teary-eyed and almost unable to speak, she said, "Me too."

I don't need more than that. I know the power and meaning of those two words. Today, they put her in deep danger and may cost her her life.

I wish she didn't love me. *Please, God. Stop her from coming!*

If I can just stay alive until KTAL reports what I've given them. When it comes out on the news, Keegan and Phillips will be so rattled that they might take off and leave me here alone. If they do, I'll find some way to escape.

It's not much, but it's the only hope I have.

I have to survive for her.

37

Casey

As I drive to Shreveport, approaching the blue dot on the map that represents Keegan's phone, I call KTAL, the station Dylan was planning to take the thumb drive to. After the robotic menu offers my options, I choose to be routed to the voice mail of Macy Weatherow.

"This is Casey Cox," I say. "Someone delivered a thumb drive to you today with evidence showing that I didn't kill my friend Brent Pace. Two police detectives — Gordon Keegan and Sy Rollins — did it and set me up so I would get the blame. If you haven't already, please look at those files. These men also killed my father and they and their partners have extorted money from multiple businesses in the area. They killed a dry cleaner last week, and a few days ago, Keegan murdered Sy Rollins, his partner."

I sound like a raving lunatic. She's going to think I'm delusional. It's such a complex web of lies and murder, and no one wants to believe a cop could do these things. They'd rather suspect me.

What will she do? Will she call the police first or investigate it herself?

"Look, I know how this sounds," I say as I drive. "But Dylan Roberts, who's a PI working on the case, took all this to District Attorney Phillips this afternoon, and now he's vanished."

My voice breaks. "I needed for someone to have the truth. I can do an interview if you're interested. I probably won't have the same number, but I'll try to call back later."

I burst into tears as I drive through the night, realizing the blue dot is taking me farther from civilization, where I won't be able to get help. "I'm sorry . . . to bring you into this, but you seem to be an objective reporter, and this is the biggest story you've ever done. Think about it. Even if I'm lying, every national news show is going to want to have you on to talk about this phone call. All I ask is that, before you decide I'm hysterical and insane, just look at the stuff on the flash drive. Just listen to the interviews, read the evidence, study the pictures. Then realize that the people we're talking

248

about are deadly. Be very careful."

My throat constricts, and I try to find my voice again. "Maybe . . . get a bodyguard." I hope she'll tell others — reporters, editors, her station manager. They can kill us one at a time, but they can't kill us all.

38

Dylan

I hear a car pulling up outside. I pray it's not Casey, that they haven't checked my phone, found the only number in my contacts list, and lured her here.

I hear the front door opening, and I get down on the floor with my ear to the slit beneath the door, hoping to hear better. I hear men's muffled voices, then a string of angry curses. They grow louder, and I hear their footsteps coming closer to the door. I get up, move across the room to the closet, and sit down with my back to the wall, my bound hands finding the carpet tack strip, my only weapon. I get back up as the key scratches in the lock, and I stand stiff, my feet apart and my teeth set, ready to fight if I have to. The door opens.

Jim Pace steps into the room.

My mouth falls open and I suck in a breath. Jim Pace, the father of Brent, my best childhood friend. Jim Pace, who hired me to find Casey and bring her to justice for his son's death.

"*Jim!*" I just gape at him, too stunned to move.

He looks fifteen years older as he stands there, shaking his head at me. "Dylan, what are you doing, man?"

"What are *you* doing?" I ask. "Are you working with these guys? Is this your house?"

"You're going rogue," he says. "Elise and I trusted you."

I tighten my hold on the carpet strip behind my back. "And I trusted you! Casey Cox didn't kill Brent, and I think you must know that. I don't understand how —"

"What?" he cuts in. "Of *course* she did." He glances back toward the door and comes farther into the room. "What are you saying?"

I'm confused now. Is he with them or not? "Your son was helping her get evidence about who killed her father, Andy Cox. They shut him up when he got too close to the truth. Keegan stabbed your son to death. Are you okay with that?"

His face changes, and his hand is shaking as he rakes it through his hair. "Dylan, son, I think you're having PTSD issues — paranoia, delusions — and they're causing us a lot of problems." He pauses and stares at the floor, as if playing my words back through his mind.

My mouth is twisting now. "Jim, tell me you weren't complicit in the murder of your own son."

"Of course I wasn't!" he shouts. "Brent's death wasn't about Andy Cox. That's . . . it isn't even possible. Why would Brent care about it?"

"Because he cared about Casey."

He's sweating now, and he's breathing heavily. I can tell that he's hearing this, considering it, for the first time. "It isn't true," he says in a voice suddenly raspy.

"Jim, it is. Why wouldn't I want to find Brent's real killers? It was Keegan and Rollins. Phillips is in it with them too, and I don't know who else, and now Keegan has murdered Rollins, and somehow, you're connected to these people?"

He reaches out to the wall and steadies himself. His eyes mist over. He looks at me with lethal sorrow and whispers, "They blackmailed me . . . I didn't know."

"You can stop this now, Jim," I say in a low voice. "If you don't, you're complicit in all these murders. And now you'll be complicit in mine."

"Nobody's killing anybody," he says on a wheezy breath. He holds his palm out to me, as if telling me to stay put. "Just . . . wait here. I need to . . . clear some things up. I'll be back. Just hold on."

He seems lost in thought as I watch him walk out. He locks the door, and I lie down and listen at the bottom of it again, in disbelief that this man I admired and trusted so much, this employer of mine . . . Brent's dad . . . is connected to this extortion and murder ring. What could they be blackmailing him for? What could be so important that he'd let them drag him into this?

I hear his voice rising outside the door. Cursing, crashing, Keegan's voice bellowing across the house. It's clear from the words I can make out that Jim really didn't know that Keegan had anything to do with Brent's death. I wonder how many others Keegan has blackmailed. It explains how he got so rich. Extortion alone didn't explain it. Elise doesn't know. She can't. She's a strong Christian woman, and she wouldn't stand for this.

"Did you kill my son?" Jim cries out, his voice echoing throughout the house. "*Did* you kill my son?" he screams. "Did you stab him to death? Did you watch him bleed until there was nothing left? Did you make me bury him?" His voice breaks off, and I hear more crashing.

I hear things breaking, grunts, muffled yells. Something shatters on the tile floor. "Did you kill Sy too?"

"Jim, you let him get into your head. None of this is true!" DA Phillips is shouting.

Keegan's voice fires back. "You don't have any say here, Jim! He's lying to influence you just when we're luring the girl here. Get a grip!"

Another crash. Then suddenly I hear all three voices rising at once. It sounds like they're coming toward my door. I hear the key in the lock, more grunts, someone swearing.

Then there's a gunshot, and I'm showered with splinters of wood through the door.

39

Dylan

The gunshot leaves a hole in the door where my head would have been if I'd been standing there, and I smell gunpowder. I drop the tack strip and get to my feet and study the hole, keeping well to the side. Blood has spattered the door.

It wasn't me they were shooting at.

I hear Keegan's voice, quieter now. "We've got to get him out of here. Help me. Now!"

They're moving away from me, and I can't hear them well. But I've heard enough.

Jim Pace is dead.

Nausea rises to my throat, and I hold it back. I'm sweating and shaking, and things fade to black, my mind disappearing into smoke, my lungs closing down, my skin burning and the feel of blood slime on my knees, soaking into the fabric of my uniform . . . I'm there, on the street in Kandahar, coughing and looking for cover, and I see my buddies on the ground. I call out to them, but I can't hear. I've gone deaf. Then I see Dex get to his elbow and try to sit up. I see his mouth moving. He's telling me something, but I can't hear him, and as I move toward him, yelling, "Let's go!" I see that he can't go anywhere. Both legs are burned to the bone, and his arm is blown to pieces.

That same blackness clouds my head again, closing over me, and then I hear gunfire, the smell of smoke and gunpowder mingling with something like ammonia, and I can't see to get out of the way. I grope for Dex, and I feel his hand closing over my arm. I have to stop his bleeding, but first I have to get him out of here. I take off my belt and tie off the area just below his knee and just above the bloody mess of his lower leg. Then I throw his good arm around my shoulders, get to my feet, and run behind our overturned Humvee, covering us from more fire.

I find his belt, still buckled at his waist where his shirt is still tucked in, and I slip it off him and tie off the other mangled leg. Gunfire keeps up its staccato song above our heads, and I know I have to take him farther. "Stay with me, man," I say, but I doubt he can hear me. I can't hear my own voice.

I throw him over my shoulders, knowing that when I grab his thighs it must be agony, but moving is his only hope.

I look back at the others. None of them are moving. They're all dead, scorched and bloody, bodies jolting as machine gun fire rat-a-tats through them.

I run blindly, my lungs burning, ears ringing, bullets exploding into objects around me. I run and pray, run and pray, and as I run, I know I probably won't be able to save either of us.

I heave, the choking feeling jolting me out of the black memory, and I'm back in the room where Keegan has locked me, where my best friend's dad is dead on the other side of the door, where I can't help Casey or even myself.

40

Casey

The blue dot leads me down a dark road past a lake. I've never been here before, but it jogs a memory. Someone I knew had a lake house out here. Who was it?

The seed of a memory seems buried too deep to sprout. I zoom in closer on my phone's screen, and I see a road up ahead that I'm supposed to turn down.

I'm very close now. As I move closer to the dot, I cut off my headlights so they can't see me coming.

I move more slowly now, hoping the sound of my tires in the gravel won't alert anyone. I won't go all the way. I'll walk part of the way.

I wish I had a gun. All this time, all this hiding, and I've never had one. The last thing I wanted to be caught with was a weapon so they could prove I was armed and dangerous. But now I need to be both.

I pull around a curve and see lights up ahead. There's a house, tucked into a wooded area. I pull the car into the trees and turn off my dome light so it won't come on when I open the door.

I need a crowbar, a knife, an umbrella, anything I can fight with, but there's nothing. There could be a tire iron in the trunk of the rental car, but if I dig around for the jack to find it, I might make noise and call attention to myself.

I should have stopped and gotten supplies. Some criminal I am.

I leave the keys in the car and walk along the muddy shoulder of the gravel drive toward the house.

The porch light comes on, and I slip behind a tree. Voices. A door closes, and I peer around the trunk and see two shadows emerging into the light. Moving closer, I hear Keegan's voice. I don't know who the other man is, but it's not Dylan.

I try to quiet my breathing. I look again as they move toward the trees. The two men move slowly, clumsily, and as they pass a lantern on a pole in the yard near a firepit, I realize they're carrying someone.

41

Casey

Rage like lava erupts inside me, and I ignore the risk and follow the men into the woods, desperate to know whether the man they're carrying is Dylan.

The sound of the night forest muffles my steps, as if God has made it crescendo just for me. Moonlight shines through the trees, and as the men pass through the beams of light, I lower behind a bush and see the faces of Keegan and another man I don't know. I can't make out the face of the dead man.

I'm close to hurling myself at them with all the rage of a lunatic when they drop him onto the ground.

My heart bangs against my chest and tears sting my eyes and knot my throat. It *must* be Dylan.

I fall to my knees as Keegan grabs a shovel leaning against a tree and starts digging. I cover my mouth with both hands to muffle my horror.

"Go back to the house and get another shovel," Keegan orders. "He keeps it in the shed behind the house."

"Do we have to do this?" the other man asks. "I'm not dressed for digging."

"You've already got Jim's blood on your pant leg." I catch my breath as Keegan lets out his good-ole-boy cackle.

Jim's blood? It isn't Dylan? Now I see that the dead man is dressed in pressed pants and a button-down shirt covered with blood. Dylan was wearing jeans when he left this morning.

It isn't him! There's only one body. He could still be alive. I turn back to the house, where the windows are lit up. He must be in there.

I move back through the woods, dodging from tree to tree as quietly as I can, the sweet sound of wind through the leaves covering me. In the darkest part of the yard, I dash from the tree line to the house and the back door . . . the one I saw them coming from.

It's unlocked. I slip quietly inside, hoping not to draw the attention of anyone else who might be inside. The living room is dimly lit with just a couple of lamps. I don't see anyone, so I tiptoe into the kitchen. No one.

The sound of scraping down the hall snags my attention. I move to the dark hall and look toward the noise.

A spot of light shines through a hole in the door at the end of the hall. I edge closer and hear the scraping again.

"Dylan?" I call out.

"Casey?" His voice from the other side of the door makes life worth living again. I steady myself on the wall as I catch my breath and try to focus through the tears rimming my eyes. "Are you all right?"

"Yes. Thank God you're here. Can you get the door open?"

I try the doorknob, but it's locked. "No, do you know where they keep the key?"

"Look in that living room area. Casey, they'll be back."

I run back up the hall into the living room and look around for a key. There's nothing on the coffee table, but on the dining room table across the room, I see a key next to a coffee cup. As I grab it, I peer out the window and see the lantern still in the trees. I hurry back to the door. "I think I found it," I say, jamming it into the lock. It gives, and the door flies open.

"Casey!" he says on a rush of breath. I throw my arms around him. But his hands are bound.

"Let's go," he says.

"Wait. I can cut your ties."

He waits just inside the living room as I run into the kitchen. I grab a knife from a holder on the counter, go back and cut his hands loose. He takes my hand and pulls me toward the front door on the opposite end of the house from where the men are. "They killed Jim Pace, Brent's dad. This is his place."

"What?" I whisper. "I knew someone I knew had a lake house here." We reach the door, but I don't go out. "Wait! I have to get a picture of the door. It's evidence we need."

"Casey!"

I run back to the splintered door and, turning on my flash, snap pictures of the bloodstains, the floor, and the walls.

I know Keegan will clean it up, but if I can show the clean cops where to use luminol to find the blood, we can prove what was done here. The sight of Jim Pace's blood makes me shiver.

"They're burying him," I say as I go back to Dylan, the gravity of that chilling through me. "They'll be busy for a little while longer. My car is that way, just out of sight." As we get out among the dark trees, I point toward the car.

"You're a genius," he whispers. I run just ahead of him in the direction of the car.

When it's at last visible in the moonlight, Dylan whispers, "I'll drive."

The keys are still in it. The dome light doesn't come on, but the door dings when he opens it. I dive in on the driver's side and climb over the center console so I won't cause another ding. Dylan gets in and closes the door, silencing it. He starts the ignition and slowly backs out of the trees onto the gravel path. The headlights are off, but the brake lights can't be hidden, and their red reflection lights the trees behind us.

He puts the car in drive and pulls carefully back toward the road. Maybe they didn't see us. But as we reach the road and turn south, I see the lantern beam bouncing toward Keegan's car as he runs to it. As Dylan gains speed, Keegan's car pulls out behind us.

"Hang on!" Dylan says. He guns the accelerator and the car shoots forward, flying toward a more populated area. I get on my knees in my seat and reach across him to grab his seat belt and clip it into its slot, then I sit down and clip my own. Dylan powers the car around a corner, then again, and I hang on.

"Do you see them?"

I look out the window and see the headlights turning behind us. "Yes. They're on us."

"Get on the floor."

I unhook my belt and fall to the floorboard. He turns sharply again, and I wonder if he knows where he's going, or if it even matters. He rounds a curve, tires screeching. A bullet crashes through the back window, past Dylan's head. He swerves.

I rise up to see how close they are.

There's only the space of three or four cars between us, and they're gaining speed. Dylan swings to the left again, then the right, and finally we're on a street with traffic. Dylan zigs and zags between cars, in and out of lanes, and I lift up and see that the car chasing us is pinned behind a box truck.

Dylan hangs a left, barely passing in front of a van, and I bump my head as I try to steady myself. He swings right, then left again, then slows. The tires screech as he makes a quick U-turn, then swings to the left again. "I think I lost them."

"Don't count on it," I say.

"Stay down. I'm getting out of this part of town." He drives for several minutes more. Then I feel him slowing.

I move back into my seat and hook my belt again, watching for any sign of lights following us. Of course Keegan could have turned them off, or he could have taken another route, planning to cut us off. I don't think he has given up.

"Are you all right?" Dylan asks.

"Yeah."

He turns onto a four-lane road and matches his speed to the traffic around us. I watch for some sign of Keegan, but no one seems to be following us. Dylan still moves from lane to lane, passing cars, turning onto side streets, going around the block, then coming back.

Eventually, he turns onto a side street with no traffic, and we check again.

No sign of Keegan.

"We have to call Macy Weatherow," I say. "I left her a message earlier."

"Yeah. Call her."

I call her at the number where I left the long voice mail, and this time she answers. "Macy Weatherow."

Relieved, I catch my breath. "Macy . . . this is Casey Cox."

"I was hoping it was you. I got your message. I've been waiting. I want to meet with you tonight. Is that possible?"

"I don't know if it's wise for us to meet

with you in person."

"Us?"

"I have a friend with me," I say. "It's too dangerous, for you and us. The district attorney is involved in this corruption, and he and Detective Keegan are looking for us right now. They want us dead. We're too much of a threat to them."

"The DA?" she says, and I can tell from her voice that she's not sure whether to believe me. It doesn't really matter if she does, as long as she reports it.

"Look, I know this whole thing seems like a stretch, but there's a story here even if I prove to be out of my mind. I'm a fugitive. I'm accused of killing several people. All you have to do is let us tell the story, and whether it turns out I'm insane or paranoid or not, you'll still have a story that everyone will want."

"Sold," she says. "All right, let's do it over the phone. I'm recording now, if that's all right with you."

"Yes, we want you to."

"Okay, let's go," she says. "This is Macy Weatherow recording this interview for KTAL, Channel 6 News, and I'm talking to fugitive Casey Cox. Casey, for the record, do I have permission to record this interview?"

"Yes," I say again.

"Casey, can you tell me again what you told me on my voice mail?"

Dylan pulls behind a dark building and parks in the shadows as I launch into our story. After I get it all out, he takes the phone, reveals to Macy who he is, and adds what happened to him today.

When we're done, Macy is quiet for a second. I worry that she still doesn't believe us, that she's calling the police and having our phone traced at this very moment. I expect a helicopter to fly overhead, or a bank of headlights to come from out of nowhere and surround us.

But finally, she says, "I talked to that dry cleaner's wife last week right after his death. I had the distinct impression that she wasn't telling everything she knew. I suspected there was something going on, that maybe she knew who killed her husband and she was afraid for the rest of her family."

"That must have been before she talked to me," Dylan says. "I told her to leave town after that."

"She must have. She hasn't answered my calls, and I went to her house the other day and she wasn't there. And while you were talking, Casey, I looked up our reports on the death of Sara Meadows. I went to the scene when it happened, and ever since, I've wondered why there was never a resolution to that case. The police never found who killed her. She *worked* for them. You would think it'd be top priority."

"Then you believe us?" I ask.

"It's just a tough sell. Brent Pace's father was involved, and the DA? Even if it's all true, making viewers believe it is going to be hard."

"Is it your job to persuade them or just report the news?" Dylan asks. "There's a body at that house, unless they've already gone back to bury him."

"What's that address?" she asks.

We look on my phone for the destination on the phone-finding app, and I give it to Macy. "Don't go there alone. You need a SWAT team."

"I think I'm going to get some of our main news anchors in to report this, but before it's aired, I'll have to call Chief Gates for a quote. Do you think I can trust him?"

"I don't know," I say. "We don't have any proof he's involved, and he may not be, but it's possible."

"Be careful with Captain Swayze," Dylan cuts in. "I think he could be connected."

"So what's your plan?" she asks.

Dylan looks at me.

"My attorney is negotiating my surrender," I say, "as long as I can be confident I won't be murdered in the jail cell. Your exposure will help with that."

"There's not time for me to unpack all you've said, so I'm probably going to air your whole interview live. NBC, my network, will want this too."

When we finally hang up, I'm trembling. Dylan gets out of the car and comes around to my side. He opens my door and pulls me up into his arms. I can feel that he's shaking too.

He kisses my hair, then I lift my face and he finds my lips. His are soft against mine, wet, and they hit me like a sedative that I'll forevermore crave. I let my worries slide away as his strength renews mine. When he breaks the kiss, his gentle sigh next to my ear tells me he feels the same.

He pulls back and looks at me for a long, stricken moment. "We did this."

I smile. "Yes, we did."

"Your name is going to be cleared and you won't have to go to jail."

"Even if I do, it's okay as long as Keegan pays."

He crushes me tighter, and I press my head against his chest. I can hear his heart through his shirt, and the rhythm soothes me. I don't want him to let me go, but I know we can't stay here.

"Let's find a place to sleep tonight. I'll get Dex to help us again."

"Maybe we should just sleep in the car."

"We need a TV and Internet. I want to see the minute they air our interview."

"But if Keegan knew about you, don't you think he knew about Dex?"

"I don't think so. If they knew, they would have tried to take him out already. I stayed with him the other night and Keegan didn't find me. I think he's still off their radar. I communicate with him on a burner."

I hope he's right. I like Dex and I don't want him to meet the same fate as Brent for helping us.

I get back into the car, and Dylan gets in behind the wheel. He gets Dex on the phone.

"Hey, buddy. Things are about to go nuclear, man." I listen as he gives Dex a recap of the day. "It's airing tonight, I hope. Morning at the latest. Listen, can you get us a room somewhere? Meet me somewhere to give us the key?"

"You got it," I hear Dex say.

Dylan tells him a place to meet that might be obscure enough, and warns him not to take any chances. We sit still in the car and wait to hear back.

"Is Dex going to be brought into all this when I turn myself in?"

"I don't think so. I think I can keep him out of it, at least until Keegan's behind bars."

My mind drifts to my sister Hannah and my mom, and how this media storm will impact them. "Do you think they'll let my family visit when I'm in jail?" I ask.

"I hope you won't be there long enough."

"You think Billy can get me out on bond?"

"Billy?" he asks, laughing. "Who is this guy?"

I give him a quick rundown on how I met him.

Dylan touches my chin, turns my face to his. "You need a better lawyer. Barbero is in over his head. Besides, he's a shark."

"I know," I say. "I just didn't know who else to call. I'll get a criminal attorney once I've turned myself in."

"I'll help your family with that unless they arrest me too."

This is starting to get too real. "They won't, will they? You were kidnapped! You were held against your will, almost murdered at least twice. Surely when a jury hears all this . . ."

"It takes a long time to get to a jury," he says.

"Okay, I understand why they'd arrest me. But you . . . The police department and the attorney general's office must know that they're culpable in this, and that none of it would have happened if they'd had a handle on their departments. You were actually investigating this."

"We'll see," he says. "I need to be out so I can help you."

I scoot closer to him and lay my head on his shoulder. "Let's not talk about it for a few minutes," I say. "Let's pretend we're a normal couple, just sitting in the night with a breeze blowing through the window, in no hurry, with no pressure . . ." My voice cracks, my throat tightening. "I just want to remember what it was like to be normal for a little while."

"Me too," he whispers, kissing my hair.

"Do you think we ever could be normal?" I ask. "I mean, you and me? Is this . . . whatever it is . . . is it just because we're in this centrifuge of danger? Would we get along if we didn't have the threat of death and prison hanging over us?"

"Yes," he says without hesitation. "Yes, we could. We will." He smiles down at me. "I've been a nightmare in relationships. I'd get involved with somebody, and she'd start expecting me to be something . . . and then I'd zone out or I'd have a bad night and not call her for days . . . or I'd be in a mood and not want to put it on her. Or I'd just be unmotivated and sullen. Eventually she'd drift off . . . or maybe I drifted off first. Happened the same way every time. I didn't think I could be with anyone in a normal way."

"Exactly my point," I say. "I've been pretty standoffish too."

"But I've thought this through," he says. "I've actually visualized it. Saturdays just hanging out, doing nothing . . . I can see it. You don't bring drama."

I shake my head, disbelieving. "Seriously? It brings *me*."

"Right, but even with all the chaos around you, you calm me down. You steady me. I'm more myself when I'm with you than I've ever been with anybody else."

Tears rim my eyes, but I blink them back. I don't want to cry. "Remember when you told me to look for God? To see where he's working?"

"Yeah."

I wipe a tear on my cheek. "I did that. And I saw him all over the place. I started trying to be intentionally grateful. Looking for the good. Seeing it."

"I'm so glad."

"Just before I was arrested in Memphis, I surrendered to Christ. I understood why he died. How I was involved in that. How it impacts me."

He looks at me in the moonlight. "Really? You told him?"

"Yes," I say, and I don't know why that makes me cry more.

He watches the tears roll down my cheeks and wipes them away. "I wanted that for you. There have been times since I've been home from overseas when I've felt like I had to cling to God. Like he was about to slip through my fingers if I didn't. But when I started on your case, I got my purpose back, and then I realized that God was clinging to *me* all along."

"I wouldn't have found him without you," I whisper.

"I wouldn't have found my way back to him without *you.*"

When he kisses me again, I feel the completion of God's plan, and all that lies before me is no longer fear. God has paved my way to Dylan.

Life is hard, and it's going to get harder. But whatever he has for me, he'll equip me to handle it.

Dylan's phone chimes. It's Dex, and he's got us a room and is ready to meet.

I put on my seat belt and we pull out of our hiding place, still watching the headlights behind us for any sign of Keegan or others. We get to the meeting place — an alley behind the local Dollar General, and we don't get out of our cars. We simply drive up beside Dex, and he passes the key to Dylan.

"Thanks, buddy."

"Take care of yourselves now. It's getting hairy."

"You don't even know how hairy," Dylan says. "Keep your eyes on the news and watch your back."

"You know I will."

As we pull away, I look back and hope I get to see Dex again. I hope I get to know him in normalcy, if there ever is such a thing for me, and I hope I get to meet his wife. Dylan has said great things about her. I think I'd like her.

We're quiet as we drive to the motel he's arranged for us.

42

Keegan

There's a way out of this. I've been in tough spots before, and I'm always able to find my way out. I do miss Rollins, though. He might be useful in a time like this, but then again, he could be like a deadweight strapped to my ankle.

In fact, they're all deadweights. Every last one of these morons I deal with. Everyone who's enjoying the abundant cash — or the secrecy they've been willing to pay top dollar for.

It all got out of control when we had to use Jim Pace's camp house. I didn't expect him to show up. A smarter man would have stayed home and let us take care of it, but there he was, trying to micromanage me. I knew when I saw him tonight that we were going to have to do something drastic.

I hate drastic. Drastic is a place you never want to be, a place that means you're failing, that you have to run a Hail Mary. Drastic means you're not on top, and I have to be on top or the engine leaves the tracks.

Jim had to know who we had in the back room, then he had to talk to him. At that point, he was the walking dead already.

When Dylan threw Brent's death up to Jim, he came back out, livid over the betrayal, like he had any right to confront me. We had to put a stop to Jim's melodramatic rant, but it was a bloody mess and I wish we'd done it differently. And how was I to know that Casey Cox was already there, waiting for a chance to go in? It's almost like we invited her.

Stupid, stupid mistake.

If I hadn't had Phillips there, angsting over his pressed trousers and his pristine reputation and negotiating for more cash for his next election to offset his heavy conscience, I would have been faster on my feet and my wits would have been sharper.

The human conscience. It's always a hindrance. It's what makes all my buddies second-guess what we do, until more cash calms them. But no amount of cash would have stopped the madness that happened tonight.

And Dylan and Casey Cox got away. It's unfathomable to me. Unforgivable.

In the back of my head I hear my father's gruff voice. *Why don't we see if we can improve that judgment of yours a little bit?*

My dad's favorite sport was rigging me up to the top floor of the barn and letting me hang there with ropes around my arms until my cartilage strained in the sockets and blisters rubbed on my skin. He would leave me hanging there for nine hours, ten sometimes, and one time he did it overnight. I couldn't breathe, the pain was so great. And my mother would let him do it. I don't know if she ever asked him where I was. She knew he was *dealing with me.* That's all she needed to know.

Then came the time that he miscalculated, and I got the best of him. And that was the end of that.

I drive through town, looking at every motel parking lot, trying to discover where Dylan and the Cox girl may have parked for the night. I have the others out combing other sections of town, but no one has found anything yet.

I slam the steering wheel. How could anybody be that evasive? Casey Cox can't be that smart, and neither can Dylan Roberts.

They've gotten lucky a couple of times, but they're about to lose their luck.

279

I'm creeping past my tenth hotel when I realize we've got no way to stop them from talking to the press. They've probably called a dozen reporters by now.

It's going to be bad.

If Casey got to the media and they report this, my path just got narrower. I won't be able to get to my plane or my Jaguar in Dallas or Candace or my yacht . . .

I have to get out of town now. I make a U-turn and turn on the blue lights installed under my grill. As fast as I can drive through traffic, I make my way to my house. I open the garage with my remote, pull in, and close it behind me. I leave the car running and jog inside.

Gail comes out of the bedroom in her robe. "Gordon, finally! I've been trying to call you."

I go into the bedroom, grab some clothes, and stuff them into a bag. "Gotta take a trip," I say.

"A trip? Gordon! Where are you going? Is it about Sy's murder?"

When I ignore her, she grasps my arm. "Gordon, answer me!"

"I don't have time for this!" I shake her off, push her away from me.

She doesn't cry often, but she clouds up now. "What have you done? It's like you're making an escape. Packing a bag and taking off, just like that, in the middle of the night?"

I can't tell her more, and even if I could I don't want to. I go to the back of our closet to the safe I have behind my clothes, and I punch in the combination and open it. I take a bag from the top shelf and start shoving in the cash from the safe.

She stands at the door behind me, unable to see what I'm getting.

"When will you be back? What about Kurt's wedding? It's coming up!"

I don't even answer her as I grab my shaving kit and stuff it full of things I'll need, then throw it into the bag. When I'm almost to the front door with her trailing behind, chattering her little annoying pleas, I turn back to her. "If anybody asks, you didn't see me, got it?"

She doesn't like that. "Gordon, you've got to tell me —"

"I don't have to tell you anything! Now get out of my way."

When she tries to grab me again, I swing my arm so hard that it knocks her to the floor. I go out the door, back into the garage. I throw my duffel bag in over the driver's seat, and it bounces on the passenger side. I head to the airport where my

Cessna is tied down.

But then I think better of it. I have to go back to the Paces' camp house and get Jim's body. I didn't bury it, and now I can't leave him there. Dylan is sure to have the place crawling with cops by morning, if they're not there already.

I drive like Dale Earnhardt, my blue lights flashing. There aren't any cops around at the turnoff. I switch off my lights and creep up the dirt road the way Casey must have. Still no one here. I go all the way to the house and pop the trunk.

I take my flashlight and go into the woods to the grave we were digging. Jim's body is still there, slumped where we left him. I get him under the arms and drag him to my car, lift him into the trunk. Then I go back and shovel the grave full of dirt, kick leaves over it.

I return to the car, toss the shovels in on top of the body, and slam the trunk. I'll find a place to dump him before I leave town. No, I don't have time. I can't waste any more time on him.

I'll just leave him in my trunk and take off in my plane.

If I don't follow a flight plan and I don't sign in with the tower, I can go wherever I want and they can't find me. I can do this.

Flying at night, I can disappear.

My mind races. Where will I go?

Maybe Ecuador, where no one will look for me and there's no extradition treaty. I'll be leaving behind everything I own and most of the cash, but this should be enough to get me going. Rollins always said it would come to an end at some point, and it made me livid because I didn't want to hear it. I never believed it.

It occurs to me that he had quite a bit of cash stashed away as well. And I know where he kept it. I head toward his house. The police have removed the crime scene tape by now, and I know where he had a key. I find it over the back door, and I go in. Idiot.

I see where the investigators have gone through his things, and I begin to worry. But when I go to the fake wall in his back bedroom, I realize they never found it. I move the things that are in the way, hiding it, and get to his safe.

I don't know the combination, but if I know Rollins, he wouldn't have trusted his memory. He has it written down somewhere around here. I just have to find it.

I look around, trying to think like he would think, and then I see a series of numbers on the underside of his closet shelf, written in pencil.

I laugh out loud, then punch in the numbers, and I hear a click. There it is, all his cash, in stacks of hundred-dollar bills. This is too good to be true.

I stuff the piles of cash into an old, dirty suitcase that's sitting against the wall. Then I carry it out to my car.

This is going to work. When I get to Ecuador I can access my cash in my offshore bank accounts. I can buy a little house on the water and start completely over. And if by some chance they've located my accounts, I can live for a long time on this cash.

I laugh hard as I drive to the private airport. Dylan Roberts doesn't have what it takes to bring this old man down. And neither does Casey Cox.

43

Casey

We park a block away and walk to the motel. The place is musty, but it'll do. Our room has one king-size bed and a sitting area with a couch.

Dylan immediately crosses the room and looks out the window to make sure there's no one on the other side of the building.

When he turns back, it's suddenly awkward. "I'll sleep on the couch again," he says, "but I don't think I'll be doing that much sleeping anyway."

"You have to sleep," I say. "After all that's happened to you, you need to rest. You still have burns . . ."

"Trust me, more has happened to you. Your gunshot wound still isn't healed. Your wrists. Your face is even still bruised."

Laughter suddenly rises up in my throat, and I abandon myself to the mild hysteria. I drop onto the small couch as gales of giggles blow over me. It's contagious, and he starts laughing too.

When I can finally find my voice, I whisper, "We're such a pair. Gunshot wounds, burns . . . What couple could say those things?"

The laughter is sweet relief, stress cascading on uncontrollable giggles. Finally, mine subsides, and I listen to the way he laughs. I haven't heard that before. I like the sound of it. His misty gaze tells me he likes mine too.

Wiping our eyes and calming our breathing, we turn on the TV to KTAL, where Macy Weatherow works. Some sitcom I've never seen before is playing. "Nothing yet," Dylan says.

"What do you think is taking so long?"

"She's confirming things," he says. "Getting quotes from officials. I guarantee you Chief Gates knows it's about to blow up by now."

"What if he's involved and he covers himself?" I ask him.

"I think we'll be able to tell by his reaction," he says. "If he demands an investigation, goes after Keegan and Phillips, suspends Keegan from the force, and contacts the AG, I think we can conclude that he's clean."

"If he doesn't?"

"If he's involved, he'll defend the force and say that the stories are patently untrue and that they can't listen to you because you're a known killer."

That makes me shiver.

"If he does that, it doesn't mean no one's going to believe you. You're very persuasive, and your story is true. The press can verify a lot of it. Believe me, the rest of the press will go crazy with it. It'll be a mushroom cloud."

I try to imagine what the news cycle will look like tomorrow.

"Go to bed," he whispers. "Tomorrow's going to be a hard day. I want you to sleep."

I nod and say, "I want that for you too."

"There'll be time for me to sleep later. Truth is, I'm not that great of a sleeper anyway."

I look at him. "Dreams?"

"Yeah. The joys of my condition. I sleep with a patch that stimulates my brain waves or something. It helps. It's part of a clinical study I signed up for."

I grow somber and stare at the TV screen. "I think you were right about me having PTSD. I have bad dreams too. And sometimes in dangerous situations, I flash back to . . . other things."

"We have a lot in common. But I feel like I'm getting better."

"Maybe I'll get better too, now that I understand what it is."

"I have a great shrink I can recommend."

I take my purse into the bathroom and dig for a toothbrush I keep there. I don't have much else. I'm still wearing the same clothes I bought at the convenience store after escaping from Keegan. I haven't had a moment to think about buying something new.

I take off my outer T-shirt and check my stitches. They're puckering red. I probably need antibiotics. I wish I could have gotten back to my car and my emergency bag in Memphis.

I shower, put my clothes back on, and blow my hair dry, wishing I could get rid of the black and go back to my original blonde before I'm blasted all over the media.

When I finally come out, Dylan has the leg of his jeans pulled up, and he's checking the burns on his calves. As if he doesn't want me to see them, he mashes the tape back down.

He's watching an *Andy Griffith* rerun now. "Still nothing?" I ask.

"No. I'm getting impatient."

"What's taking them so long?"

"Maybe they're waiting till morning."

I sigh. "What if they don't run it? I'm starting to think maybe somebody got to them."

"They will. Trust me." He gets up, walks to the window, and peers out again. "Can you imagine what Keegan's going through right now?"

"Somebody else is going to have to die," I whisper. "He wants it to be us."

"But this time he has no choice," Dylan says. "He's out of options. If I were him, I'd probably take off. Disappear. There'll be a manhunt for him like there was for you."

"Well, we know where his favorite haunts are."

Dylan goes into the bathroom, then returns still fully clothed and sits on the couch as I get under the covers on the bed. He dozes first. His head is rolled back on the sofa, and I smile at the sound of his rhythmic, comforting breathing. I try to forget that my future depends on this night, and that our freedom may be taken from both of us tomorrow.

I drift off to the sound of his sleep, and the dreams I dream are of him and me folding laundry — and laughing like we did earlier tonight. I hang on to it as long as I can.

44

Keegan

I drive out to the tarmac, and I'm getting my stuff out of my car and loading it into my plane when Phillips appears out of the shadows.

I jump. "What are you doing?" I ask. "You almost gave me a coronary."

"I knew you'd come here. You have to take me with you. We have to get out of town."

"I'm not taking you," I say. "You're on your own. Every man for himself." I load my bags of cash into the cargo bay, then throw my bag of clothes in.

"I'm only in this because of you," he says. "You owe me."

I swing around and grab him by the throat and slam him against another plane. "I don't owe you anything," I bite out. "I got you elected. I brought down chaos on your opponents, and my money financed your campaign." I want to choke him, but I throw him down.

He scrambles to his feet and comes at me, and I kick his legs out from under him. As he falls, I kick him in the ribs. He grunts and tries to fight back, but he doesn't have the skills. He's worked in an office his whole life. He thinks he's going to take me on?

Suddenly lights over the runway and tarmac come on. Either someone is coming in for a landing and activated the lights, or someone in the tower has spotted the fight going on at my plane.

This isn't how I expected this to go.

I may not be able to fly now. I can't very well expect to get clearance with Phillips lying there, and by now they may be looking for me.

I grab my bags out of my cargo bay and throw them back into my car. I get behind the wheel and consider what to do about Phillips. I quell the instinct to run over him. That won't help.

And leaving him behind won't help either, if someone in the tower saw our brawl. I get back out and lift Phillips. He struggles, but I put him in the passenger seat of my car and slam his door. Then I get back into my seat.

"What are you doing, Gordon?" he says, still clutching his ribs. "Where are you taking me?"

"To your car. I don't want you calling attention to us by bleeding on the tarmac."

"I need a plan, Gordon. Tell me what to do. I'm not going to prison."

"You're the big lawyer. Figure it out."

"What's your plan?" he demands.

"Getting rid of you!" I bellow.

"Fine," he says. "Just shoot me. Bury me like you did Sy."

Though it sounds like a great idea, I don't have time for it. I can't fit another body in my trunk. I find my way to his Mercedes and stop there. I lean across and open his door. "Get out."

"Seriously?" he says. "Gordon, you've gotta help me!"

"Out!" I yell in his ear. "Now!"

He stumbles out of the car, his arm around his rib cage, and I don't even bother to close his door. I just step on the accelerator and take off. The thrust makes the door close by itself. I drive out of the airport, scared I'm going to be surrounded by a SWAT team any minute now. I drive through neighborhoods and back roads, stopping only once to steal a license plate to put on my car. If there's a BOLO for me, there must be about a thousand cars that look like mine out on the road.

The tag will give me some cover to get out of town.

I don't know where I'll go.

45

Casey

Dylan and I doze off and on. Several times throughout the night, I rouse out of my sleep and sit up in bed and look across the room. Sometimes he's up, pacing back and forth, and other times he's lying on the couch wrapped in his blanket. The TV still plays in the background, but no one has reported our news yet, at least not while I've been awake. Finally, I see the sun beginning to peek through the bottom of the blinds, and I know it's almost morning. The theme music of the morning news show on Channel 6 plays.

I sit up in bed and look over at Dylan. He's asleep, so I don't want to disturb him. Instead of the usual morning anchor, I see Macy Weatherow. I suck in a breath and sit up.

She looks deliberate, intense. I know this is it. "Dylan," I say.

He looks up at me with sleepy eyes.

"She's about to report it."

He sits up and jerks his cover off of him.

I turn up the volume as the music stops playing. The camera zooms in on Macy. "We have breaking news this morning regarding the Casey Cox case."

Dylan jumps up and goes to the window again, peers out. Macy begins her report, rattling off a short intro, then they play parts of my phone call, which they've transcribed on the screen. I listen to my own voice, a voice that the media hasn't heard before now, and I try to put myself in the shoes of every person out there who will view this today, and try to decide if I'm believable. I don't know if I am or not.

"That's good," Dylan says when they go to commercial. "You did great." He holds out a hand for me, and I get out of bed, aware of my wrinkled clothes and my bed head. He doesn't seem to notice. He pulls me down next to him on the couch.

When the news comes back on, he puts both arms around me and rests his chin on my head as we watch. I feel his heart beating against my head as I listen to more of our interview.

The anchor comes back on, along with the normal morning host, and he interviews

Macy about her call with me. She tells him that their network is going to be reporting it this morning, that I'm expected to turn myself in today, and according to Chief Gates, there will be a press conference later this morning where he will discuss the things I've revealed.

I look up at Dylan. "What should we do? Should we stay here or go somewhere else? Should we call Barbero to come here? Should I go ahead and turn myself in?"

"Not yet," he says. "Tell him to fly here and you'll turn yourself in as soon as we hear Chief Gates's statement and know what we're dealing with."

"Maybe you could call Chief Gates now?"

"No. I can't trust him to be honest with me. What he says to the press will tell us what we need to know. We have to wait."

"Then let's stay here," I tell him. "I think if we go out we risk being seen. Everyone will be looking for us now. They know we're in town."

"Yeah, let's just stay like this. I'm liking it."

I smile and lay my head back against his chest as they come back from commercial and play more of our interview. When they break again, he says, "I wonder what's happening with Keegan."

"I'm sure he's desperate by now."

When NBC opens its *Today Show,* they immediately launch into the same breaking news report. My blood pressure has just shot up a few points, and my heart is racing as if I've done a cardiac workout.

But I feel unburdened, and sitting here like this with Dylan is a miracle. I don't want it to end.

46

Dylan

I hold Casey as we watch the press conference at noon, crowded with reporters and a bank of microphones for Chief Gates. Every cable news station is covering it live. It is now that we'll have a sense of what Casey is in for, and whether I will face charges as well. Casey is shaking as we watch to see whether Gates will defend his detectives and deny what's been reported — trashing Casey more than she's already been trashed — or do what any clean chief of police would do when his underlings are accused of corruption and murder.

I've already heard a report that Keegan is still at large, and I glance toward the window, expecting him to go out in a spray of bullets as he comes after us. But the parking lot is quiet.

I turn back to the TV. As Gates comes down the front steps of the police department, the camera zooms in on him, and I study his face. He looks pale and tired, and he clears his throat as he gets up to the mikes.

"Thank you, everyone, for coming," he says. He puts his notes on the podium and shoves his glasses on. The man is nervous. His hands are shaking as he straightens a mike. "Last night, I received a call from Macy Weatherow, a news reporter from KTAL, who was planning to go live with an interview she'd just had with Casey Cox. In the interview, Miss Cox stated that she had evidence that two of my detectives, as well as the Shreveport district attorney, for starters, had been involved in an extortion and blackmail scheme and massive cover-up that included multiple homicides. One of my detectives was among the murdered." His voice breaks off, and he stops to clear his throat.

"Casey Cox claims that she is innocent of the crime she's been indicted for, and alleges that these individuals were the actual killers. The reporter sent me copies of the files Miss Cox sent her as evidence."

He stops and looks out at the reporters. The pause almost sends me over the edge.

"He's going to deny it," Casey whispers.

Gates goes on. "After reviewing those files

299

and the things Cox said in the interview . . . and after consulting with special agents of the FBI, as well as the Louisiana attorney general and the governor, I have suspended Detective Gordon Keegan pending our investigation, and other suspensions will be forthcoming as we determine who else may have been involved in this alleged scheme. We have issued an arrest warrant for Detective Keegan. His location is unknown, but he is believed to be armed and dangerous."

Casey leaps up as Gates gives the number for a tip line. "He believes it!" I grab her and swing her around.

"The indictment against Casey Cox is being reviewed by the attorney general, and if needed, we will empanel another grand jury to review her indictment. I'm deferring to the attorney general on her charges."

I'm still holding her, and I feel her stiffening. "It's okay," I say. "He has to do this. He can't just drop the charges when there's already been an indictment. They'll get there."

Gates pauses, rubs his mouth. "It is not easy to admit that there is corruption within my own police department, and I do not take these matters lightly. But be assured that I will do everything within my power to see that any crimes committed by my police

300

officers will be prosecuted to the fullest extent of the law."

That's just what I hoped to hear. It tells me he's stepping up, doing what's right, admitting to the wrongdoing on his force.

"I encourage you not to turn this into a witch hunt. The FBI is now involved in this case — or these cases — and they will uncover the truth, whether it leads to more police officers or back to Miss Cox herself.

"Meanwhile, Miss Cox has agreed to turn herself in to this department. She will be charged with multiple crimes, including evading an arrest warrant, identity theft, and obstruction of justice. I will follow the recommendations of the AG regarding other charges. Please address your questions about District Attorney Phillips to the governor and the attorney general, who will be holding a press conference this afternoon."

When he leaves the podium without taking questions, I look down at Casey. "I don't think he's involved. He seemed genuinely grieved over the whole thing."

"No defensiveness," she says. "He met it head-on. And the FBI being involved is a good thing."

"Right. It's all public now, and the ones who are involved will be running scared.

But I don't like the charges he said you'll face."

"I can handle it," she says. "It'll be okay."

I take her in my arms and hold her tight, absorbing her warmth. I don't want to let her go. She's a perfect fit. "You'll be out soon," I say against her hair. "They'll have to overturn your indictment. If they get another grand jury, they'll surely let you go."

"I'm just worried about you," she says. "Gates didn't mention you at all. And Keegan still wants you dead. He needs both of us dead."

"You're right. He's insane enough to keep trying. But I don't think even that would get him out of this hot water. Keegan's ship has sailed. It's just a matter of time before he gets what he deserves."

47

Casey

Barbero and his wife, Marge, flew into Shreveport this morning and hired a wheelchair van. Now the plan is for us to meet them behind the mall. Dylan parks the rental we're still driving and gets into the van behind me. We take the back seats, and Barbero keeps the van idling and turns his chair around. His mood is jubilant.

"So you're the infamous Casey Cox," he says. "Honestly, I knew there was something different about you."

"You did not," Marge says. "You never said a word." She looks at me over her seat. "Don't listen to him. He didn't have a clue."

"I'm sorry I lied to you," I say. "But it's all out now."

"No disrespect," Dylan says, "but she has to have a criminal attorney."

"Of course she does," Barbero says. "I'm not a fool. I'm just a litigator. I don't know anything about criminal law. But she was right to call me. I'll do the best I can for you, Liana, and I do appreciate the exposure."

"Casey," I correct again.

"Right, sorry." He laughs with Marge, and I can see that they're both enjoying this too much.

Dylan doesn't seem amused. "So how is this going to work?"

"They have an arrest warrant out for Keegan," Barbero says. "They tried catching him at the private airport last night and at his house. But he evaded authorities."

"So you think he's still in town?" Dylan asks.

"I think he's probably wishing he were somewhere else. His face is all over the news now. He's gotta be desperate."

"Don't underestimate him," Dylan says. "We need guarantees about Casey's safety."

"Yours too," I tell him, but he ignores me.

"Keegan wants her bad. We need specifics. Firewalls and barriers. She needs to surrender in a closed-off area. Nothing public."

Barbero laughs again. "I'll have her protected like the president of the USA."

Again, Dylan doesn't respond with a smile. "This is serious. If you can't take it seriously, we will find another attorney."

Barbero looks at me. "This fella's a keeper."

"That's the truth," Marge adds.

Barbero forces the smile from his face and gets his game face on. "I hear you, Dylan. I'm not gonna botch this. I don't intend to leave here with egg on my face. And I like this girl. I don't want her hurt."

Dylan takes my hand, and I see the worry and fear in his eyes, but not for himself. Only for me.

"Dylan, I think it's you he'll come after first," I say. "I'll be guarded. You won't. I want you to stay with us."

"He can't," Barbero says, and looks at Dylan. "Chief Gates wants to see you ASAP in his office. Before she surrenders."

"No!" I say. "Keegan is hoping for this. So are his friends."

"This is way beyond you two being witnesses," Barbero says. "He could kill you, but it wouldn't help. The media has all the evidence, all the witnesses, all the roads leading a couple dozen directions. The DA being involved? That's massive. No, they have to see that killing you won't put an end to this."

"But Keegan's a psychopath," Dylan says. "He doesn't care if it puts an end to it. Neither of us will be safe until he and his coconspirators are caught. I have to find him."

"No, you don't," I tell him. "Dylan, I don't want you anywhere near him! The entire police force and the FBI are looking for him. It doesn't have to be you."

Dylan thinks about it for a moment, then he breaks my heart. "I'll go see Chief Gates," he says. "Then I'll decide what to do next."

Tears spring to my eyes. "You're a stubborn man."

He squeezes my hand. "I solve crimes, Casey. I'm good at it. I can find him."

I press my thumbs against my tear ducts as the futility of all this overwhelms me. "Then will you try to convince Chief Gates to take care of my family? Hannah and her family and my mother all need to be moved to a safe location while Keegan is still out there."

"If I still think Gates is with us after I meet with him, then I'll use his resources to find them a safe house. If not, I'll find them a place on my own."

I hug him goodbye, knowing that in the next few minutes, everything is going to change. I may never touch him again. He kisses the top of my head, my forehead, my lips, and I melt in his kiss and pray that it won't be the last one. It would seem so cruel to have him ripped from me that way, after I've discovered the joy of knowing him.

Dylan pulls back and wipes my tears. "We're going to be together again," he whispers. "It'll be all right."

I can't speak, but I nod.

He slides his fingers down my arms, across my hands, to my fingertips. He lingers there a minute. Then he reaches for the door, breaking our connection, leaving me feeling untethered. *Help me, Lord.*

I watch him walk to his rental car. He gets in and looks back, lifts his hand in a wave. Then he drives away.

Barbero has locked himself back into place behind the steering wheel. "Ready?" he asks.

"Yes."

As we drive, I pull a small mirror out of my purse and examine myself. I think of putting on some eye shadow or lip gloss, but then I realize that I'm not Grace Newland or Miranda Henley or Liana Winters. I'm Casey Cox.

It's time for the real me.

48

Dylan

I have trouble getting close enough to the police department to park. There are news vans glutting the street on every side of the police station, and press are clustered there like flies on a melting candy bar.

They're all waiting for Casey.

I park in the lot of an insurance company two blocks away and walk to the police station. I push through the media, and a cop tries to stop me before I get to the steps.

"I'm Dylan Roberts," I say in a low voice. "Chief Gates has asked to see me."

He makes a quick radio call inside the department, then lets me go by. I trot up the front steps, eager to get this over with so I can be where Casey is when she turns herself in. I pull open the door. There's a charge of excitement in the air as cops stand in the front room looking out the glass doors toward the media, enjoying the drama. They don't notice me. I head down the hall toward Chief Gates's office. The secretary rises to her feet the second she sees me and scurries around the desk and into his office. "Chief, he's here."

Chief Gates doesn't wait for me to come in. He's at the door in a split second. "Get in here!" he says.

I hurry into his office as the secretary comes back out, and the chief slams the door shut. "Sit down!"

This is not looking good. I almost tell him he has no reason for the attitude, that he should be thanking me for exposing these monsters, but I stay quiet to see where this goes. I take my seat, and he goes back around the desk, drops into his own chair so hard that it slides back a foot. "I could arrest you for aiding and abetting a known fugitive, obstruction, conspiracy . . . But the truth is you're the blasted hero in all this!" He says it with venom, as if he's livid. "So do you want to tell me why you kept all this from me?"

I don't let him ruffle me. "Because I didn't know if you were part of this or not. It's kind of hard knowing who I can trust when so much of the police department seems involved."

"*Seems* being the key word," Gates says.

"Let me get this straight. You don't think the chief of police needs to know that some of his major detectives are murderers? That they're extortion artists? That they've made millions blackmailing people? That there are massive cover-ups that reach out to the highest level, including one of my captains *and* the district attorney? Are you kidding me?"

I sit there — arms crossed — rubbing my finger across my lip, waiting for his ire to die down. "Then you believe Casey's allegations?"

"Believe them? Most of the world believes them. They came to the attention of the reporter before they came to my attention. How is that proper protocol, Dylan?"

"I told you why."

Chief Gates looks pained. "We haven't found Jim's body yet. I'm hoping you were wrong about his death."

"I'm not."

He leans back in his chair and holds his head as if he's got a splitting migraine. "You can't tell me that Jim was involved in this."

"He was," I say. "He didn't know about his son's investigation into it or about them killing him, but he was involved in a lot of the other stuff. They were blackmailing him. I don't even know how many years this has been going on or the extent of his involvement, or what they were holding over his head. But he told me it was blackmail."

"I thought I cleaned house when I came on," he says. "I didn't know I fell right into his trap."

"Keegan's?"

"Yeah, Keegan." Gates shakes his head and gets back up, walks to the window, and looks out at all the press assembling in front of the building. "He's really good at what he does. He came to me as soon as I was appointed. Chummed up to me, offered his help in cleaning house, said there were a lot of cops that needed to be let go. Planted suggestions about things they had done. I let him plant those things in my head and it redirected me. Kept me from ever looking at him."

I'm feeling less antagonistic now that I know he really does believe me. "Did you seriously not get any complaints over the years? Were there no businesses that complained that they were being shaken down? Were there no victims' families who came forward and wanted to talk to you?"

"Honestly, no. The dry cleaner who died, his wife put in a call to me, but by the time I called her back she must've lost her nerve and she never answered the phone. I never could get in touch with her. And Rollins . . . I knew he drank. But it seemed like whenever he was working on a case he was sober, so I just let it go. I did fire four or five guys when I first came on the force, but now that I look back, they were some of the ones that Keegan directed me to fire. He made it sound like he was looking out for the brotherhood, trying to keep everything pure. He seemed like he was at the top of his game, and convinced me he was one of the best ones I had. I'm not proud of being duped that way."

"So what are you doing about it now?"

"I have arrest warrants out for Keegan, Phillips, and Swayze, and we're questioning some others that I'm pretty sure are involved, now that we've been investigating for the last ten hours."

"So what does that mean for Casey?"

"She's going to be charged with a few things, but I think they're going to rescind the indictment for murder."

"She doesn't deserve to serve even one day in jail," I say. "She was only trying to survive."

"She fled prosecution. She stole identities, Dylan."

"She couldn't let him find her. Surely you can see that."

"Her lawyers can bring all that up in court. A judge or jury might give her a pass because of her circumstances. Look, I'm just doing my job here. Because of the scrutiny and the suspicion against everyone who wears a badge here, I have to go by the book. Believe it or not, there are some of us who still want to do the right thing. Some of us who still think law enforcement is one of the most important things that keeps our country anchored."

"Yeah, there are some of us who think that."

"I'm sick that this happened on my watch, Dylan, and to be perfectly honest, I should probably resign. But I'm not leaving the police department in that kind of turmoil at a time like this. I'm going to stick with it at least until we get this mess cleaned up, and then I'll reassess. But I need you being perfectly honest from this moment on about all of this. I need you going over everything you know with me. I don't want to get my information from the news."

"Understood," I say. "But before we get to work, I want assurances. I want to know that Casey is safe. I want the list of people who have access to her while she's in custody to be limited. Only the people you absolutely trust."

"We're putting her in lockdown," he says. "Her attorney is hard-nosed. He's negotiating every detail of her surrender, making sure we don't make her a bull's-eye for Keegan."

"The PD has handed her over to him before."

Gates sears me with a look. "If you'd told me the truth, Dylan. Not part of the truth . . ."

"You wouldn't have believed me. You said it yourself. You've fallen for his schemes before."

His voice breaks. "There's enough blame to go around. Let's not get sidetracked. Casey's going to be safe. And hopefully she'll be bailed out soon and get out of here. Believe me, the sooner we get rid of the media, the better."

"Her family isn't safe either," I say. "We need to move them to a safe house."

He sighs. "All right. The state police just acquired a new house. Keegan wouldn't know about it because we haven't used it yet. I'll call them and get access. Let the family know to pack, that we're coming."

"I want to take them," I say. "I want to make sure they're safe. I promised Casey."

Chief Gates folds his hands. "That's another thing, Dylan. Your relationship with

Casey is a huge concern of mine."

I stiffen. "My relationship with her is none of your business."

"Actually, it is. I hired you."

"I figured you tore up the paperwork when you called me off."

"I didn't. You're still on our payroll. Your relationship muddies the waters."

"Then I'll quit. I'm not hiding anything anymore. Everything is on the table. We can tear up those papers. You don't have to pay me a cent."

Gates groans as his phone buzzes. He picks up, listens, then says, "I'll be right there." He looks at me. "She's a few minutes out."

My gut hitches. "You're not going to make her walk through those people, are you?"

"No. Barbero made sure. I have to go. You can go with the patrol officers to move Casey's family. That's fine. But we need to talk about one more thing."

"What?" I ask.

"I'm obviously going to need to replace some of my detectives," he says. "I think you've proven that you have what it takes. Besides, you could pass the detective exam hands down. I've got to give you the test as a formality, but I'm promoting you to detective. I need you working immediately to help me strategize how we're going to clean house and how we're going to round up every single person who's involved in this cover-up and all these crimes."

I'm flabbergasted. I wish I could call Casey and tell her about this. She would be as stunned as I am. "Thought you didn't trust me."

"Wrong, Dylan. You're about the only one in this outfit I do trust. I need you."

"Okay, then," I say. "I would be honored to come to work for the police department, as long as you don't try to dictate my love life."

He studies me. "So you and Casey are serious? In all this mess, you've had time to build that kind of relationship?"

"I don't want to get into that with you. If it's an issue, I don't want the job."

He lets out another sigh. "You just have to understand that we're not going to change the way we handle her based on your feelings for her. We have to go textbook on this."

"That's fair," I say. "She's innocent, after all."

"So go take care of her family. Then get back here and help us with all this."

When he reaches out to shake my hand, I shake. "You got it, Chief."

I feel a little more buoyant as I walk back down the hall.

49

Casey

I have to hand it to Billy. He's done a good job working out my surrender. He arranges for us to have a police escort as we head for the department to turn myself in. As six police cars encircle us with their sirens blaring and their lights flashing, I feel a little sick.

I watch the sides of the road, looking for someone with a grenade launcher, and scan the windows for gun barrels. Keegan could ram his car into us and explode a bomb. He could simply have a dirty cop in one of the cars guarding us, or a guard at the jail who would let him get to me.

Even if I'm safe from Keegan, I'm scared. The whole time I've been running, I've told myself it was because I didn't want to be murdered if Keegan caught me, but now that it's just jail that I face, I'm still scared.

"You okay, Casey?" Barbero asks as he follows the police cars toward the department.

"I guess."

"You look pale," Marge says, glancing back. "Did you eat this morning?"

"No. My stomach wasn't very steady."

"You look like you're about to pass out."

"I'll be okay," I say.

We round the corner a block from the police department. I see all the vans and the news media from more than the local outlets. It's press from all over the place. How did they get here so fast?

The police cars escort us around back and pull into a driveway that leads to the jail. It's blocked off so the press can't get there.

"Where are they taking us?" I ask.

"Into the sally port. When you get out, the doors will be closed. They won't be able to film you."

"Thank you," I say.

"Listen, Casey," Billy says. "I don't want you to talk to them unless I'm with you. Understood? The minute you talk without me, it's like waiving your right to have an attorney present. If you say you won't talk without one, they can't question you further unless you start it back up yourself. Clear?"

"Yes, but I don't have anything to hide. I want to tell them what I know."

"And you can. But I want to direct this

conversation and make sure you don't get yourself in more hot water. Until you get a criminal attorney, I'm going to look out for you."

"So you think I could still be charged with murder?"

"Not if we can help it. For now, let's get you booked, and you just be quiet until I tell you that you can talk. We've got to stay in control of this."

In spite of his assurances, when we reach the garage under the building, some of the cameramen run to get as close as they can. A scratched yellow garage door slides open. Barbero pulls his car in behind the police cars that are still flashing their lights. It goes dark as the door closes behind us. Barbero unlocks his wheelchair and turns around, and his side doors come open. He rolls onto the hydraulic lift that lowers him to the ground. I get out of my seat and step down too.

Immediately the officers in the car in front of us are out of theirs. As they approach me, I hold out my wrists for them to cuff. But they don't.

They walk me inside. Things get rougher as they put me through the paces of book-ing, as if I'm as much a criminal as a gang thug with two dozen murders under his belt. I send up a quiet, tearful plea to God to help me not to care about this. It won't hurt me to be humbled. I think about Jesus when he was in the custody of the authorities, being paraded before the religious leaders. But it was worse for him. He was beaten and spat at until he didn't even look like himself. Compared to that, this is nothing.

They lead me to the camera, and I stare straight ahead, knowing this will be the picture that defines me for the next years of my life if I have to stay. They fingerprint me, roughly rolling my fingers across the ink pad. Instead of putting me in a holding cell, they take me to an interview room with a lock on the door.

They park me there at a table with Billy by my side and leave me there alone with him. A few minutes later four detectives come in. They look like they've been up all night.

They introduce themselves, then two step out, and I know the others are watching through the window. The other two slide their chairs up to the table.

They ask me what I'd like to drink, and I tell them a Diet Coke. Within a few seconds someone has brought me one.

I can do this, I tell myself. They don't seem hostile. It may be they're inclined to believe me after all that has happened. But I'm talking about their friend here, their coworker, and some of them could be among Keegan's men. I wonder how Chief Gates has filtered them out to make sure they're not in on Keegan's crimes.

I look around for the camera that is inevitably there, and I see it across the room from me up in a corner, filming everything we do. That actually might be my safety net.

50

Dylan

Once I know Casey is safe and that she's spending the afternoon in the interview room — and after I've gotten her family settled in the safe house — I join the police at Jim Pace's elegant cabin and walk them out into the woods where Casey saw them taking Jim's body. Jim isn't there.

They bring the dogs out of the canine van, give them a whiff of Jim's clothing from the house. The dogs roam around picking up his scent, but never finding him.

"Keegan came back to get him," I tell them.

They go through the house, checking out my story about where I was held, the blood on the door, the carpet strip I pulled up, the switch plate I loosened before Casey arrived.

The CSIs take over the scene as the rest of us go back to the police station. I watch through the window as they interview Casey, as if it's a movie unfolding. I want so badly to go in there and help her with the story, but she's doing a great job laying it out. They have all the information we gave the press on a thumb drive, and they've been investigating it all morning.

Keegan's house is a crime scene.

His wife is sitting in another interview room, and his son Kurt is on suspension until he is debriefed.

But Keegan is nowhere to be found.

51

Dylan

There's a sense of urgency as we strategize about finding Keegan. Two more detectives — Robinson and Parker — and a crime scene investigator have been suspended from the force as we zero in on those involved in his schemes. It turns out that Keegan doesn't have that many friends in the department. Those who are left are glad he's gone, or they're putting on a good face. The truth is that they're all under scrutiny, and if they even display an attitude, they're likely to come under investigation.

They probably don't appreciate me coming in here with authority, but I don't have time to worry about that. I have a job to do, and lives depend on it.

I stand in front of the whiteboards in the Major Crimes room, where I've copied the one I originally did on my paper roll. I've added what has happened in the last few days and hours. All eyes are focused on it. Though I'm not yet a detective, they all treat me like I'm one.

"We've put out a BOLO for Keegan's vehicle," Stamps tells me. "I figure he's going to ditch it as soon as he can. I've got patrol officers checking out every rental car company to see if he's come by there. He's got a distinctive look, so I think his picture will alert people."

Though the media is all over him, plastering his face to kingdom come, I don't doubt that he can escape. "Are we still watching the airport?"

"Yes," he says. "They've been watching it since this morning. The TSA is alerted to watch for him on commercial flights too."

I try to think like Keegan would think. When he realized he couldn't find us and that things were about to go south, he would have tried to get to his plane and leave the country. But if he feared being caught there . . .

He could get out of town, but if he even suspected he'd be all over the news by morning, he would try to find a way out of the country. It's his only hope.

Then it hits me.

"I need to see the classified ads in every

aviation magazine in a three-hundred-mile radius."

"For what?"

"Maybe he drove to another town and bought a plane."

"But this came out first thing this morning. I don't think he could have bought one in the middle of the night. If he'd bought one this morning, the seller would have surely called it in when he saw him on the news."

I still get on my computer and pull up the website for Trade-A-Plane, which lists aircraft for sale all across North America. Keegan owns a Cessna 180. He would have wanted what he was familiar with. I type in 'single engine Cessna 180,' and up come five planes. One is in Canada, another in Las Vegas, so I rule those out. The other three are here, in the South — one in Mississippi, one in Arkansas, and one in Texas. I print out the phone numbers for those sellers, and I call the closest one. The seller in Texas tells me no one has called about his plane.

I try the one in Arkansas. Again, the seller hasn't been contacted.

I call the one in Raymond, Mississippi. There's no answer, so I look at the listing and find a secondary number. I dial it, and a woman answers the phone.

"This is Dylan Roberts from the Shreveport, Louisiana, police department. I'm calling about the plane you have listed."

"Yes. Really, it's my husband you need to talk to, Jake Gibbons, but he isn't here. You could call his cell."

She gives me the number I called first, and I tell her he didn't answer. "Could you just tell me if he's shown his plane to anyone today?"

"Yes, early this morning. He was meeting some guy at seven o'clock. Guy called at six and said he had cash, but he needed Jake to show the plane to him right then. Jake hasn't come home."

I look at my watch. It's three o'clock. "Did you expect him home afterward?"

"Yes. I knew he was probably taking the guy for a test flight, but he would have called me after to tell me how it went. He's been trying to sell it for the longest time, so I was anxious to hear. Why are you calling?"

"We're looking for someone we think may have been in the market in that area. Would you take my number and have your husband call me when he gets home? It's very important."

She hesitates. "This person . . . do you think he's dangerous?"

I don't want to alarm her, so I don't tell her he's the one she's probably seen on the news all day. "Do you happen to have the number the buyer called from?"

"No, he called Jake's cell phone."

I was afraid of that. "Just have him call me, ma'am. Thanks for your help."

I hang up and yell, "Pretty sure he was in Raymond, Mississippi!" As the others come to my desk to hear more, I dial the Raymond, Mississippi, police department and ask them to go check on that plane at the tiny Raymond airport to see if it's still there.

I'm still filling the other detectives in and writing that bit of news on the whiteboard when my phone rings. It's the Raymond police. "We thought you should know what we found."

"Is the plane still there?"

"No. But we did find Jake Gibbons."

"You did? Where?"

"Dead in his car. Strangled."

I jump out of my chair. "Do you have security footage?"

"We're getting it now."

"I'm e-mailing you a picture of the guy we're looking for. I need to know if it's him. And while we're on the phone, I need to know the number of the person who called Gibbons at six this morning."

I hold while he goes to look. He finds the cell phone and checks the dead man's recent calls. He reads the number off to me. I give him my e-mail and ask him to send the video so I can see it for myself.

When I hang up, I go to the whiteboard and write the number the buyer called from. Maybe this will lead us to Keegan.

52

Keegan

This plane isn't fit to be flown. It's burning fuel twice as fast as my plane, which cuts my range in half.

Flying from Mississippi, I couldn't be sure that I'd make it south across the Gulf to the Yucatan peninsula for fuel. Even in my plane, that would have been iffy. So I've had to navigate west, hoping to stop to fuel up just inside of Mexico. Now I'm thinking my best bet is to land somewhere around Corpus Christi.

But I wasn't prepared for this. I balance the chart on my knee and try to find a small private airport where I can self-announce. Since I'm not contacting Houston Center and I've turned off my transponder, I'm trying hard to stay under the radar. I have to find a small airport that doesn't have a tower, one that's self-fueling, so I won't have to come in contact with anyone who will recognize me, like I did this morning.

That Jake Gibbons guy, he had it coming. I was waiting for him in the parking lot of his airport, fully willing to pay cash for his plane. But when I walked toward him in the parking lot, I could see on his face that he had already seen me on the news. His expression changed, and he muttered some excuse to get back in his car. As he reached for his phone, I opened the car door and took it out of his hand, and before he could react, I had my hands around his throat. When he stopped fighting back and I let him go, I checked for a pulse. He was dead. I reclined his seat so it looked like he was taking a nap and wasn't immediately visible to others who might come and go. Bought me a few hours.

And saved me a wad of cash, which is good since this plane isn't worth the price he was asking.

On the map, I find a small airport just west of Corpus Christi, and I follow the coast of Louisiana on my way to Texas. Once I stop to fuel up, I won't have to stop again until I'm well into Mexico.

As I fly, I scan the sky for other planes and listen to the radio for other flights in my area. I don't like flying without guidance from a tower, but it is what it is.

I set my GPS with the coordinates that will take me to that little airport, then I unzip my duffel bag on the seat next to me, and I dig through for a baseball cap. I pull it on and look in the mirror. With the sunglasses, maybe people won't immediately think I'm the guy whose face is on the news.

This never should have happened. I never should have been exposed. I was careful, covering my tracks, staging evidence, and paying people for their help . . . That slippery girl and that mental case never should have been able to find me out.

I blame Rollins and Phillips and the others who weren't as careful as I was. Or maybe it was Candy. Maybe she was loose-lipped in Dallas, bragging about our relationship, and somehow word got back to Dylan Roberts.

As I fly, I go back over the evidence they have on me now. Besides what they're already reporting on TV, they'll eventually find Jake Gibbons in his car. Will they realize I'm the one who took the plane? Will they arrest DA Phillips? Does he have the backbone to not expose everything else we've done? Will they find Jim Pace's body in my trunk at the Raymond airport?

There's no way I can allow myself to be seen before I'm out of the country, and even then, I'll have to keep my head down as I make my way down Central America and into Ecuador.

Now that I see how much fuel I'm burning, I'm wondering if I should have planned things differently. Maybe it would have been wiser to go to Cuba instead.

No time for second-guessing now. It'll be okay. Everything usually works out for me.

I find the box of cigars I shoved into my bag and pull one out and put it in my teeth. I grab the matches and light it.

It calms me and reminds me that I need to celebrate. I got all that cash from Rollins, every penny he made under the table, and I can live well somewhere else. I'm almost home free. Dylan Roberts and Casey Cox haven't won. I have. I'm always the one who comes out on top.

I take the cigar out of my mouth and laugh out loud. What am I worried about? I'll be in Corpus Christi in another hour. I'll fuel up on my own, and nobody will pay me the slightest attention. I'll hop into Mexico, refuel at Mexican airports during the night, and be in Ecuador by morning.

Even with the shorter range in this plane, my plan will work.

I'm almost home free.

53

Dylan

I'm studying the map and trying to figure out whether Keegan might head for Cuba or down into Mexico, when a Raymond police officer calls me. "Thought you might be interested in this," he says. "Jake Gibbons's wife mentioned that the Cessna Keegan stole has some problems. It's burning fuel faster than it should, which is why they've had a hard time selling it."

"So he has to stop earlier than we thought to refuel."

"Sounds like it."

As I get off the phone, I look at my map. If Keegan is headed for Cuba, he would have to stop in Florida to refuel. If he's going down to Mexico, he would have to go by way of Texas. He would probably have to stop somewhere in the southern part of Texas to refuel.

There are a couple of FBI special agents

here now, working with us to get up to speed. Special Agent Griffin has been on the phone. He clicks it off, then steps toward me. "We've contacted the Air Route Traffic Control Centers for Class B Airspace to let them know to look for a plane that might not have contacted the tower and might have its transponder off."

"That's not narrow enough," I tell him. "There are planes that don't even have transponders. If I were Keegan, I'd be looking for a small airport that doesn't have a tower and has self-fueling. That way he doesn't risk having to talk to somebody who might recognize him."

Agent Griffin gets back on his phone and puts out an alert to private airports in all the Gulf states. He also calls other agents working this case and orders them to put in calls to the private airports in case they don't see the alerts, starting with Texas and Florida.

The other agent, named Bilao, yells across the room, "We just got a ping on Keegan's phone! The number he called Gibbons from this morning."

"Where is he?" I ask.

"He's just west of New Orleans."

"He must be going toward Texas." I hustle back to my desk and open the aviation chart

I've pulled up on my computer for south Texas. I try to figure out where he might have to land to refuel.

There are small airports all over southern Texas. Dillinger, one of the detectives in the unit, looks over my shoulder and I show him how to identify the small airports.

"There are a lot of them," he says. "How will we narrow it down?"

"He would choose one that's self-announcing."

"Meaning?"

"It means there's no one there watching him land. No tower to talk to. Pilots have to announce their landing on the radio in case there are other aircraft in the area about to land on the same runway. And an airport that small usually has self-fueling pumps. He might never have to interact with any-one." I print out the map on my screen, jerk it off the printer tray, and, with a red pen, circle all the small airports that fit that criteria.

"This one," I say. "I would choose this one, just outside Corpus Christi. If he's burning fuel as fast as we hope he is, he wouldn't try to make it all the way into Mexico. He'd have to stop around Corpus. This airport is perfect. This is the one I'd choose."

The FBI agents get on the phone with Houston Center, the tower that tracks the planes in that region. With their radar, they locate a plane that hasn't contacted them and doesn't have its transponder on, in the vicinity where the phone pinged off the tower.

"I think we've got him," Bilao says.

54

Keegan

By the time I locate the small runway west of Corpus Christi, my bladder feels ready to burst. I can't wait to get out of the plane to relieve myself, but I can't go inside to use the facilities because someone there might recognize me.

I'll have to find a place outside.

I self-announce my landing on the radio, knowing it's not going to be picked up by most people listening. Then I begin my descent.

My landing is a little bumpy because this plane is about ready for the garbage heap, but I get the job done. I taxi to the tarmac. There's a small hangar with a couple of planes inside, and about half a dozen planes are tied down outside. I see the gas pumps and taxi toward them.

Cigar in my teeth, I get out of the plane. I open the fuel cap and reach for the pump. I need a credit card, and that gives me pause for a minute. The ones in my wallet are in my name. I lean back into the plane and dig through my duffel bag for my fake passport and my alias credit card.

I get back out and stick the credit card in, and when it's approved, I put the nozzle in and start filling the tank.

"Put your hands over your head and get down on the ground!"

I swing around. I'm surrounded. SWAT team guys with "FBI" on their vests and helmets stand at all angles, ready to spray bullets into my brain.

No! It's not going to end this way!

"Hands over your head, Keegan," someone repeats. "Get down on the ground!"

I know they're going to shoot me if I go for my gun, but something deep inside me rages to the surface. As one last act of defiance, I pull the nozzle out and spray gas toward the three guys closest to me. Then I drop my cigar. Flames whoosh up as a bullet slashes through me, twisting somewhere in my side. My head hits concrete.

My own clothes catch fire and I roll, trying to put out the flames. Searing pain in my flesh mingles with the nerve-scream of that bullet through bone and muscle.

Before I know it they've put out the fire

and are on top of me, my face down on the pavement, the smell of gasoline and gunpowder making me heave.

They remove my gun and the knife in my pocket . . . cuffing my hands behind my back . . . knocking my forehead to the pavement. I'm bleeding and frying . . .

I feel consciousness slipping away . . . in . . . out . . . and things blur like the hazy fumes of the fuel.

55

Dylan

A cheer goes up in the Major Crimes Unit as the FBI sends us video of their takedown of Keegan. It's all there — his fight to the end, his alias credit card, which may lead us to his offshore bank accounts, the trail of bodies on his way to get out of the country to escape prosecution.

Chief Gates is in the room as we celebrate, and I see that he's more somber than the rest of us. He's slumped in a chair behind Keegan's desk, which has been cleared of his possessions, all taken into evidence.

"You okay, Chief?" I ask.

"Yeah. Just not in the celebrating mood. All of Casey Cox's and your allegations are true. Right there, for everybody to see. There's a trail of dirty cops on my watch. It's about to get ugly."

"At least he can't kill anybody else." I turn back to Special Agent Griffin, who's still with us. "What were his injuries?"

"Gunshot wound on the right side, missed his lung, grazed some ribs. Burns on his arms and legs. He can be patched up and flown back here on an FBI transport.

"Also, we got the surveillance video of the Gibbons homicide. It shows Keegan meeting him in the parking lot, then following him to his car and leaning in. He's not going to shake free of these charges. We have so much evidence against him now that he can't squirm his way out of this."

Chief Gates gets a call and walks out of the room. I wonder if I can get permission to go into the jail and give Casey the good news.

I step out into the hall to follow the chief. I catch him on the stairs. He's just getting off his phone.

"Chief! Can I talk to you?"

He turns. "I have good news for you, Dylan."

"More?" I ask.

"It's about Casey. I was just talking to the AG. He saw the surveillance video and has reviewed all the evidence against Keegan, and he's considering dropping Casey's indictment for Brent Pace's murder."

"Considering? This should be a no-brainer."

"Just be patient. Casey will go before the judge tomorrow morning. She'll still have a few minor charges even if they drop the murder charge, but my guess is he'll set a low bond for her."

"I want to be there."

"Feel free. And when she's released, you can take her to the safe house to join her family. She probably should stay there until we locate the rest of those involved in this."

I want to dance, to laugh, to hug Casey. Instead I try to look professional. "Thank you, sir."

He shakes my hand. "No, thank you, Dylan. We couldn't have done all this without you today. Even the FBI told me you'd come through for them. I hope they don't hire you out from under me."

"I'm here as long as you want me."

"We need you. We have a lot of rebuilding to do. It's going to take an army of geniuses to dig out of this mess. At least I'll have one to start with."

I think of my mother, my father, my uncle . . . all those who have told me I'm worthless. I don't care if they never learn the truth. I know it, and God knows it, and so does Casey.

That's all the validation I need.

56

Casey

I expected to be interviewed all day today, but they've left me alone in my cell. The time ticking by is ramping up my anxiety. If there were something to distract me, it would be easier. But in lockdown there's no TV, no radio, no books.

I spend a lot of time praying, and I force my mind to focus on gratitude. As Dylan was the first to point out to me, if I look for God, I'll see where he's working.

I'm thankful for the six-inch mattress on the metal bench bolted to the floor, and the blanket they've issued me. I'm thankful for the ill-fitting socks and the fact that I can pull my arms inside my jumpsuit and keep them warm. I'm thankful that they allowed me to shower this morning, and that the nurse practitioner looked at the wound that's healing on my shoulder and took out the stitches Dex sewed into me when he patched me up and gave me antibiotics. I'm thankful that Dylan is working in freedom to help find Keegan.

I'm thankful that the guards have been kind, that one of them stood guard when I showered, that no one else has been allowed near me. I'm thankful that one of them said she remembers my father, and that he deserved better than he got.

I'm thankful that they've allowed me to call and talk to my mom and Hannah. I'm thankful that they're in a safe house where Keegan can't get to them.

And as I doze into a light sleep, I thank God most of all for Dylan. I know he's working behind the scenes to help me. I feel safe in this place, no longer burdened by my load.

Yes, time ticks slowly, but I trust that resolutions will come soon enough.

57

Dylan

I want to check on Casey, but I can't get clearance to see her, and they're not interviewing her, so I can't look in. Instead I go check on her family. As I'm heading to the safe house, my phone rings. It's Special Agent Griffin.

"Dylan, I wanted to let you know that we found Jim Pace's body. It was in the trunk of Keegan's car, in the parking lot at the Raymond airport."

Though his death doesn't surprise me, I can't help thinking about his poor wife finding out about this. "Has this been released to the press yet?"

"No, not yet. We wanted to notify the family first."

"I'd like to go with whoever notifies her. I'm a friend of the family."

"I was about to go tell her myself. You can meet me there."

I'm somber as I drive to the Pace house, thinking of how I loved going over there when Brent and I were kids, how the place always smelled like cookies, how it was synonymous with happiness to me.

I get there before Griffin, and I sit alone out front, remembering how high we used to climb that oak tree in the front yard. There was a tire swing his father had rigged up with a rope as thick as my arm, and we spun on it for hours until we were so dizzy we couldn't walk straight. The swing was cut down years ago.

I feel a fierce longing for my old friend. I miss him. I never got to say goodbye.

Griffin pulls up, and I blink back the mist in my eyes and get out of the car, wiping all expression from my face. I try to sort through what Elise might know from the news. Jim's name hasn't been released yet, and they haven't revealed that any of it happened on the Pace property.

Elise answers the door when I ring the bell. "Dylan, I didn't expect to see you. I've been watching the news. I don't even know what to say. Nothing is what I thought it was. Why haven't you called me?"

"I'm sorry. I've just been so busy with it all. I thought maybe Chief Gates was keeping you informed."

"No. It's like everybody's avoiding my calls."

I introduce her to Agent Griffin. She has company — two women — and she introduces us to her sister and her niece and takes us into the kitchen to sit at the table I've eaten at so many times.

As she sits down, she says, "I know you have a lot to tell us about the case, but I'm afraid Jim isn't home. He left to go out of town the night before last, and I haven't been able to get in touch with him to tell him about all this. I guess he's been busy. He hasn't answered any of my voice mails or texts."

I swallow the knot in my throat and reach out to take her hand. "Elise, that's why we're here. It's about Jim."

She tips her head and her eyes suddenly get a defensive expression, and she draws her hand back. "Please don't do this to me again."

I can't speak, and I look at Griffin. He's opening his mouth to say it himself, but I find my voice. "Elise, I'm so sorry, but Jim is dead. He was shot last night."

The two women are on her instantly as she crumples in her chair. "No!" she says. "He's not. It's a mistake."

"I'm so sorry," I whisper.

She covers her mouth with her hand and sobs into it, and tries to get up, but she falls back. "No . . . What . . . Tell me how this happened . . . Who did this?"

Now I let Griffin take over. "Mrs. Pace, your husband was being blackmailed by Gordon Keegan. Because of that, he was complicit in some of Keegan's crimes."

"No!" she shouts, cutting him off. She gets up, stumbles away. Her sister tries to bolster her, but Elise turns to me. "It's that girl. She got to you. She's brainwashed you somehow. This isn't true. None of this is true!"

"Elise . . ." Her sister pulls her into her arms and holds her. "Honey, you knew something wasn't right. He had so many secrets."

"Not this!" she screams. "He wasn't involved in killing our son. He loved him."

I quickly take the reins again. "Elise, he didn't know about Brent. He would've never been involved in that. I told him about Keegan's involvement in Brent's death myself, and I'm absolutely positive it was news to him. He confronted Keegan. That's when they shot him."

She stares at me for a moment, her face twisted as if none of it makes sense to her. "So you're telling me that Jim didn't have anything to do with killing our son, but that he was involved with those other deaths, the extortion, the money laundering? What was he being blackmailed for?"

"I don't think we know yet," I say, trying to soften the blow. I would give anything if I could spare her this pain, but it feels like I'm wielding the weapon that will kill her.

I watch all life drain out of her. Her face loses its color, and her lips blanch. Her legs buckle and she drops to the floor. I spring up and go to her side as her crying niece kneels on the other side of her. I check her pulse, and her heart is racing in triple time. Griffin calls an ambulance while I try to revive her. Her eyelids flutter open, but she seems disoriented, confused. She lacks the strength to sit up.

Have I given her a stroke?

I wait there with her until the ambulance arrives. Her vitals slowly come around as they load her into the back of it. Her blood pressure is rocket-high. They think it was a fainting episode and they say something about sedatives.

I watch as they drive her away, praying that God will somehow help her through this darkness.

As much of a victory as it is to have Keegan exposed, I know there will be some who

still have to grieve.
  Maybe I'm one of them.

58

Dylan

Because I'm still homeless, I spend the night in a motel near the safe house where Casey's family is, but I don't sleep well. Thoughts of her in that jail cell plague me.

When I get back to the police department the next morning, Keegan is being booked after being flown here on an FBI plane. He's been treated for his gunshot and his burns, and now he's waiting to move into his new digs.

He has dressings on his arm, like the ones I've had on my legs, and he holds his arm carefully because of the sutures in his gunshot wound. But he hasn't been humbled. He wears a sour expression, and the veins in his temples are protruding. He talks to the booking guards as if they're his old friends. But no one engages with him.

When he catches sight of me, he yells across the room. "Hear you got a job out of this whole thing, Dylan. No conflict of interest here, is there? Trumped up this whole thing — threw everybody you knew under the bus — so you could get a job. When they dig through this mess, they'll find out the things you did. You and that girlfriend of yours. Watch your backs, guys."

Everyone in the area turns and looks at me, waiting for me to react, but I don't. Gordon Keegan has no power over me. Soon he's going to be in a jail cell, and the life he's chosen will be lived out the way criminal lives often end. He'll be around others like him who've murdered and assaulted and stolen to feed their own appetites. He'll die in captivity, like I was supposed to at the lake house.

I turn my back on him and walk upstairs toward the detective unit. Kurt Keegan is coming down the stairs. He looks pale and weary, as if he hasn't slept since the news broke. I slow my steps as I approach him, not sure what to say. "You okay, man?"

He stops and looks over the rail toward the booking office, where he knows they have his father. "Just trying to help my mom through this. It isn't easy for her."

"Not for you, either."

"He's getting what he deserves." He rubs his mouth, and I can see the tears stinging

his eyes red. "I just handed in my resigna-
tion."

"Why?"

His voice is shaking, and I know he's on
the edge. "Everybody's going to suspect me
for the rest of my life. I'm his son."

"If you were involved you'd have been arrested with him. I'll put in a good word for
you. Don't leave. We need you."

"No, I'm done," he says. "For now I'm
going to work for my future father-in-law's
business. He's a good guy. Trusts me. Needs
help with security. I can do that."

I can see that his mind is made up. "I'll
pray for you, man. I'm so sorry."

"He killed all those people," he whispers.
"I knew he didn't have a heart. Now I know
he doesn't have a soul, either."

"He does have one," I say. "It may be cal-
loused, but he's accountable for it."

Kurt doesn't seem able to speak. He
reaches out to shake my hand, then pats me
on the shoulder and heads down the stairs.
I say a silent prayer for him that this tragedy
in his life won't sour the rest of his years.
His wedding is coming up, and this will
overshadow it. I pray that God will protect
his and Grayson's joy as they become
husband and wife.

Later that day, I learn that Keegan is

about to be arraigned, even sooner than Casey. Because the press circles like vultures and the district attorney's office is plagued by charges of corruption, they've expedited this process to show they mean business. I squeeze my way into the courtroom and sit in the back row, trying not to draw attention. The gallery is full of press members.

Keegan is wearing jail clothes — a red jumpsuit indicating violent crime charges — and he has shackles on his flip-flopped feet as he is taken before the judge. His lawyer stands beside him — one of the ones I've seen on the news locally. The gallery is so quiet that you can hear feet tapping.

The judge reads Keegan's charges: extortion, blackmail, obstruction of justice, kidnapping, homicide . . .

My mouth goes dry as the charges are read out, and my heart is hammering. Keegan stands stiffly before the judge, his head tipped back arrogantly, as if this isn't fazing him.

"Do you understand the charges?" the judge asks.

"Yes, Judge."

The attorney takes over. "Your Honor, we request a preliminary hearing, at which time a plea will be offered. The nature of these charges, and the public attention to this, warrant that."

"All right. We'll set a date for the preliminary hearing."

"And, Your Honor, we'd like to request that you set bond for my client. We have every reason to believe that he can be trusted to appear in court."

My heart freezes, and I hold my breath. If they let him out, then it all continues. He could still come after us. Casey won't be safe anywhere.

"Bond is denied," the judge says, and I let out that breath. "Defendant will be held pending the preliminary hearing."

I want to cheer as they escort Keegan out of the courtroom. He doesn't look into the gallery. He simply keeps his eyes down and makes his way out of the room.

I don't like the idea that he's going to be incarcerated in the same building where Casey is, even if he is on a different floor in a separate part of the facility.

I have to get her out of here.

But time ticks by too slowly.

59

Casey

The prison phone system is a racket. I try calling the last burner phone Dylan had, but I don't expect to get through. In order for a call to go through on a cell phone, he has to buy a ton of minutes for like four hundred dollars and put it on his credit card. There's no charging by the number of minutes we've talked.

Even my sister has had to give the automated system her credit card number so I can call her and my mom on Hannah's cell phone. I've promised to pay them back as soon as I get out.

I don't know how most inmates can afford to talk to their families at all.

Now I wait as the phone rings, and miraculously, Dylan picks up. "Hello?"

I wait again as the automated message tells him that it's a call from the Caddo Parish Jail, and that he should enter a code if he's purchased minutes, or press the number one to give his credit card. People often get flustered and frustrated as they scurry around trying to get the proper information together to punch in. I had to give my sister four tries before she got it right.

But Dylan simply types in a series of numbers, then the voice says, "You are connected."

"Casey," he says, his voice full of relief.

"How were you able to connect?" I ask.

"I signed up for the minutes. I'm so glad you called."

"Okay, I'm impressed."

"How are you? Are they treating you okay?"

"I'm fine," I say. "They have me in lockdown, which is kind of boring. But I can live with boring."

"They're trying to keep you separated from the population. We want you safe."

"Yeah, it's fine. Do you know anything that's happening?"

He tells me about Keegan being arrested and brought in, and denied bond, and how they've found the plane owner's body and Jim Pace's. My heart sinks for Brent's mom. She's lost so much. Her son, her husband. How will she survive this?

Though I'm relieved that Keegan is where he should be, a desperate sadness falls over me at the thought of her grief.

"I'm hoping they'll get you before a judge later today or tomorrow. They're waiting for paperwork and a press conference from the attorney general."

"I'm still in red," I say. "They still have me classified as violent."

"Everyone there knows you're not."

"Have you talked to Billy Barbero?"

"Yes. He's been contacted by this famous attorney who wants to represent you. Sid Jameson."

The name rings a bell. "Who is he?"

"A celebrity attorney. He got that woman off who drove her car with her child in it into a lake, then jumped out and let her baby die. Remember?"

I shiver. "I don't want to be represented by someone like that."

"I thought that too, at first," he says. "But, Casey, if they don't do the right thing, you need somebody like him. Somebody whose ego is involved in fighting for you. The public scrutiny will make him do the best thing for you."

"But I don't need all that, do I? I'm really innocent. Besides, I can't afford it."

"He offered to do it pro bono. Barbero is

on the way to the airport to pick him up now. Jameson is a publicity hound. That might work in your favor. It's worth talking to him."

"But if I go to court tomorrow, can I just use Barbero?"

"Yes. You don't have to offer a plea tomorrow. Barbero can ask for bond."

My voice catches, and I try to steady it. "I want you to know that if I don't get released, I'm okay here. I can do this."

"You can do anything," he says. "Remember a few months ago when I told you that you were the bravest person I know? I still mean that."

My brave girl. My dad's endearment hangs in my heart. "Thank you, Dylan. You're the bravest man I know."

"I didn't think it was even possible to miss someone this much," he says.

Once again, I can hardly speak. He gets quiet too.

Finally, I ask, "So how is it being on the force?"

"It's great," he says. "It was especially great helping them find Keegan. I want to help rehabilitate the image of the force. Keegan has done unspeakable damage."

"To a lot of people," I say.

"He's going to pay. His days of getting

away with everything are over."

I think of my father, and of Brent's promise snuffed out so prematurely.

No amount of punishment would be enough for a man like Keegan.

The next morning, I get up early and ask if I can take a shower, and they take me into the bathroom where I use the harsh, all-in-one shampoo to wash my hair. Then I let it air dry as I go back to my cell. We're passing the elevator when the doors open and two guards rush out. They go into the guards' station and I hear them excitedly telling the other guards, "District attorney just killed himself!"

"What?" the guard with me asks. "Are you serious?"

"Yes. He was in C Block. Managed to cut his carotid artery and bleed out before anyone knew it had happened."

"Was he in the cell alone?"

"Yes, but he wasn't on suicide watch. Not sure what he used, but . . ."

The voices fade as I'm escorted down the hall to my cell. I look back as my door opens. The guards seem as excited as if they've just won a lottery pool.

I step back into my cell, and the door is locked behind me. So the DA is gone. He can't hurt anyone else.

But I can't help feeling the pain of his family. The shame of his death along with the horror of knowing what he was involved in. How will they ever overcome it?

I get on my bed and pull my knees up to hug them, and I pray for all the people who will be impacted by that man's choices.

Later that morning, I'm loaded into the van with the others going to court. It's a relief to hear the buzz of women's voices around me as I take my seat.

"You Casey Cox?" one of the women asks me.

I look back at her and nod. Half of her head is shaved, and she has a tattoo of a mustang on her scalp.

"How'd you hide all that time?" she asks gleefully, as if I'm a criminal celebrity.

I turn back to the front without answering.

"You can't talk?" the woman blurts.

"Not about that," I say.

"Leave her alone," someone else tells her. "She ain't done nothin'."

The woman behind me is suddenly distracted by my defender, and as they go back and forth, I let my mind drift as we drive the short distance to the courthouse. The press swarms around the front steps. The van turns into a small garage and takes us into another sally port, where it lets us out.

They lead us all single-file into a holding room and tell us they'll take us into court when it's time.

There's a guard at the door, but she's reading something on her phone. After a moment, she steps out of the room.

Something whams me from behind, and I'm knocked to my face. I flip around, trying to see what hit me. One of the inmates is straddling me and her rough hands close around my throat, choking me.

I swing my arms and fight, trying to get her off of me, and I manage to loosen her grip. She swings and hits me in the eye, then comes back down and her knuckles smash against my lips. Her hands close around my throat again.

Some of the women are screaming for help, and the guards rush in and wrestle her off me. I get to my feet, gasping for breath and wiping blood from my eyelid and my lip.

I hear someone chewing out the guard for stepping out, and things seem to move in slow motion as they take me out of the room and to a bathroom so I can wash my face. My eye and bottom lip are swelling. I pray there aren't cameras in the courtroom.

Two guards sit one on either side of me

after that, and in a few minutes, they tell me it's time.

I don't want my family or Dylan or the press to see me like this, bloody and swollen, but I can't prevent it. I walk in, my head down until I'm facing the judge.

The bailiff whispers something to him, and he frowns and adjusts his microphone. "Miss Cox, I've just been told what happened in the holding room."

Billy wheels up beside me. "Your Honor, we asked that you keep her out of the general population, and this is why. This is ludicrous."

"I agree," the judge says. "Miss Cox, I'm very sorry."

Billy keeps going. "Your Honor, in light of this situation, surely you see that my client should be given bond. Her murder charges were dropped by the state's attorney this afternoon . . ."

I catch my breath. Relief pounds through me.

"Her remaining charges are only misdemeanors, and she's suffered so much that you must see how unwise it would be to hold her in the same population where her tormentors are also being held."

I look at the floor, resigned to having to get back into that van with those women, where it could happen again. Keegan has probably paid someone off. He's not going to go down without a fight.

When the judge grants bond at ten thousand dollars, I look up at him, stunned. Billy whispers, "You only have to put a thousand dollars down. We'll get a bail bondsman here within the hour."

"That means . . ."

"You're about to be released."

I burst into tears and turn to see my family and Dylan sitting together in the courtroom behind me. They're celebrating and hugging, but then they see my face, and their smiles fade. My mother bursts into tears. I hate it. I didn't want them to have to live with this.

I want to go to them, but I haven't been released yet.

"When you're released," Billy is saying as he wheels beside me to wherever the guards are taking me, "we're going to take you in front of all those cameras and let the world see what they did to you."

I don't want to do that. I just want to lie down. I feel bruises forming on my throat.

"We'll wait right here until they process you out," he says. "You won't have to go back that way."

"Not in the van?" I ask, my voice raspy.

"Not with those women?"

"No. They'll release you from here."

I close my eyes and let the tears flow, and thank God for what he's done.

A little while later, when my bond has been paid, I'm allowed to put my clothes back on and have my possessions. I step out of the back room and see my family waiting. They rush to hold me, and I'm passed from Hannah to my mother to Jeff, and then Jeff passes little Emma to me.

I weep as I kiss her — shocked at how big she's gotten since I saw her last — and she looks up at me and studies my face, perplexed. I cover the side where my eye is swollen and play peek-a-boo. She seems to recognize me then and grins, her little dimples cutting into her cheeks.

I had forgotten her dimples!

Dylan steps through them, and still holding Emma, I step into his arms. He kisses my hair as he holds me, but he's not smiling. "What did she do to you?"

"Tried to strangle me," I say, shifting Emma to my good side. I smile at her as she touches my face.

"A Keegan stooge," he says. "I could hurt someone. But I just checked, and if it's any consolation, it's all on videotape. The woman is in for second-degree murder. A hundred dollars was put on her books today. We think it was payment for what she did."

"My life for a hundred bucks?"

"It's like gold in jail. There were probably other payments promised."

I don't know why I'm so emotional, but I can't stop my tears. I hug Emma against me, hiding my tears from her. "Are we going to be safe? I don't want to bring danger to my family."

"We're going to keep you in the safe house for now. All of you. I'll take you there myself."

I hug him again and whisper in his ear, "Will you be able to hang out with us there?"

"Just try and get rid of me," he says with a grin.

60

Dylan

I've just gotten Casey and her family to the safe house when a phone call from Elise Pace comes. I didn't expect to hear from her, but she asks if she can come visit me at home and talk. I tell her I still don't have a place to live, but I agree to meet her at a restaurant.

I'm curious what she has to say.

She shows up at exactly four o'clock, a perfect meeting time since the restaurant is almost empty. I don't know whether or not to hug her, but she leans over and hugs me and presses a kiss on my cheek.

We sit down, and she squeezes my hand. "I'm so sorry about your apartment burning, Dylan. I really don't think Jim knew about any of that. He wouldn't have allowed it."

"No, I didn't think he did."

Tears rim her eyes. "It's wrong, what happened, on so many levels. I wish he were still here so I could ask him what he was thinking, giving in to blackmail. Bringing all this on us."

I don't know what to say, so I just stay quiet.

She dries her eyes and sits up straighter. "Don't worry. I'm not going to fall apart again." She draws in a long breath. "I wanted you to know that I've been digging back through financial records, trying to figure out what part of our finances was criminally gained, what part was legitimate income. Back about fifteen years ago, Jim went through a rough patch in his business. He'd made some risky investments, and he lost a lot of money. I think it must have been then that he sold corporate secrets to a rival company. Keegan was probably targeting him to blackmail for something — anything — because Jim was rich. By the time Keegan figured out what Jim had done, Jim was the CEO of the company he had betrayed, and he had investors and shareholders to answer to. He couldn't let that get out. If Jim had just told me he was in trouble . . . I didn't have to live in that big house. I often wondered if it was best to bring Brent up in that way. I would have been happy living in a regular neighborhood and downscaling our life. But I never got the chance to weigh in on that, because he never told me we were having problems."

"I know you always made Brent your priority over everything," I say. "You were just a great mom. That's how I thought of you."

She bursts into tears again and squeezes my hand. "I can't tell you how much that means to me, Dylan." She looks up at the ceiling tiles. "I miss Brent so much. All this . . . if I could turn back time and know what was going on. If I could intervene somehow."

"What could you have done?"

"I don't know," she whispers. She forces her posture straighter again. "I really didn't come here to do this. I came to tell you something else. Something good. At least, I hope you'll think so."

"What?"

"I wanted to tell you how sorry I am for thinking that girl — Casey Cox — did this to Brent. I'm proud of you for figuring all this out and exposing everything, even when it meant going against Jim and me. Brent would have wanted you to do that. I know he would."

"He sure wouldn't have wanted the wrong person accused of his murder."

"No, he wouldn't. I feel like I was part of the reason Casey was put in all that danger."

"Well, by that logic, you're part of the reason she got out of it. If you hadn't hired me, if God hadn't given me clarity and discernment about the evidence, then she might still be hiding, or she might be dead by now."

"I want to do something for her. For you."

I shake my head. "No, Elise. We don't need anything. You have enough to deal with."

"No, I was thinking about what I could do. I've taken all the money that looks like it came from illegal means, and I have a trustee who's finding victims' rights groups to donate it to. But out of the money that was in Brent's trust fund, I wanted to give you a gift."

I smile. "You can't," I say. "I'm a police officer now. I can't take gifts from you."

"Then it's a gift to Casey. I think she was a good friend to Brent, and she helped find his killer." She reaches into her purse and pulls out a check. She writes Casey's name in the "Pay to the Order Of" blank, then slides it across the table to me. "I thought it might help her with the down payment on a house or something. I know you're in love with her. And from what I've seen of her, I can see why. She's strong, Dylan. She has integrity. And I want the two of you to have what you deserve."

I look down at the amount, and I'm blown away. It's not just a down payment. It's enough for an entire starter home. "Elise, this is too much."

"No, it's not. Brent had all this money just sitting there. I'll sell his apartment, his car. I don't want to spend it on myself. It's just too . . . you know. I want it to go to something that would have made him happy. You were the best friend he ever had. Maybe Casey was the other one. I think he would be thrilled to see the two of you together."

I look down at the check, not sure Casey will accept it. "I'll have to run this by the department, make sure it doesn't somehow go against policy, even if it's Casey's. Like, for instance, if I did marry her, it would come to me too, and I don't want to create any problems. The department is overcompensating for all the corruption, so we have to play by the rules."

"Marriage?" she asks, smiling. "Was that a hypothetical, or *do* you plan to marry her?"

I can't help smiling. "I haven't proposed, but I can't see my future without her."

"Then you'd better get on that."

"Yeah. Maybe I'd better." I chuckle lightly, and she seems to enjoy that. Her eyes light up.

"It's just . . . I've never been with her when things were normal and boring, when life was going along like it does without someone about to kill us. She hasn't been with me like that either. I'm thinking we need some time to hang out like that, when we can see if we still like each other when things aren't so intense."

"I know you pretty well, Dylan. You're not an adrenaline junkie. I think you'll be fine together. Don't waste too much time. Life is really short."

When she leaves, I stare at the check and wonder what it might be like if we did shop for a house together. If we moved in and bought furniture, watched TV and cooked and did laundry . : . The mundane, daily activities seem so pleasant when I think of doing them with her.

Maybe Elise has a point. Maybe I shouldn't waste any more time.

61

Casey

Dylan insists on staying with my family at the safe house, which makes my freedom even sweeter. The three-bedroom house is guarded by state police, but Dylan doesn't trust anyone, so he plans to sleep on the couch.

My sister bought products for the multi-step process of getting the black dye out of my hair and bleaching it back to my normal shade of blonde. When that's all done, I feel more like myself.

Dylan plays with Emma and me on the floor, and I delight in her ability to walk to me. It's like I haven't even been away. She still loves me and comes to me willingly. When Dylan catches my eye, I have to look away because tears are ambushing me.

"You okay?" he asks.

"Yeah. Just thinking . . . God is good."

"Yes, he is." He scoots over next to me

and kisses my cheek, and keeps his eyes on me. "Your laughter is so healing."

"Yours too," I say.

Hannah buzzes around the kitchen, talking nonstop and catching me up on all that has happened in the last few months. When Jeff puts Emma to bed, Dylan sits with us as we watch *Monty Python and the Holy Grail,* and I'm surprised that Dylan knows the same lines I do.

When everyone goes to bed, I try to as well, but I lie awake, unable to sleep. Finally, I get up and go into the living room. I find Dylan sitting on the couch with his computer on his lap.

"What are you doing?"

He looks up, his face lit by the screen. He pats the cushion on the couch next to him. "Couldn't sleep?"

"No. It's weird. You would think I'd sleep like a baby tonight. Maybe it's because you're here."

"I'm supposed to bring you comfort."

"You do, but it's not the kind of comfort that makes me want to sleep." We smile at each other, a smile that does relax me. "Besides, I was thinking I need to wash a load of clothes."

I take a load to the laundry room and dump my clothes into the washer, and he brings me some popcorn before I've located the detergent. He pulls himself up onto the counter as I set the washer and start it. I smile. "I love that sound."

"Really? You're easy to please."

"It sounds like peace. Like . . . you don't wash clothes when you think someone might kill you. You only do it when things are normal, right? When you're safe."

"I never thought of it that way."

"I love laundromats. The warmth in them. The noise of the machines. The way they smell. People who aren't in a hurry, just waiting for their clothes to dry."

"I like them too," he says. "Always have."

I take a handful of popcorn and wonder when I last had some. It's such a luxury. "So what were you doing on your computer? Working?"

His eyes seem to soften even more. "No, I was looking for a place to live. You want to help me?"

"Sure," I say. "I have to do that too, eventually."

We go back to the couch and sit next to each other, and I peruse the choices with him. "Wow. I guess you can afford a lot more than I can now that you have a steady gig."

He grins. "I was waiting until I got you

alone to tell you. Plus I had to get clearance from Chief Gates, but he gave it to me this afternoon."

"Clearance for what?"

"To give you this." He pulls a folded check out of his pocket and hands it to me.

I open it and catch my breath at the amount. "What?"

"From Elise Pace. It's part of Brent's trust fund. She wants you to have it to get a place to live."

I just stare at the amount. "I don't want to profit from Brent's death."

"I know," he says. "But to her, it's a gift from Brent himself. It was his money. He would be sorry about what happened to you. You spent the money your dad left you. You have injuries, lost wages . . ."

"But still —"

"Use it. It made her feel better to give it to you."

"Well, I do want her to feel better." We both grin.

We look through the houses that Dylan has brought up, and flip through the rooms. We seem to have the same taste. Simple, homey. Shabby chic, though he would never call it that.

We both fall in love with the same house, but I tell him he should get it. It's perfect for him. He clicks on the fenced backyard. It has a fort-like swing set.

We both get quiet, longing.

Finally, he closes the lid.

"What?" I ask. "You don't want to look anymore?"

He shifts on the couch and says, "I want to look at you."

I smile, basking in that.

"The thing is, Casey, I don't really want to get a house . . . without you. I don't want you to get one without me. I want us to do this together."

"Live together?" I ask. "Because I don't think that's —"

"No," he cuts in. "I know this isn't a very romantic way to do this. I should make a grand gesture, give you a story to tell your friends and family if you want to. I should have had a little box ready, and a speech and everything."

He slips off the couch and kneels on the floor, and I don't know what he's doing, so I get down there with him, thinking he's picking up toys or something.

But he has another idea.

"Casey, I know this is soon, and maybe you won't feel the same, and if you don't, that's fine. We can slow down all you want. But if you do feel the way I do . . ."

I'm starting to understand what he's doing. "I do," I manage to say.

"I feel like you're already a part of my future, and I want to start our future right now. Today, if we can. Tomorrow or the next day if there's a waiting period."

I whisper a laugh. "What are you asking me, Dylan?"

He laughs as if he's botching it big-time. "I'm asking you to marry me, Casey. I'm asking you to be my wife."

I rise up on my knees and touch his face, and tears roll down my face as I whisper, "Yes! Make me your wife!"

He kisses me then, and I feel his heart beating in his neck, and the love in his touch is greater than any ring he could have shown me. I can't stop crying as he pulls back and looks at me.

"I'll get you a ring," he whispers.

"No, I don't want one. I just want you. I want to marry you as soon as it's legally allowed. No big hoopla. I don't want people looking at me and the press going nuts. I just want Hannah and Jeff and my mom there. I want to go house hunting and get furniture and make a home with you. I want to be safe with you, and have a normal, boring life."

"A normal, boring life," he whispers, as if

it's the best thing he's ever heard.

It turns out there's a seventy-two-hour waiting period in Louisiana to get married, but we apply for the marriage license the next morning. Then Hannah goes shopping with a bodyguard to buy me a dress. She comes back with a white gown and a veil that she got off the rack at a local bridal store. Dylan surprises me by bringing home a rented tux.

The day before our wedding, his pastor comes to see us at the safe house. He counsels us for three hours before granting his blessing and telling us he'll see us when he performs our small ceremony. We swear him to secrecy, not wanting anyone to get wind of it.

The hour our waiting period ends, the preacher is there, and he performs the sweetest wedding ceremony I've ever heard in my life. It's as if a movie score is playing over my life as we exchange our vows, seal them with a kiss, and are pronounced husband and wife.

That night, Dylan doesn't have to sleep on the couch. Curled in each other's arms as man and wife, we celebrate our love and sleep more soundly than either of us has ever slept before.

62

Casey

Gordon Keegan has seen better days. He shuffles into the courtroom for his sentencing, shackles on his feet and his hands cuffed together in front. He's got two black eyes, his nose is swollen and cut, and his cheekbone is gashed. Dried blood festers on it.

For six weeks, he's been in the population with people he helped put away, whether rightfully or wrongfully. They each probably have a case now if they have good lawyers who can help them untangle the mess of their convictions, based on the fact that a known liar and criminal was the one who arrested them. I don't like that aspect of Keegan getting caught, but I suppose it can't be helped.

I sit among the other victims, including Elise Pace, who looks like she's lost at least thirty pounds and aged about twenty years since her son and husband were taken from her. On the other side of me is Sy Rollins's sister, and next to her is Sara Meadows' brother-in-law and her neighbor and best friend.

When the judge makes Keegan take his seat, he looks over toward us. Our eyes meet, and I don't let myself look away. I hold that gaze.

The judge drones on about the nature of his crimes. "And now I'm going to give a few minutes for the victims' families to testify, starting with Miss Cox. Are you ready, Miss Cox?"

I get to my feet and look back into the gallery where my husband is sitting. He nods at me, encouraging me to go on.

I step to the podium with my printout of the remarks I want to make. I had to type them up because I didn't want to leave anything out.

I clear my throat and swallow. "My father, Andy Cox, was an honorable, hardworking, trustworthy police officer. He was also a strong family man and the best father a girl could have."

I look at Keegan and realize he's not even watching me. He's looking down at his fingernails as if there's something there that's more important than what I have to say. "I've come to terms with losing him thirteen years ago," I say. "What I have trouble coming to terms with is how I found him. You murdered my father in cold blood. He fought you, and there was evidence of that at the crime scene. You covered up that evidence, then called it a suicide and let our family face that stigma. But worse, you staged the body for me to find. I was twelve years old, and the worst thing that had ever happened to me before that was my cat dying when I was six. My dad insisted on burying her in the backyard, and he had a very solemn funeral service in which he told her how much she meant to us. He did it all for me, because he wanted me to be okay with the very first death I experienced."

My mouth shakes, but I force myself to go on.

"Fast-forward six years. I had gotten an A on a math paper that I didn't expect to pass, but my dad had stayed up with me into the wee hours the night before, studying for it. I couldn't wait to get off the bus. He had come home early to meet me and see how I had done. His car was in the driveway, so I bounced off the school bus and hurried to the door. I ran inside, yelling, 'Daddy!' "

My throat constricts and the words cut off. I don't want to go on, but I have to. "I

384

found my dad hanging there in the middle of our living room, dead."

I look at Keegan, and he looks up at me. His eyelids are heavy, dull, and he seems to be taunting me, saying, "What are you going to do about it?"

Well, there's plenty I can do. I think of leaping on top of him, strangling him with my bare hands. I could do it.

And then I pull myself back, draw a deep breath, and send up a prayer asking God to forgive me, because I have no right to hate Keegan the way he hated me. I ask that Jesus will come down on me and grant me the grace to go on.

I go back to my page. "We all know that you're a murderer," I say, "but I want people to know that there's something wrong in your brain. You are the very definition of a psychopath. You can't be healed or rehabilitated. It's only by a full transformation by Christ that you can change at all. But the Bible says there is a point where God turns you over to a depraved mind, and I think that's what has happened with you."

Is he laughing? He's looking down at his legs now, hiding his grin behind his steepled hands, but his shoulders give him away. My lips grow tighter, but I keep going.

"I want you to know that while you were hunting me, you underestimated one thing. You underestimated God. And justice does win."

I head back to my seat, and I see Dylan looking down at his knees, wiping the tears on his face. I sit there feeling a sense of relief and calm wash over me as Elise stands up and says her piece, and then the others, each of them in turn, one by one.

When it's over, the judge pronounces his sentence. "Gordon Keegan, I sentence you to six consecutive life sentences without the possibility of parole." A gasp falls over the gallery, but Keegan doesn't flinch or move. He already expected it. His attorney probably convinced him to accept life instead of death by lethal injection, by pleading guilty.

I watch as they get him to his feet and shuffle him out of the room. He is still holding his head high, still prideful, daring anyone to cross him. I'm sure there are inmates at Angola who will take that dare.

When the court is adjourned, I make my way out of the room and go around the back way where I know they'll be loading him into the prison transport van. I watch as they tighten his shackles and his handcuffs and shuffle him out to the van. There's media all around, taking pictures and shouting questions as he does his perp shuffle. I watch through a window as he gets into the van, watch as they drive him away.

It's not until the van is out of sight that I look away. As I turn, I see Dylan waiting at the end of the hall. He's got his hands in his jeans pockets, and his eyes are red. He looks at me like he's worried about me, but I walk to him. Just as I'm about to reach him, he opens his arms and pulls me in, and we hold each other for a long moment.

Then he takes my hand and leads me to the front doors, where we've agreed I will walk outside to the bank of microphones. I'm ready to talk to the press.

I want them to know that Keegan hasn't defeated me. I am stronger than I've ever been. I have more. I'm loved more.

I have already overcome.

A NOTE FROM THE AUTHOR

Do you choose to be miserable? Lately, I've noticed that a lot of us do. Our culture divides us, and hatred is at an all-time high. We feed our anger in multiple ways throughout each day. We look for opportunities to be offended and feel slighted. We anticipate that we will be treated badly. We shame and are ashamed; we judge and feel judged; we assign guilt and feel guilty. We blame and assume wrong motives of everyone around us. We are pessimistic, and we mock those who hope. Everything has the look and feel of smoke and mirrors, but we deny reality. We doubt truth when it's obvious and heartily embrace falsehoods.

Over the last couple of years, I've been spending a lot of time with my grandson Liam, who is four as I'm writing this. The other day we were at the playground, and another child refused to answer him when he tried to make friends. It hurt his feelings, and on the way home, Liam said, "He must not know that Jesus told us to be kind to one another."

It hit me that so many of our cultural ailments could be solved by embracing the simplest biblical principles — things that my four-year-old grandson understands. *Be kind to one another, treat people the way you want to be treated, rejoice with those who rejoice, mourn with those who mourn, share what you have, don't judge people for things you do yourself, love one another, put others before yourself, serve others, forgive those who sin against you, pray for your enemies.*

If we applied these things to those who rubbed us the wrong way, our culture would be so different. Instead of slapping each other down for daring to differ, we would respect one another and be willing to listen. We wouldn't assume people are evil just because we don't understand them. We wouldn't let others tell us how to feel. We would investigate things on our own and dig for truth.

We would never be convinced to trash people over social media because we're trying to make a point or because we have a cause. We wouldn't hammer our points home over and over under the guise of enlightening the less intelligent, because we would realize our relationships are more important than our opinions. We would *consider* others, not target them.

The Bible tells us many ways to combat misery. Seek God's kingdom first (Matthew 6:33); love because you're loved (John 13:34); overflow with hope by trusting in God (Romans 15:13). Philippians 4:8 says, "Finally, brethren, whatever is true, whatever is honorable, whatever is right, whatever is pure, whatever is lovely, whatever is of good repute, if there is any excellence and if anything worthy of praise, let your mind dwell on these things. The things you have learned and received and heard and seen in me, practice these things; and the God of peace shall be with you."

Misery is a choice. Sometimes it's my choice. Is it yours? What if we chose not to be miserable? What if we made a conscious effort to spend less time with the things and people who make us miserable? What if we chose to trust God instead? After all, He loved us enough to send His son to die for us, so that we wouldn't be stuck in the mire of our sins, but would have abundant life.

We can trust Him. He knows what's coming. He's the one who knows the whole picture. He's the one who loves us and doesn't want us to be miserable. He gave us

ways to find joy.
Let's choose that instead.

ACKNOWLEDGMENTS

A few years ago, I had a dream of writing a series about a female fugitive. I wanted to model it after the David Janssen "Fugitive" TV series from the 1950s. In those episodes, Janssen plays Dr. Richard Kimball, who's blamed for his wife's murder. He's searching for the notorious one-armed man who killed his wife while he was hiding from the investigators catching up to him. In every episode, someone discovers who he is, and he's forced to flee again. I wanted to pay homage to that TV series by having a female fugitive who has similar issues and has to keep uprooting herself from the communities she becomes part of. From that concept, my mind fleshed out one of my favorite characters ever — Casey Cox.

From the very beginning, I had support from my team at HarperCollins Christian Publishing, and I owe them special thanks for that. Daisy Hutton, who was the fiction publisher at that time, embraced the story right away, as did Amanda Bostic, my acquisitions editor. During the writing of this last book in the series, Amanda became the fiction publisher, and she continued her support of this series without a glitch. She also allowed me to work with Dave Lambert, who has edited about fifty of my books over the last twenty-three years. My agent, Natasha Kern, was also a huge encouragement as I wrote these books.

From the cover designs (have you noticed that the three covers make a puzzle?) to the copy on the back, to what goes inside, to the marketing and publicity that got the books into my readers' hands, every single member of the HarperCollins fiction team — and others outside the HCCP family who helped make these books successful — did a fantastic job. It's one thing to write a series, but it takes a lot of people to put it into a form in which readers can find it and have a great experience reading it. Thank you to all of you who helped with these books.

And to my fantastic readers out there who launched the series straight to the *USA Today* bestseller list, I owe you my deepest gratitude. You make my work so satisfying.

God is good, and you are among his greatest blessings in my life.

DISCUSSION QUESTIONS

1. How do you feel about Casey's and Dylan's future? Do you think they will be right for each other even when things go back to normal?
2. How do the characters react to things that would make others miserable? Would you react the same?
3. What motivated Sy Rollins into committing his crimes? What motivated Gordon Keegan?
4. Discuss God's role in this series, and how the characters have evolved spiritually.
5. Although Casey and Dylan still have PTSD when the series ends, how have they helped each other with their trauma?
6. Discuss Keegan's capture and whether he got the justice he deserved.
7. Have you ever been in a situation in which you couldn't trust anyone?
8. Imagine the future for Dylan and Casey. What do you think that will look like?

9. What overriding themes have resonated with you during the If I Run Series?

ABOUT THE AUTHOR

Terri Blackstock has sold over seven million books worldwide and is a *New York Times* bestselling author. She is the award-winning author of *Intervention, Vicious Cycle,* and *Downfall,* as well as the Moonlighters, Cape Refuge, Newpointe 911, SunCoast Chronicles, and Restoration series, among others.

www.terriblackstock.com
Facebook: tblackstock
Twitter: @terriblackstock